HEATHER GRAHAM

Kiss of Darkness

ISBN-13: 978-0-7394-7380-1

KISS OF DARKNESS

Printed in U.S.A.

To Rich Devin, Lance Taubold, Ripper,
Eddy and Jack (and, okay, the duck!),
to Tammy and Brian Russotto and Little Sly,
and Laura Mills-Alcott,

With love and thanks.

And very especially to Bayley Crow—
flooded out by Katrina to meet
Rita and Wilma down in south Florida!
—and her folks,
and the incredible city of New Orleans.

Thanks!

Please visit New Orleans. This wonderful city,
with its unique heritage, still needs our help.
The Gulf area in general remains desperate,
but we can help by pouring our tourist dollars into
the shops, restaurants and hotels of this region.

Prologue

The land was drenched with blood, after years of desperate fighting, and there would be more.

The knight sat atop his horse at the side of his king, watching as the troops rode through the valley below. Behind them rode Father Gregore, the warrior priest who had so often accompanied the new king on his quest to obtain and hold his domain, murmuring in Latin.

The king cursed softly. "Damn them. So many," he added, turning to his knight. "After all these years, the feeble son feels he must prove himself to be the equal of his father. Sweet Jesu, will we forever be fighting this scourge? If the invaders reach the village, we will see a savagery beyond anything we have witnessed yet, not to show strength, as it might have been with the father, but because he longs to give the lie to his very weakness." He spoke with disgust and a hard-won right to bitterness.

The breeze shifted, bringing with it a chill. The

knight looked up, noting the sky. Darkness would come early, and according to the priest it would come earlier still today, for what Father Gregore called the Demon Moon would be upon them that night. Gregore was a great astronomer, as well as a healer. Many men had survived the field of battle because of his prowess.

Gregore was an interesting man, to say the least. He had studied for the priesthood in Rome. His father had been a highlander, an ambassador to the papal court. His mother, according to local legend, had been a witch.

Father Gregore had acted strangely throughout the day, cursing and muttering much more than usual. Now, as they assessed their enemy's strength and planned their defense, he seemed stranger still. The knight respected the priest, though he was wary of his many incantations, intoned in a language bearing no resemblance to anything the knight had ever heard. A chill ran up his spine—an unusual sensation. He had faced ruthless enemies on the field again and again. He had watched his kinsmen and friends fall. Long ago, he had set his mind to the task with the knowledge he could never look anywhere but straight ahead, that there could be nothing but the fight for freedom to guide them.

"He rides with the Devil's own henchman," Father Gregore muttered savagely.

The knight forced the sounds of the priest's voice from his mind and focused on the scene below. He pointed to the glen and the river, and the great tor beyond. "There," he said softly. "There is where we must stop them."

"They'll attack by day," the king mused.

"I don't think we dare make that supposition," the knight said.

The king sat very still. "My household rests in that glen."

The knight was very aware of that, as well as the fact that the king had a number of illegitimate children. He had married for love; his bride had braved her own family's disapproval for her husband. But there had been long times when they had been parted.

One of the king's by blood, a daughter, had quite recently come of age. She attended the queen, who bore her no malice. Like her father, she was fierce, loyal and dauntless. Like her mother, late of the Isle of Skye, she was beautiful. She was adept with a small bow, and had used her weapon successfully against the enemy. Her wit was as quick as her shot. Bold with her laugher, her ability to tease and seduce, she epitomized everything the knight fought for: the fierce, wild spirit of the land. A challenge, proud and independent, she had captured his mind along with his heart. Sometimes, sleeping on the rocky ground, he closed off the sounds of the night and the smell of blood. He felt himself seduced anew in his mind, a hint of the scent of her skin and the feel of her flesh teasing him in his dreams.

He turned to the king. "They will not wait." He pointed skyward to the rising moon. "It's Father Gregore's Demon Moon. They will see by its light, crimson and shadowed as that may be."

The king gasped suddenly and caught the warrior's arm. The knight looked down to the glen below, and his breath caught, as had his liege's. There was suddenly a great burst of laughter among the men there as what had apparently been a small scouting party made a triumphant return. Horses burst through the pass, hooves pounding, the riders shouting loudly enough to be heard by the force looking down on them.

"A prize. A prize for our great king!" a man roared.

And then the knight saw. The king's daughter Igrainia, his own true love, bruised and muddied, straight and defiant still, was seated before one of the raiders, who shoved her from the horse at the feet of the very man who was now their most hated enemy. Yet thrown hard, the wind knocked from her, she rose quickly, her chin high as she looked into the eyes of their foe.

Their enemy stared at the girl, then at his men. "The others?" he inquired.

"Dead," the rider said, and spat. "At her hands."

"And the queen?"

"Escaped—while this one mowed down our men."

"And the so-called king of these outlaws?"

"Nowhere to be found."

The enemy king, sly though not brave, cruel if not strong, assessed her, then looked around slowly. He raised his voice high, shouting so his words were an echo in the strange and eerie light that already seemed to be rising around them. "She shall die a traitor's death! By the full rise of the moon, she shall die."

The knight's horse pawed at the earth of the cliff. The king again set a hand upon his arm. "Hold."

"I will go alone," the knight said. It felt as if his blood were boiling.

"Demon Moon," the priest muttered behind him. "She is lost already."

The knight ignored him. "I will not let her die without a fight," he told the king. "She is your flesh and blood. Too many times she has risked herself to save others. I cannot let her die without a fight."

"You cannot die needlessly. They know that we are near, that we are listening," the king said. "We must plan."

The knight looked at the king. "There is a way." He pointed out the river, which was but a rill upstream, the jagged cliffs opposite their position.

The cairns to the northwest, where they could escape through labyrinths, the enemy could not know.

The king listened gravely. Other nobles and knights came closer. The plan was decided.

"Pay heed," Father Gregore demanded suddenly.

The king looked up, a deep frown creasing his forehead. He gave the orders to his men to circle to their positions, then rode to the edge of the cliff again.

The knight followed him. His stomach quickened.

Below, they were playing a taunting game with the king's daughter, tossing her from man to man. She didn't cry out. Her life had taught her stoicism.

A man grabbed her, pulled her close, then let out a scream as she bit his lip and kneed his groin. "My God, I'll kill her!" he shrieked, drawing his sword.

The enemy king laughed. "So quickly? You are no match for her. But we ride this night with one who is."

"The Devil's own appears," Gregore muttered. "But you must hold," he warned the knight.

The enemy king lifted a hand as, from the throng of cavalry and foot soldiers, strode a man. He was taller than others, a black cloak around his shoulders and a painted black helm upon his head. He walked with confidence, approaching the girl.

The knight's blood quickened; he gritted his teeth, fighting desperately for control.

This man had long been a servant of the enemy.

The knight had met him in battle before, knew that at least once, he had inflicted grave damage upon him.

He remembered when they had last met. They had fought savagely, so savagely that he had believed he had killed his opponent, for he had managed a thrust to the throat. He had seen the blood gush and spill, the man fall, his life choking from him, his final words a curse and a vow that revenge would be his.

But rumor said that his foe had refused to die. That he had called upon Satan himself for succor.

Some whispered that Satan had sent one of his concubines to the earl. That she had given him a kiss, and therein sealed his pact with the Devil. He had not died, and the word that went across the country—terrifying his friends, it was said, as well as his foes—was that he had become invincible.

He was referred to now, in tones of awe and fear, as the Master.

And now that loathsome being had the king's daughter in his power.

She would fight. The knight knew this in his heart. A feeling like death itself stole his breath. She would fight, and she would die. He had no prayer of reaching her, of perishing in her defense.

But she did not fight; she made no move. She merely stared at the damned warrior as he approached.

The man lifted his helm, his face shaded by the

growing red moon. He seized the girl, drew her close beneath his cloak.

Suddenly she came to life. She screamed and raged, fought hard and somehow drew away, clasping her neck. With stunning speed, she stole the sword from the noble at the king's left side. She swung it high and strong, despite its staggering weight. The cloaked man moved back; the warrior at his side was not so quick, and he died in agony.

Before she could strike again, a dozen men were upon her. She was instantly captured and bound, dragged to a tree, where faggots were quickly set. All the while, she swore in defiance. She cursed those who would murder her. "You will die," she promised the enemy king. "You, too, will die in an agony of fire. Your insides will burn, as your soul races toward the fires of an eternal hell!" she shouted.

The black-cloaked figure turned, staring at the surrounding countryside. "See, Ioin? My power is greater now than any you will ever know. She is mine. Come, save her now, if you dare."

The fire was lit.

Father Gregore crossed himself, muttered a prayer and drew his sword.

The knight knew he could wait no longer. He would defy the king.

But atop the tor, the king gave the signal to his haggard army.

And from the heights, they rode down upon the enemy. Battle cries split the air, and they rode like the berserkers, those maddened Viking raiders whose blood ran in the veins of so many there. The enemy outnumbered them, but they were part of the land beneath their feet, and many of those who rode with the enemy were paid for their services and had no heart for the battle.

The knight could smell the fire.

And in his mind, he heard her cry his name. It wasn't a cry for help, but one of loss, of sadness beyond life, beyond the grave. In reply, he called out her name, and his fury created a sound like thunder and seemed to shake the earth. He strode through death, defying it, ignoring it. He reached the tree and burst through the flames, ignoring the scorching of his own flesh. He slashed through the ties that bound her, and she fell, still, silent… lifeless…into his arms.

A roar of pure rage escaped him. He looked for the cloaked man, but did not see him.

The enemy rushed him, and he was forced to lay her down. He sensed the death at his back, and he turned, raised his sword, parried and slashed without stopping.

He felt the darkness, deep, overwhelming. Crimson. He spun once more, ready to swing with wearied arms, fighting the burning in his muscles.

But there was no one. Nothing. And she…

She was gone.

The enemy swept closer again, and, stunned, he was nearly taken. Only instinct saved him. He turned in time to smite his opponent, and the battle grew ever more frenzied. He fought on, heedless, his mind numbed.

Swords clashed again and again. Battle-axes split skulls. Soon the footing was treacherous, blood mingling with the dirt. Then came the blast of a horn, and the battle paused. The man before the knight smiled—just before he died. Then, keening on the breeze, came the eerie sound of unholy laughter.

It had been a trap. A trap from the beginning. They had seen only a fraction of the troops riding with the enemy. More were arriving, storming through the pass.

The knight turned in time to slash the throat of the infantryman behind him, who had meant to stab him through the back. He saw the king, and rational thought took over once again. He strode over blood, bodies, limbs, and reached the place where the king fought. Savagely, he battled by his ruler's side, willing to fight unto death, until he was overwhelmed.

Because death would be welcome. She was dead, his soul cried. Dead and gone. All that was left was to find her remains.

"Go!" the knight roared above the clash of steel.

A cohort was there with a horse. The king's follow-ers thrust him behind themselves, forcing him to the horse. A pipe played, and the defenders began to slip away, heading for the caves and tunnels they knew so well. The battle continued to rage. They could not all escape; someone had to remain so the others might survive to fight another day.

The knight looked up briefly. The moon was full in the sky, as red as the bloody field around him. The mist that had fallen was the same crimson shade. It was as if he stood in a fog of blood. And in his heart and mind, he was dead already.

His time had come. He did not damn God or fate. *She* was lost, and he could only pray that there was indeed a heaven, that he would find her there. He had killed, true, but his cause had been a righteous one.

He closed his eyes for a split second, then opened them, roared out a warning and strode into the melee.

They fell before him, man after man. He knew his rage at that moment was not for the future, not for a dream.

It was for her.

He didn't know if blood or sweat dripped into his eyes, for he moved in a red haze. He was dimly aware of someone near him, the sound of an incantation.

And then a blow against his head sent him down, spiraling into darkness, an endless bloodred night.

* * *

He opened his eyes. There was darkness, there was shadow.

There was sensation.

He hadn't expected this. Had God spurned him?

Warmth surrounded him. He heard the crackling of a fire. He blinked and realized he was not dead after all.

A massive shadow loomed on the wall, then resolved itself into Father Gregore. The man came to his side, bringing water. The knight swallowed, his head cradled by the powerful hand of the strange priest.

"The battle…?" he asked.

"It is over. Long over," the priest said. "Sip slowly."

The knight looked around. They were in a cave. He couldn't tell if it was morning or evening, early or late. He knew only that the red mist was gone. Gone, too, was the scent of scorched flesh, the awful smell of blood and death.

Gone, too, was the woman he had loved.

"How long have I been here?" the knight asked.

"A very long time."

"My lady… I took her from the fire. And then she was gone. I've got to find her."

The priest looked at him, studying him for a long time. "Yes, you do," he said softly.

"I must hurry," the knight muttered.

The priest stopped him. "You must heal."

"But...I have to find her."

"A little more time won't matter," the priest said, and sat back. The glow of the fire touched his features. "You have to help me heal you. I am not entirely a miracle worker. There will be time."

"But she is in danger."

"Yes. She is your quest. Her immortal soul cries out."

"Then—"

"There is time, my son. Much has happened. There's much I must tell you. Much you must learn."

The fire snapped and crackled and the knight looked into the priest's eyes....

It was only then that he began to understand.

1

Jessica Fraser listened to the music, the cool jazz tones. She had closed her eyes, and despite the voices, the scraping of chairs and clinking of glasses, she could filter everything else out and hear the music. She wished she could just give way to it, forget the night, forget work and her upcoming flight—even the very good friends surrounding her. From the moment she had first come to New Orleans, years ago now, she had been in love not just with the city's sense of history and pulsing life, but with the sounds, especially the music. Tonight, for a few minutes, closing her eyes, she was alone. All she could feel was the music, as if it had entered her body and soul, and soothed her.

Of course, few people actually considered Bourbon Street to be *soothing*.

Yet even as she listened to the music, savoring the feeling of calm, a sense that all was not well startled her. She opened her eyes and looked around, plagued by a sudden and yet very disturbing feeling that she was being watched.

"Hey, did you hear me?" Maggie Canady asked, nudging Jessica.

"I'm sorry. What?"

"What you need to design," Maggie said, "is a bathing suit for people with a little more body than they want to show."

"Oh, Maggie, just get one of those tankini things," put in Stacey LeCroix, who helped Jessica with both her B and B and the designing she did, both sidelines, since Jessica's real livelihood came as a practicing psychologist. Stacey was young, cute and thin as a reed.

Maggie sighed. "Honey, a tankini doesn't do a thing in the world for too much rear and thunder thighs."

Jessica couldn't help but laugh as she looked across the table at Sean Canady, Maggie's husband, a tall, well-built man who combined a look of complete authority with a handsome, strikingly rugged face, an asset in his job as a cop. "Please tell your wife she doesn't have thunder thighs."

Sean pushed back a thatch of thick blond hair and looked at his wife. "Maggie, you don't have thunder thighs."

It was a curious complaint, coming from Maggie, who tended to be far more serious and spent her time worrying about the fate of the world. She had been much occupied in the past months dealing with problems in the parish, the "coming back," as they called it, of New Orleans. On top of that, she was a stunning woman with burnished auburn hair and hazel eyes that seemed to flash with gold. She was usually last person to feel insecure about her appearance. Maggie knew there were real evils in the world, but she tried not to worry about the possibilities—natural and otherwise—unless she had to.

Maggie sighed deeply. "Who knows? Maybe I just gained a bit more thigh with each of our three children. But I dream of a comfortable, good-looking bathing suit. Jessica, can't you come up with something? Hey, Jessica—are you with us?"

Jessica started; she had been looking around, certain she would find someone watching her. But no one seemed the least bit interested in her or her table.

Maybe it was just the odd restlessness that had settled over her before she had even reached the club tonight, a restlessness she hadn't been able to understand.

"Um…of course." Jessica said, forcing her attention back to the conversation. "If you want a bathing suit that covers more of you, I can certainly design one for you."

"It's going to make for a really weird tan line," Stacey warned.

Jessica looked at her assistant. Stacey was wonderful. She was a fireball of energy, just over five feet tall, but confident and even fiercely assertive at times— *assertive*, not aggressive, Stacey had once told her.

"This whole conversation is…" Jessica began, but caught herself before saying *inane*. She winced, wondering at the impatience she was feeling. It was as if she needed to be somewhere, doing something, but she had no idea where or what. Maybe she was just on edge about heading out to the conference.

Jessica turned to see a man heading toward them. Bobby Munro, Stacey's latest boyfriend, was one of Sean's fellow cops, tall, dark-haired and good looking.

He nodded at Sean. "Lieutenant."

"Bobby, I thought you had to work," Stacey said.

"I do, private party, around the corner," Bobby said. "I just came to wish Jessica a good trip. And say hello to you, of course." He stood behind Stacey, bent down and kissed the top of her head, then looked at Jessica. "You be careful, huh?"

Jessica groaned.

"It's just a conference," she said. She considered asking the others if they had been seized by any strange feelings, if they felt that eyes were secretively scrutinizing their every move, but forced herself not to. Sean was a cop, for God's sake. If he saw or even *felt* anything, he would certainly say so. She was just on edge because going to a conference in Romania wasn't exactly her usual thing.

Bobby waved and left, and once he was gone, Sean leaned forward again.

"You're awfully tense for someone heading off to a simple professional conference," he said. "Hell, Jessica…it's a foreign country."

"It's not a trip into the deepest jungle, Sean. Romania is very much a part of the modern world," she said.

"We should be going with you."

Jessica waved a dismissive hand in the air. "Don't be ridiculous."

"I—" Stacey began.

"I need you here to take care of things. I'm just going to a conference."

"Still," Sean observed, "you're awfully tense. Do you want a drink?"

"I'm not tense," Jessica informed him quickly. Yes, she realized, she was. She had practically snapped at Sean. She was tense—and she had no idea why. "I'm sorry. It's just that …" She stared at her friends. She just couldn't sit still any longer. She stood suddenly, feigning a yawn. "Guys, excuse me, will you? I leave tomorrow, and I guess I'm a little on edge."

"I knew it." Sean said. "You *are* worried about your trip."

"No, just antsy, I guess. But I think I'll head home," Jessica said.

"I think I'll leave, too," Stacey said, rising. "It's too bad you're not going on a real vacation. You need one. You aren't yourself tonight. Maybe psychologists need psychologists more than anyone else. Maybe you should be taking a trip to a mountain cabin. This is just more pressure, and very strange. I mean, seriously, who ever heard of a psychologists' convention in Romania?"

"I'm an experienced traveler, so don't worry about me. This will be almost like a vacation, I'll do all kinds of wonderful touristy things," Jessica assured her.

"Will you go to Dracula's castle, walk in the mist-shrouded woods and listen for werewolves?" Maggie asked.

"Exactly," Jessica said, smiling. "I'll be back in a week."

Sean laughed. "I hardly think Jessica needs to worry about vampires and werewolves. For God's sake, she's from New Orleans, land of voodoo—and all the crazies who *think* they're zombies and vampires."

"He has a point," Jessica assured Maggie.

"I know, it's just that…I don't know. I just don't like it."

"I'm going, and it's going to be a great experience. I'm grateful you all care. I love you, and good night." Jessica hugged them all, then left, walking past the stage on her way out. She lifted a hand and waved to Big Jim, the trumpet player.

He was a huge man, his skin was like ebony, yet he played his instrument with a delicacy that belied his size. There was an angel's touch in his music. He also had great instincts about people and situations, perhaps handed down by his family, many of whom were known in the local voodoo community.

Like Sean and Maggie, he'd befriended her when she'd first moved to the parish. He looked at her now, shaking his head with a sigh. Then he quietly mouthed the words to her, "Be careful."

She mouthed in reply, "*Always.*"

He still didn't look happy. But then, Big Jim's mother had been a voodoo priestess, and he was a definite believer that things weren't always what they seemed. She lowered her head, hiding the secret grin that teased her lips. Bless him. He was such a good guy. Just like a big brother.

Band member Barry Larson, lanky, in his thirties, a transplant from somewhere in the Midwest, covered his mike with his free hand. "Hey, gorgeous. You have a good trip and come home safe, okay?"

"Of course."

He smiled deeply. He was nice, a little bit geeky. She'd been afraid when she first met him that he'd had something of a crush on her, but he'd never said anything and over time had become a good friend.

She left the club, glad that the French Quarter was back to its busy, even a little bit crazy, self. It was just around eleven, a time when the streets were at their busiest. She quickly walked the three blocks to her house, then, at her gates, paused for a minute. There was a stirring in the air. Rain tomorrow, she thought, and looked up at the sky.

She didn't like what she saw. As she hurried toward the front door, she reminded herself that Gareth Miller was in the cottage at the rear, once the old smokehouse. Gareth was great. In return for a place to live, he kept an eye on the place, and on her and Stacey. He was a quiet man, kind of like a reticent hippie, with his slight slouch and longish, clean but unkempt hair.

He was another of the good friends she'd made here, and her home was safe in his keeping.

Even so, she paused again halfway up the walkway, staring heavenward. Again the sense of urgency assailed her, a feeling that she needed to be moving quickly.

Maybe they're right. Maybe I do need a real vacation, she thought. Or maybe I'm just losing my mind.

She almost laughed aloud at the idea of a vacation when she was feeling this terrible need to hurry, to get ahead of something....

Of some*one*?

Too bad. There was nothing she could do about it now. The plane would leave the next day, and she would be on it.

Jessica couldn't sleep. She lay on her bed, strangely aware of time passing.

In the middle of the night, she walked outside to her balcony, which faced the street. She loved her house, and it was sheer luck that she'd been able to buy it. Amazingly, the winds and flooding from hurricane Katrina that had devastated so much of the parish had done very little damage to the Quarter or her house. The house was quite large, and she was able to keep it because, with Stacey's help, she ran it as a very selective bed-and-breakfast. Her practice, which she ran out of the house, was a good one; in psychology, she had found the perfect vocation. And, on the side, she designed one-of-a-kind costumes for various Mardi Gras krewes.

From a distance, she could very faintly hear the sounds of music and laughter, carried on the breeze from the French Quarter.

She looked at the sky again. Absurdly, it appeared as if there was a hint of red in the night air. A hint of red that seemed to grow stronger as she watched and the darkness seemed to take almost physical form around her.

"Ridiculous," she told herself.

She imagined herself with a shrink. "I don't actually see the dark...I *feel* it."

For a moment, a chill seized her as the darkness seemed to loom, like a hint, a warning. A deep red darkness...

It made her feel as if she was being hunted. Stalked.

She stepped back into her room, locking the balcony doors, trying to fight the feeling.

But she was oddly afraid. As she hadn't been in ages.

She stayed awake, staring at the sky, certain the darkness was turning a still deeper red as she watched.

Her friends had felt it, too, she thought. That was why they've been so nervous about her trip.

This was ridiculous, she told herself. When the conference had been announced, it had immediately intrigued her. And now she was committed to speak. She had to go, and that was that, even though her initial excitement was gone.

What the hell had changed? she wondered. Or was it all in her mind?

Suddenly, she felt dizzy. The world before her seemed to shift and change. She was no longer in her bedroom but outside, staring up at a high ridge, and atop the ridge stood a man. He was exceptionally tall, a cape billowing around him in the breeze.

And he was the epitome of evil.

Evil that was stalking her. An ancient evil that

lurked somewhere in a strange and distant memory that couldn't be.

The Master.

The name flashed unbidden to her mind. She banished it immediately.

The vision faded. She was home again, in her own room, the peace and beauty barely disturbed by distant sounds from the street, the scent of magnolia blossoms heavy on the air.

She was losing her mind, she told herself impatiently. She needed some sleep.

The next day, alighting in Romania, she felt a chill the minute her feet touched the ground.

A disembodied voice announced arrivals and departures in a multitude of languages. The bright lights of the airport were all around her.

Yet she felt as if the world had darkened behind her, as if a shadow were following her. As she walked toward Customs, she stopped, swinging around, certain that footsteps right behind her were closing in on her. Panic almost overwhelmed her. She was convinced she was being followed, that she could feel hot breath—fetid breath—at her nape. Chills shivered up her spine.

She thought she heard her name whispered by a deep, mocking voice.

But when she turned, there was no one near her.

Busy people, bored, anxious, were hurrying through the airport. No one seemed interested in her at all.

It was night again before she reached her final destination. And there, in the exquisite historic hotel, she felt the darkness again as she walked to her room.

She locked the door securely behind her, then waited, afraid, watching the door, wanting to believe she had worked with one too many an antisocial paranoid and their fears had simply rubbed off on her.

Nothing.

She turned away.

Then there was a sound, a clicking, as if someone were trying the door. And again, the whisper in her mind of her name. And something more.

Laughter.

You can't hide. Wherever you go, I will find you....

"Are you coming with us?" Mary demanded, her expression seductive as she sat on the edge of Jeremy's bed at the former seventeenth-century monastery, now a youth hostel, where they were staying. "I can't believe I got the invite. Some girl on the street just came up to me and started talking. It's a *private* club. There's not even a sign on the door. She says people will be there from all over Europe. It's in the ruins of some old cathedral. There was a Hungarian couple in the café, and they said it's

almost impossible to get into the local club scene, especially the "castle" vampire parties. But *I* got an invitation. And get this. They supposedly brought in
a famous dominatrix to be the hostess. Celebrities
even come to Transylvania to show up at these
parties. I guarantee you, it's the coolest thing we'll
do all year."

Mary was gorgeous, an energetic pixie with brilliant blue eyes and a cascade of wheat blond hair.
Jeremy was old enough, however, to know that going
out with *him* hadn't suddenly become the focus of her
life. She wanted to get into this club, but she was
scared, and she wanted friends with her.

In high school, he might have dropped everything to do what she wanted. Though he'd never
been a first-string player, he'd made his way onto the
football team just because she was a cheerleader.
He'd learned the guitar because she loved musicians.
He'd never set out to be one of the in-crowd, but
somehow, in his quest for her approval, he'd become
one. He'd kept his own brand of morality, though,
and that had somehow made him more desirable—
to all the girls but Mary.

He had to admit, he'd chosen to attend Tulane,
in New Orleans, largely because of her. But he was
past that. He was twenty-two, ready to graduate—
with honors—and either accept a decent job offer,
or head off to grad school. He had gained four inches

since his eighteenth birthday, and time spent in the college gym had actually given him shoulders and a chest. He was serious and studious, something Mary had always teased him about, but something other girls seemed to appreciate. Once, he had worshiped Mary, now he saw her from a clearer perspective, but he still loved her, just more realistically, so he'd agreed to join her on this trip for their last spring break. Still, this wasn't exactly like visiting England, or even France or Italy.

This was Transylvania. They had started in Bucharest, explored Walachia before heading into Sighisoara and dining in the ancient home—now a restaurant—where Vlad Tepes, the man who'd become known as Dracula, had been born. They had strolled medieval towns, visited dozens of churches, heard about history and architecture. Their guides had all spoken English. The Romanians were no fools. Americans were willing to spend lots of money to travel, to feel a part of myth and mystery—and buy souvenirs.

There were twenty students in their group, and luckily everyone got on well. Even better, they had crossed paths with an international convention of psychologists a few days earlier, and one of them was Jessica Fraser, who he'd met when she'd given a lecture at school. She had spent her free afternoon with them, and even claimed to remember meeting him. He had to admit, he'd developed a little bit of a crush on her. In fact, compared to her, Mary had started to seem kind of shallow and not at all interesting.

He had an uneasy feeling about this invitation of hers, too. He'd heard a little about the kind of parties she was talking about. Rumor had it that on top of the usual bondage scene, they were run by a group of people who actually believed that they were vampires.

"Mary, I don't like it."

"Don't be a wuss, Jeremy. I'm a journalism major. Think what I can do with this story."

Mary's idea of journalism had landed them in several uncomfortable situations already. For about six months, he'd had an out, because he'd gotten into a serious relationship with a pretty English major. But she'd left the school when her mother got sick, and never returned. They had called each other every night for a while. Then the calls had become fewer and fewer. Even their e-mails had dwindled, until they'd finally drifted completely apart.

So here he was in Transylvania, and here was Mary, ready to use him again. No, that wasn't fair, he told himself. She'd always been a good friend.

"I just don't think it's a good idea."

She laughed. "Oh, Jeremy. Come on. You've been mourning Melissa too long. What's the matter? Are you afraid you might get laid?"

"Mary," he murmured. He hated it when she talked that way, no matter how liberated the world was supposed to be.

"Please, Jeremy. I've read up the recent surge of private sex clubs—there was an article in the paper a few months back about one right in New Orleans. No sign on the door. People come from all over, because they can do what they want to do there."

"Yeah. Have silly rituals and slice their thumbs and suck each other's blood. That's pathetic, Mary."

"No, it's not. No one is allowed to push anyone else into doing anything they don't want to do. The woman who wrote the article said she wasn't hit on as much there as at a bar."

"Maybe she's old and ugly. And if there was already an article—"

Mary sighed. "Jeremy, I want to take this story national. An exposé—what's going on here and in the States. Look, I'm going, with or without you. I won't be going alone. Nancy agreed to come. But we need a guy. I mean, we'd like to have a guy with us. And, if you don't go, what are you going to do? Play some dumb computer game all night?"

"Mary, I designed that game, and it's going to get me a good job."

To his amazement, she took his hands, pleading. "I want this story so badly, Jeremy. Please."

"All right, fine. I'll go."

She jumped up, a brilliant smile on her face. "I knew you wouldn't let me down. Ever."

"Listen, Mary, when I say we have to leave—"

"We leave. Fine. Now, quit worrying. I always land on my feet."

"How do we get there?" he demanded.

"It's too cool. We head up that path toward the mountain, and we get picked up by a carriage." Mary shook her head, smiling. "I still don't know why that girl invited *me*. I guess I'm just lucky."

I guess you're just beautiful, he thought.

But he wanted her to be happy, so he kept his mouth shut. He'd go, but he still didn't like it.

He was still unhappy when Mary went to her room to change for the night. While she was gone, he went outside. The psychologists were all in the restored judicial palace across the street, now a four-star hotel.

He walked into the lobby and asked for Jessica Fraser, but she was already out for the evening.

What the hell was making him so uneasy?

Nervous enough that he wouldn't dream of letting Mary go alone.

And nervous enough to dread the fact he was going to go.

He hesitated, then left a note.

A precaution.

Someone needed to know where they had gone.

2

In the shadows, PowerPoint flashed a new image on the screen. The ancient lecture hall was filled, and Bryan MacAllistair was amazed that the many students gathered here from around the world had listened to him thus far in rapt silence. He was nearing the end of his lecture, only a few more points to make.

"This is an eighteenth-century sketch of Katherine, Countess Valor, considered one of the greatest beauties of her time. She was charged with crimes so vile that the court records were sealed. Later, they were lost to a fire. Was she a real monster, or herself a victim of evil? Like Countess Bathory, she was a member of the aristocracy, and one of the many women to find riches as a mistress in the court of Louis XIV. History records a cult within his own house, members of his royal court who became involved in witchcraft. The lady in question is actually the focus of another lecture, but she has a connection to this area. She was condemned for witchcraft and murder but, miraculously, made an escape. Some say she turned to smoke and escaped between the bars of the Bastille. At the time, witch hunters could still make a living, and the price on her head was so high that she was hunted across the continent. The accepted belief was that she had made a pact with a demon, perhaps even Satan himself, in the guise of a fiend known as the Master. The Master, the legends say, is an anglicized form of an ancient Babylonian evil, a being sprung from the womb of the lamia, one of the very earliest vampire myths, a woman who sucked the life from infants. It's said that Katherine escaped here, to Transylvania, where the Master had gained a foothold, seeking his help, his power.

"But perhaps this creature had become infuriated with her previous disregard of his power in her own pursuits, for he did not come to her aid when she reached these fog-shrouded mountains. The witch hunters found her here. She had run hard and fast, but with no followers, she had no guard to watch over her as she slept. The witch hunters came upon her, and they immediately axed her beautiful neck. The story goes that there was a hideous outcry from her deadly lips, and she spilled more blood than might have filled the veins of a dozen good women. Not satisfied that the removal of her head would keep her evil at bay, they chopped her into pieces, then burned those pieces in an inferno they kept going for thirteen days and thirteen nights, thirteen being the number of members in a coven, the number of diners at the ill-fated last supper, when Christ was betrayed. At any rate, there was little doubt she was dead when her pursuers finished with her.

"Did she in life really consume the blood of countless virgins in order to perform magic not only for the nobility but for the king himself? Or was she the victim of jealous rumor, and did time itself create the monster? That is the question we all must answer for ourselves."

He waved to the crowd of spring-break students who had filled the old guildhall and headed down from the podium. As he walked, he was met with a thunder of applause. He hurried down the aisle, anxious to escape. Ostensibly, he had come to teach; he was actually on the trail of the monster.

When he'd found out he was coming to Transylvania, he'd promised his friend, Robert Walker, dean of history at the local university, that he would give a speech. But he'd had to sandwich it in between his commitments and now he was running late.

He had done a lot of traveling lately, he reflected, watching what seemed to be the awakening of an ancient evil.

He left the guildhall behind and reached the large

village square. And there, despite his haste, he paused and looked up. The sky seemed to be roiling. There was a moon, not a full moon, but a crescent. It gave scant light, and even that was extinguished when the clouds moved over it.

There was a hint of red in the moon's glow, and even in the shadows when that glow was gone. He didn't like the night. He'd spent most of his life traveling, studying the evils one man did to another in the name of belief.

He picked up his pace, eager to reach his hotel.

In the lobby, he paused, feeling the sense that something…someone…was there. He turned around. Nothing. No one. It didn't matter. He'd received enough of a warning when he'd been in London. He knew what he was facing.

"Professor, your key," the young man behind the desk said.

"Thank you," he murmured.

Again, he looked around the lobby.

Then he reminded himself that he was out of time, and he hurried up the stairs.

Jessica sipped her wine, staring at the fire burning in the grate. The flames fascinated her, rising, falling, lapping at the ancient stone of the hearth. Gold, red, even a touch of blue…

"Don't you agree, Miss Fraser? That society itself

has created so many of the difficulties our children face? Society and the modern world, with its bombs and wars?"

She stared across at the sturdy German professor who had spoken to her. They had been talking about dealing with teenage angst. She blinked, realizing she didn't have the least idea what he had said in the last few minutes. That morning, she had given her speech. She had been asked to speak about teenage fantasies, and setting troubled youth on the right path. The German had been quizzing her endlessly, it seemed, apparently quite taken by her ideas.

She had to get out.

Why? she taunted herself. Why was she so eager to escape into the night when she was suddenly afraid of shadows?

Confront your fears. It was one of her own doctrines.

"A very difficult time, yes," she agreed, and rose, smiling. Watching the fire had been like an opiate. She felt positively serene.

Surrounded by…normalcy.

"Excuse me, will you? It's a bit late, and I'm feeling a bit jet-lagged suddenly. Good night."

The desperate urge to escape—even to hide— was on her again. She had to force herself not to run out of the restaurant.

She looked at her watch, disturbed to see it had

grown later than she had expected. She started briskly walking across the square to her hotel.

Confront your fears. She had done so, hadn't she? She would do so.

In the middle of the square, she found herself pausing. She looked up at the sky and shuddered. The night was red.

She heard something and swung around. Her breath eased from her lungs. It was just an old couple, hand in hand, out for a stroll. She turned and started walking again. Her nape grew cold. Ice cold. It felt as if the darkness was following her. Looming ever closer…just a breath away. She spun around. The square was empty. She quickened her pace, trying to be calm, logical, attempting not to give in to sheer insanity and run.

Light blazed from her hotel. She was almost running as she neared the entry.

A man was exiting, arm in arm with an attractive woman. They were laughing. Lights shone behind them. Jessica recognized the man; he was an American movie idol. She gave no sign she recognized him, but thanked him as he held the door, then hurried in.

The shadows were gone. The darkness was gone. She let out a breath, shaking her head. She was letting her imagination get the better of her. She strode to the desk, smiling as she asked for her key, the old-fashioned kind that was always kept by the concierge. He gave her the key, along with a note.

She read the message left by the college student she had run into earlier, a deep frown creasing her forehead. She looked at the stately concierge, with his graying hair and upright stance. "Where is the police station?"

She felt it again. There, in the bright light of the lobby. *Felt* it. The darkness, so black, and yet….

Red.

It was time for her to act.

Literally.

"Oh, my God!" Mary said. "That must be her, the dominatrix the Hungarians were talking about."

Jeremy stared at the woman. She couldn't be missed, and not only because of the black leather mask hiding her eyes. Her hair was pitch black, her skin fair. She was wearing black leather pants that clung to her form, showing little, but somehow emphasizing the perfection of her hips and thighs. When he forced his eyes upward, he saw she was also clad in a sheer black blouse over high, full breasts—he had to look twice to realize she was wearing a skin-toned top beneath the blouse. She was completely and decently clad, but the outfit still had an erotic appeal. In this case, more was less. He tried to stop staring. The sight of her was kicking his libido into overdrive. It was a strange feeling.

But then, strange feelings had been coming on ever since Mary had first talked to him about the party that afternoon.

She had been thrilled all during the ride in the black carriage, drawn by two black horses, that had taken them deep into the woods. The carriage had felt like something out of an old-time horror film, as had the ride through the fog-drenched trees. Nancy, a cute redhead, also in the journalism school, had been every bit as excited. She had stared out the window every few seconds, saying, "Can you believe this?"

She said it again now as they stood there, just inside the entry.

"Can you believe this?"

Mary nudged her. "Nancy, don't gawk. We'll look totally out of place."

Jeremy was fairly certain they didn't look as if they belonged to begin with. The girls had dressed in miniskirts and boots, but it was cold out, so they were also wearing tights and sweaters and heavy coats. He was in his usual tourist garb, jeans and a sweater. But here…

People were in every manner of dress. And undress. Several wore traditional vampire capes, but they weren't in the majority. A few of the women were topless. One, a redhead of about thirty, was naked. She wore nothing but a belly-button ring and a silver belt. An extremely well built black man strode by, and he, too, was in the buff, except for a flapping loincloth. A few of the men smoking and drinking at the bar wore coats—at least some people in the place recognized the fact it was cold out.

And, to be fair, there were a number of men and women in very ordinary clothing. The kind that actually covered their bodies completely. As he watched, a middle-aged man at the bar adjusted his fake fangs.

"Where's the girl who invited you?" Jeremy asked.

Mary shook her head. "I don't see her. It's a big place. She must be somewhere." She led them toward the crowd by the bar.

"Americans," the woman in black leather said, suddenly materializing in front of them. Strangely, Jeremy got the idea that she wasn't particularly pleased. A look passed across her face in a fraction of a second that made him shiver.

Then it was gone. As if it had never been.

"Americans," she repeated. "You were invited?"

Her English was heavily accented. She rose, walking toward them. She was strikingly beautiful, with perfect features, dark eyes. He wondered if in real life she might be a model.

Actually, she didn't walk. She sauntered, every move entirely languid and sensual, her eyes filled with an amused confidence that both set a fire in Jeremy's gut and also a warning. She eyed Nancy and Mary with a smile, then turned her attention to Jeremy, sliding a hand down his arm. Again, he was strangely excited, and yet…he didn't feel she found him particularly exciting. In fact, it was almost as if she were putting on a performance. But for whom?

Of course, her whole life was probably an act, if she was indeed the dominatrix, as Mary believed.

"A woman I met in town invited me. She told me to bring friends," Mary explained quickly, then introduced the three of them. Jeremy noticed that the woman didn't introduce herself in return.

Again something indefinable passed through the dominatrix's eyes, so quickly that he decided he might have imagined it.

Must have imagined it.

She went on with that same sensual amusement, as if she were educating the totally innocent— which, of course, in the circumstances, she was.

"Children, let me point out the playrooms. Beyond the bar, the movie room. We have a comprehensive selection of exceptional quality, men and women, women and women, men and men… whatever might appeal. Up the stone stairway…the pleasure rooms. Just beyond that, my personal domain. My dungeon. Visit me later, if you dare." She smiled at Mary and Nancy. "Have you been bad?" she inquired in a throaty, teasing voice. "Do you need confession? We can arrange for that, too.

But first, you must have a drink. The special tonight is a Bloody Mary. Mary…how darling, just like your name," she said, eyeing Mary again. "Tonight, everything is on me." She laughed softly. "We'll find a form of payment. For now remain at the bar. Watch." She stared at the three of them for a long moment. "*I* will tell you when it's all right to move, do you understand?"

"Yes," Jeremy said, relieved. He had to admit, he was more than uneasy.

He was…scared.

She leaned close to them. "Always know the way out," she said.

"Always know the way out," Nancy repeated. Jeremy wondered if he had sounded almost mesmerized when he had spoken, the way Nancy did.

The dominatrix seemed pleased with the response and smiled again.

She exuded a sleek sensuality, along with something smoldering and fierce. She escorted them the rest of the way to the bar and spoke to the man behind it. "Drinks, please. Right away. For my American friends."

The bartender was tall, lean, dark-eyed, perhaps in his early thirties. He nodded, then hurried to do her bidding.

They sat at the bar to wait for their drinks. Looking around, Jeremy thought it might have been almost any bar anywhere—except for the naked people and the masked woman. Next to them, two men were discussing something in French. At the end of the bar, a good-looking man speaking German was trying to pick up a pretty blonde.

He turned to say something to the dominatrix, but she was gone.

"This is so exciting." Mary whispered.

"Yeah. A thrill a minute," Jeremy murmured.

"Stop being such a weenie," Mary told him.

"You know," Nancy murmured, "we're not going to learn much if we spend all night just hanging out at the bar. We need to look around."

"That woman just told us to stay here," Jeremy said firmly.

"She also said we should watch," Nancy argued. "We'll see more if we look around."

"She said to stay at the bar," Jeremy repeated firmly. "And to always know the way out."

Mary giggled. "Maybe they're worried about police raids."

He had a sickly feeling the dominatrix had been worried about something far more serious.

"Look, Jeremy, that woman is gone, and we can't just sit here all night," Nancy said.

"We need to split up," Mary added. "No one is going to talk to us if we stick together like the Three Musketeers."

"We should stay together," Jeremy warned uneasily.

Mary laughed softly. "You shouldn't want us hanging on to you. Our hostess seemed to be pretty into you."

Jeremy didn't know why, but he had the feeling the dominatrix had quickly assessed him and found him too young and far too naive. He looked over the heads of the Frenchmen and saw that she was back at the bar. She was behaving casually, chatting with the bartender, speaking to people as they came and went from room to room, and yet...

She seemed to be watching.

For what?

"I don't know about you two, but I've got to see the pleasure rooms," Mary said, sliding off her bar stool.

"I'll check out the movie room," Nancy said.

"I don't know about this," Jeremy protested. "I can't be with both of you."

But they ignored him, already moving. He saw the dominatrix. She had noted their movements, and she didn't seem pleased.

Jeremy immediately lost sight of Mary, who must have run up the stairs. He found Nancy hovering at the back of the movie room. He stopped where he was, taking the overstuffed couches and the haze in the air from cigarettes and pot. On a large screen, a porno flick played. Two women were seducing one man—and each other. As he watched, one woman held the other down while the man bared his teeth and bit into the immobilized woman's neck. She seemed to go into instant throes of ecstasy. Blood lust apparently led to wild arousal.

Despite all the flesh on show, the movie didn't begin to arouse him. He realized he was far too tense to feel anything other than an unsettling sense of alarm.

A girl rose from one of the couches and approached Nancy, taking her hand. Nancy followed her back and sat down.

Jeremy decided that Nancy could fend for herself. The woman who had approached her was slim and not more than five two. Nancy was giggling and over twenty-one. If she wanted to live on the wild side in pursuit of her craft—or using her craft as an excuse— it was completely her call.

He made his way to the stone stairway and hurried up.

They should have stayed together at the bar, as they'd been told, and just watched.

He reached a long hall lined with doors.

The hall itself seemed far longer than it could possibly be. Perhaps it was the dim lighting and the way the far end of the hall was almost completely dark, adding to the illusion that it went on forever.

On and on…as if in an impossibly long shot for a horror film.

Except this was real.

He told himself that he was only giving in to fear and letting his imagination run wild. Look. All he had to do was look.

No one was in the hallway. He had no idea which door Mary might have chosen.

As he stood there, he felt rather than saw a shadow. No, not a shadow, exactly, a sense of greater darkness. As if something large had cast a pall over the meager light offered by the candles that burned in medieval sconces every ten feet along the walls.

A lump formed in his throat. He was tempted to turn, run back down the stairs and out into the night. Of course, if he did, he had no idea of where he would actually wind up. They had been driven through a dense, fog-shrouded forest, and they hadn't passed another living soul until they had reached this place, which, from the outside, had appeared to be nothing more than a ruin on a cliff. Yet the urge to run, escape, flee to any other place on earth, tore at him with an urgency that defied all logic.

He would not yield to it. Mary and Nancy were here, and while they were welcome to whatever pursuits they chose, he couldn't abandon them to this...

"This danger," he whispered aloud.

Because somehow he knew that his unease was justified. He felt a raw sense of instinctive panic taking hold in his gut.

The shadow was there, real, palpable, evil and malignant.

It was just a shadow, he tried to tell himself. A result of the candlelight, the intense darkness of the night...

"Where are all those psychologists when you need them?" he mocked himself out loud.

He felt the most intense desire to keep looking over his shoulder. There was something there. Something pursuing—no, stalking—him. Slowly, playing with him. He could feel it. Feel the danger, like a gazelle on an African plain suddenly aware that a lioness was silently slipping up behind it....

He spun around. He was alone in the hall.

It was simply the time and place, he told himself. He was in the land of legends, with a bunch of no-life idiots who liked to play at being vampires. It was silly; it was sad.

But fanatics could be dangerous.

And still he felt he was facing something that didn't remotely resemble a *human* danger.

He turned back, staring at the doors.

And felt it again. There was a shadow, something...evil.

It was laughing at him, he thought. It knew his fear, thrived on it, and laughed....

They had to get out of there.

"Mary?" he called aloud—almost screaming it. He no longer cared what anyone thought, what ridiculous expectation the girls had for journalistic success. They had to get out.

"Mary?" he called again, and opened the first door.

It was simply too fascinating. Mary was pretty sure she was standing there in wide-eyed wonder. No matter how sophisticated she might have considered herself to be in her own world, she knew she must appear like a lamb in a forest here. Still, this was the kind of thing that made for a great story. People loved to share such wanton and carnal experiences—vicariously. They wanted to be shocked and appalled. They were curious, and satisfying their curiosity sold print. And she? She intended to sell. People were always intrigued by sex and violence. It was unlikely that she would be traveling to any major war zones, so that left sex.

Well, sex and fantasy. The vampire fantasy. It kind of made sense that some guys wanted to act like they were vampires, because vampires had power over women. And some women loved the idea of being taken, dominated....

There was certainly fantasy here, combined with masks...and sex....

First she had stumbled on an intimate ménage à trois. They hadn't noticed her in the doorway at first, they had been so...involved. Then a husky voice had suggested she join in. Certain her face was a thousand shades of red, she had apologized and moved on.

Another door had led to an empty—but prepared—chamber. And *chamber* was the right word, not *room*. The space had been decorated to resemble an ancient dungeon, with shackles on the wall, and whips and chains laid out on a table, ready for use.

She had studied the place as dispassionately as she could, trying for journalistic objectivity, but then, uneasy, she had hurried on with a little shudder. Definitely not her scene.

The third room she found amusing. A very tall, well-muscled man was dressed in a very pink, very lacy nightie, heels and a garter belt. He was admiring himself in a mirror. She excused herself, trying not to laugh as she departed.

But she didn't feel actually scared until she opened the fourth door.

There was no reason for her fear, really. The room was empty and almost completely dark. Where candles and lamps had burned elsewhere, the only light here spilled in from the hall. When she first opened the door, she saw nothing at all. Then it seemed as if a pair of eyes, *fire-colored eyes*, stared at her from the deep recesses of the room.

As the light filtered in and her eyes adjusted, she realized it was just a man, sitting alone in the dark. Again she excused herself and hurried on. But even as she closed the door, it seemed as if the darkness still cloaked itself around her. The hall hadn't changed, and yet it had. It had darkened. As if a giant shadow…

Don't be silly, she told herself. The candles in the wall sconces were just burning down.

But it seemed as if something chilling had settled in her bones. People. She needed to find people. It didn't matter what they were doing. He-men dressing in pink lace and frills, writhing bodies involved in an orgy…anyone.

She opened the next door. There was soft light. Comfortable chairs. One wall seemed to consist entirely of a giant television screen. From somewhere, music was playing.

She walked in. "Hello?"

No answer. For a moment she felt faint. Dizziness seized her. She closed her eyes. She couldn't believe it, but she was afraid she was going to black out.

She fought the feeling, wondering just how strong her Bloody Mary had been. She opened her eyes. Somehow, things seemed slightly askew, as if something had changed in the few seconds when her eyes had been shut.

The sense of fear was still gripping her heart.
Run. Go!

She found herself sitting down. The TV came on, and the scene was arresting. A beautiful woman sat at a dressing table. She was in an elegant silk gown, brushing her hair. The room appeared Victorian, though the dressing table had art nouveau elements. There was a large wardrobe with the same elegant wood carvings, and a four-poster bed. Drapes floated in, wafting on the breeze with the same surreal whisper as the brush made, stroking through the woman's long pale-gold hair.

As Mary watched, a shadow seemed to materialize at the window.

She was afraid. Very afraid. She wanted to run.

And yet she could not. It was as if she had frozen in her chair.

Even as the shadow appeared at the window, she sensed another shadow rising behind her. She could feel the darkness, could feel the chill, the ice, whispering along her spine, as if arctic breath were teasing at her back.

There was nothing there, she insisted to herself.

It was evil, cold, a whisper in black and red....

Whispers didn't have colors....

This one did. Black, like an abyss. But touched by something...crimson.

Like blood.

Get up, Mary. Run! she warned herself.

But she couldn't. She could only stare at the screen. The shadow had drifted in through the flowing drapes and was gaining greater form. Materializing.

Her eyes widened. She wasn't watching TV, she realized. No movie was playing. She was looking through a one-way mirror. The scene was in the next room, and it was really happening.

It had to be a parlor trick, a magician's act. The shadow was becoming a man. Materializing from the mist, like a vision from every tale told about the evils found in the Carpathian Mountains of Transylvania. It couldn't be real. It was an act, performed by employees of the private club, something done with smoke and mirrors. Not real.

She would not watch anymore.

But she couldn't move.

Her limbs were far too heavy. And cold…she was so cold. The chill had traveled from her nape to her spine, from her spine to her limbs. She was frozen as surely as any ice sculpture, her eyes glued to the tableau unfolding before her.

The mist had become a man. Tall, dark, sensual, with burning eyes. Slowly, step by step, every movement filled with…*hunger*, he approached the beauty at the dressing table….

Mary thought she couldn't get any colder. But still, the sense of darkness and a fetid whispered breath of cold behind her became stronger and stronger.

Then it was as if she became aware of herself again. She looked down, and a frown creased her forehead.

She looked up. She wasn't staring at a scene taking place in the next room.

She was staring at a mirror.

Somehow *she* was the blonde at the dressing table.

And there *was* a man in black behind her, a man with burning, demonic eyes, with breath as fetid as the grave, as cold as death itself....

From somewhere, she heard her name being called, breaking the chains of ice that held her.

And as the shadow-man smiled and approached, teeth—fangs—gleaming she began to scream.

"You say you have no time tonight," the Australian complained. "All right, I accept that, but just tell me when. I'm rich. I'll pay you anything. When may I hire your services?"

The dominatrix was only half listening. She could already have damned the man for distracting her until she lost sight of the American and his blond companion. She gave him her full attention for a minute. "I'm sorry. I never know how long I'll keep the club open in any one place. I don't plan that far ahead."

"But—" he began in protest. He was tall, rich, handsome. He could probably have his pick of dozens of women. He'd come for the excitement, the difference, the ever so slightly naughty, the out of the ordinary.

If only he knew how lucky he was not to receive her attentions.

"You'll have to excuse me. I have an appointment," she said, then turned and hurried toward the stairs.

Then she heard it, very faintly. The sound of a scream.

"Wait!" the man protested, following her.

No more time to be polite.

"I said, excuse me." She gave him a hard shove, and he fell back, smiling. She shook her head. Apparently she'd just made the man's night.

She turned and sailed up the stairs.

Nancy had begun to grow uncomfortable.

It was one thing to play at being sexually daring, quite another to feel she was trapped. And alone.

She'd taken a seat on the couch next to a petite, ever-delicate woman of around her own age. But the hand that held hers now might have been made of iron. They had chatted casually at first about the beauty of the countryside and, the way Americans loved to visit more than any other nationality, because they were such legend hounds, not to mention the kooks who thought they were vampires, and, worse, the ones who had convinced themselves they actually needed to drink blood.

The woman told her that she had spent many years living in Amsterdam, had visited the States frequently, and was particularly fond of a village in the Ukraine. Nancy realized, as they whispered and the porn flick played, that her second drink was making her exceptionally drowsy. She wanted to move, to escape a situation that was becoming uncomfortably intimate, but she didn't seem to have the will or the ability to get up. It occurred to her, in the back of her mind, that the woman had never even mentioned her name.

She'd held Nancy's hand, smoothed back her hair. Nothing too forward at first, and Nancy had thought she could get the woman to talk about this place and what went on here, information she could write about later. Did drugs flow freely? She hadn't been offered any. Then again, what the second Bloody Mary was doing to her was more than a little frightening. Her companion began touching her more intimately, and she didn't seem to have the wherewithal to stop her. The woman's fingers lingered on her knee, crept up under her skirt. The soft, hot brush of her breath seemed to caress Nancy's throat and her earlobes, yet when Nancy looked, she seemed to be inches away.

"I...I...I'm not gay," Nancy whispered.

Her companion laughed softly. "You think you need to be gay to experiment and explore?"

Speaking seemed to take a tremendous effort. "It's just not...not what...I need to leave now."

"Don't run away now. I can show you a good time you'll remember until your dying breath. Pleasure so exquisite—"

"I have to go."

"Very well. Go, then."

The woman wasn't touching her at all, Nancy realized. She could have risen. There was nothing on earth stopping her.

Except...

Except everything was too heavy. The room was too heavy. The darkness was too heavy.

Her limbs were like boulders.

Fingers teased her hair and throat. A touch so light, so seductive, that she couldn't help responding to it.

She had to get out. Had to rise, had to run.

"There, on the screen," her companion said. "Watch. My friend is in this one."

Nancy stared at the movie.

They had gone from a sex tape to a very different scene, something both far more beautiful and far more disturbing. There was a woman, her every movement languid, elegant. Gossamer fabric floated around the woman. Her hair seemed to swish across the screen like silk. The film was provocative in a way that the simple thrusting and panting that had preceded it hadn't been. Nancy couldn't stand, couldn't protest. She could only watch. She felt tears forming in her eyes and she was suddenly scared.

She thought she heard a whisper, but her companion wasn't talking, only watching the screen.

Still, Nancy was sure she heard words.

Come, sweetheart. Show me your throat. Let me taste all that life rushing through your veins....

Nancy heard her companion moan softly and turned to find the woman looking at her, so at ease, so pleased.

Like a cat with the canary already between its paws.

"Watch, now."

And she did, because she had no other choice. Her heart was beating so loudly that she could hear its thunder. Somehow she knew that the woman at her side could hear it, too.

"There." The woman pointed, and Nancy stared.

There was something dark at the right-hand corner of the screen. A mist, red and black...darkening, becoming...something....

A man. A low-brimmed hat hid his features. He was tall. He walked slowly up behind the woman.

The woman turned. Mary.

A soft gasp escaped Nancy. She tried to form a protest.

"Yes," her companion hissed. "Yes, soon..."

Mary turned.

Saw the man... and screamed.

On the screen, a door burst open. Jeremy. The

man looked up, his face shadowed except for his eyes, which glowed like fire. And he had fangs.

The man was undisturbed by Jeremy's presence. He strode toward him, laughing.

"Yes," the woman beside Nancy hissed again.

Nancy turned, and her eyes widened in horror. The woman had changed. She had grown. Her eyes were glowing with a pure fire. And her teeth…were no longer teeth.

They were fangs.

Terrified, sure she was hallucinating, Nancy forced her eyes back to the screen.

The man had reached Jeremy, still laughing. He threw his arm out, his hand connecting with Jeremy's face.

Jeremy went flying, slamming back against the doorframe.

Nancy's eyes darted back to the woman. She saw the fire in her eyes, felt her own terror rise. Watched the fangs, dripping with anticipation.

And she could do nothing but weep in her soul. The woman's touch, her eyes…it was as if Nancy had been stung by a paralyzing spider. She could not prevent her own demise. She could not even cry out, only hear herself scream in terror inside her head.

Then there was a shattering sound. As if someone had burst into Mary's room through a window. The sound changed everything. Or maybe the arrival of whatever...whoever...had caused the that sound. Nancy felt something stirring in her, a sense of herself, of strength. She stared at the screen. There was someone else in that room now...a presence. Broad-shouldered, tall, dominating. A man, and something about his appearance...

What?

Changed everything. Evened the playing field. Gave her...hope.

He was wearing a large, low-brimmed hat and a floor-length leather trench coat, like an old railway frock coat. And he carried what appeared to be a longbow.

The man moved with the speed of lightning, stringing his bow in a blur.

He stood still for a moment, a bastion against the insanity.

"No," gasped the woman at Nancy's side. "No." she repeated, a whine of protest and even of horror.

Nancy no longer had any idea what was real and what was not, but she, too, knew that everything had changed.

The man had burst not just through glass but through the spell that had been upon them, the miasma...

The evil.

3

The dominatrix reached the room. She hadn't been prepared for this, hadn't believed...

She threw open the door, her heart thundering with fear, with anticipation. What had been conjecture was now proved to be true. *He* was there.

But someone else was there, as well. Someone unknown to her, yet she sensed his power.

She straightened, hesitating, knowing she had to make a split-second decision.

And then she saw the other man more clearly. Not his face, for his hat was drawn too low, but she saw the longbow, the way his head was bent, eyes on his target.

She backed away.

Who? What?

Then she heard screams coming from below.

Screams of shrill, uncanny terror.

All hell had broken loose.

Indecision tore at her for a moment.

Alone. She shouldn't have been alone.

She should have seen to it that she had help with her. But she hadn't really known what would happen here. So she *was* alone.

What to do?

Whatever was happening here, there was a force at work to counter evil, while down below...

The screams continued.

She turned and ran.

She could move, Nancy realized. The sound of the shattering glass had somehow freed her.

She stood, screaming—aloud, this time.

On the screen, the arrow was fired. It caught the fanged monster in the shoulder. The creature hissed, then gave an ungodly roar of fury.

It seemed to echo and echo....

A hand fell on Nancy's arm. She looked down and shivered. Not a hand, a talon. She looked again at the woman who had tried to seduce her, who looked even less human than before.

Her grip, again, was powerful.

Chaos broke out. People were rising all around. Some, like her, were screaming...fighting.

And others—like the woman beside her—were shrieking in fury, attacking.

Something seemed to fly into the room. A shadow, the essence of darkness and speed. As Nancy stood, a continual scream flowing from her lips, the woman was ripped away from her.

"Get out!" The command was harsh. Male? Female? She couldn't tell.

She was all too willing to obey, however. She ran for the entry, terror lending her speed.

Behind her, someone cried her name. She was afraid to turn, even though she knew it was Mary calling out to her. She was afraid to stop.

Mary caught up to her, still dressed in the gossamer gown. In the back of Nancy's mind, she knew it was cold out and that her friend would freeze.

Tears were streaming down Mary's cheeks. "We've got to get out."

Someone shouted behind them. They heard a cry of savage fury, saw a body go flying across the room and slam against the bar. They heard a snap, the sound of bones breaking.

They stumbled for the door and burst out into the night. Mary stopped dead still. "Jeremy is still in there."

She turned. Nancy grasped her by the shoulders. "You can't go back in there."

"Jeremy tried to save me," Mary said. Her teeth were chattering.

Someone burst through the door behind them, someone they had seen at the bar. He practically shoved them out of the way, then stopped, staring wildly around.

He turned back. He was large and well muscled. His eyes, however, echoed their own terror.

"Got to get away," he said in German-accented English. He started to run, then stopped, stripping his jacket from his shoulders, throwing it toward them. Nancy caught the jacket and automatically wrapped it around Mary's shoulders. The German man continued to stare at them. "Get away," he said tonelessly.

"To where?" Nancy wailed.

But the man was gone, running blindly toward the forest.

"We've got to go, too," Nancy said.

"Jeremy," Mary repeated.

Others began to burst out the door. Like the man before them, they began racing madly toward the mist-filled forest.

Nancy dragged her friend in the same direction, though Mary felt like lead. Nancy stared at her and realized that she was in shock. Her eyes were wide; her teeth continued to chatter. She was as pale as ash.

Nancy knew she had to move for the both of them. She dragged Mary with her, heading toward what looked like a trail.

A new sound made itself heard, but what it meant didn't register in her mind. She just knew they had to get away.

"Come on, come on," she pleaded. And then, at last, Mary began to move. Through the mist, Nancy saw the trail more clearly. She staggered toward it.

Jeremy was in agony the minute consciousness returned. The bursting pain in his head was overwhelming. He tried to open his eyes but couldn't. He became aware of movement, of shouts, of a fight.

He heard grunts of ferocious determination and raw anger. Something fell, close to him. He forced his lids open. He could see figures...men, flying at one another. Something else landed at his side.

Eyes open. Steady his head. Ignore the agony.

Get to his feet.

Using the wall, he managed to rise. Once he was up, he fought a savage wave of nausea that threatened to cause him to black out again. There was a thud. And then...

Silence.

He turned, aware that he needed to flee, but he stumbled. Someone was striding toward him. He screamed, throwing up his arms, too exhausted to fight.

His mind cried out that he should remain standing. But his body gave out, and he began to fall.

Nancy found a place under the trees where at least the blast of the wind was blocked. She remained in terror that any minute they would be attacked by a monster, but she knew she couldn't possibly walk all the way back to the village with Mary. Her friend's feet were bare. She all but needed to be carried, and Nancy didn't have the strength for that. She lowered her head, suddenly recognizing the newest sound.

Sirens. Thank God! There were police, even here, deep in the shrouded forest, in this no man's land of darkness and mist….

The police would find Jeremy.

"Miss?"

She froze. The voice had come from behind her. Terror snaked up her spine once again. She couldn't turn.

It had been a man's voice, deep, husky. There had been nothing threatening in it, but still…

"Tend to your friend. The police are on the way," the voice continued.

She spun around. There was no one there. Wait! On the ground, by the tree. *Jeremy.* As she stared at him, he groaned.

She raced to his side. He groaned again. She fell to the forest floor, taking his head on her lap. "Jeremy, you're alive. Speak to me. Are you hurt? Hang on, the police are coming."

He blinked and opened his eyes, staring at her as if he didn't know her for a minute. The he blinked again and tried to sit up, groaning. "How did I get here?" he murmured. He gripped her by the shoulders. "Mary. Where's Mary?"

Nancy pointed. Mary was seated against another of the sheltering trees, staring straight ahead, her eyes blank even as they were wide open.

Jeremy stared at Nancy, then touched her cheek, and struggled to rise. He made it halfway and crawled over to Mary.

"Mary?"

She didn't seem to see or hear him.

"Oh, Mary," he murmured, taking her into his arms. She didn't protest or respond. After a moment he set her against the tree again and looked at Nancy. "Help me. I've got to make sure the police find us."

Nancy helped him stagger to his feet. "Stay with Mary," he commanded.

Blood was trickling down his forehead. Nancy started to say something, then didn't. What did it matter? They had to have help.

In the silence after Jeremy left, she became aware of the screams of terror, still echoing, audible even over the sirens.

A minute later, through the trees, she saw the police vehicles drive up. Suddenly the night was aglow with flashing lights.

The police seemed to be everywhere, helping those who had stumbled outside, those who were injured and those who were in shock.

"It's going to be okay now, Mary," she whispered gently, hugging her friend. She wondered if she should get Mary up, try to force her back toward the house. But as she sat there, shivering, she saw that Jeremy had found help and was bringing the police toward them.

She began to weep.

As she did, she looked up at a sky streaked with black and red....

At a night sky that seemed to bleed.

Jeremy didn't go to the police station with some of the others who had been rounded up, screaming and in panic, outside the old castle. He'd been whisked off to the hospital, like Mary, because of the head wound he'd sustained.

It didn't get him out of having to deal with a police officer.

Detective Florenscu sat in a chair by his bed, dark eyes brooding, brow creased with a frown, as he listened to Jeremy's account of the events.

Then he shook his head. Behind him, another officer cleared his throat. Florenscu looked back at his partner, and sighed. "Mass hysteria," he said in English.

"I am not hysterical," Jeremy argued. He winced. His head still hurt if he talked too loudly.

Florenscu sighed. "We searched the place thoroughly. There were no signs of vampires—because vampires do not exist. But even in a small village, there is crime. And here, with so many tourists, men and women of unsavory character are drawn to our streets. Our only chance of finding them is with the help of the victims. With *your* help."

"I've told you what I saw," Jeremy said softly, closing his eyes.

"Please, you must keep trying to remember everything. Tomorrow you can go through books of photos for me."

"Ask Mary," Jeremy said.

"I'm afraid no one can ask your friend anything. She remains in shock. She doesn't speak, she just stares."

Jeremy roused himself. "She'll come out of it. She has to."

Florenscu shrugged. "When she is more stable, we'll see that your friend gets home to the United States."

"Nancy?" Jeremy whispered.

"She is waiting. You may speak with her now." Florenscu rose. "She says someone brought you out to them in the trees. Who?"

"I don't know. I wasn't conscious."

"You have no idea?"

"No." Jeremy shook his head. He winced. That wasn't true.

"The man who fought the vampire," he said aloud.

"There are no vampires," Florenscu told him. "My men have recovered a large amount of alcohol and drugs. They are demons enough."

"There was a vampire," Jeremy said determinedly.

Florenscu sighed wearily. "This is Transylvania," he said with a shrug. "Everyone wants there to be a vampire."

"I'm not lying."

"No. You are not lying. You are mistaken. But you are trying to be honest with me. So, tell me, what about this other man?"

"He stopped the vampire."

"With a stake?"

The weary humor was apparent in Florenscu's voice.

"With a longbow."

"Touched with holy water, I imagine."

"I wouldn't know. All I know is that he saved my life."

"Well, that is good. Let us hope I can find him and get some real answers."

Florenscu rose and turned to leave at last, his partner following him. The minute he was gone, Nancy burst in. She rushed to him, all but throwing herself on him, then drawing away quickly. "I'm so sorry. Did I hurt you?"

"Hug me whether it hurts or not. You're warm and alive."

She sat down on the side of his bed and looked at him, troubled. "They don't believe me. Not a word I say."

"It's a little late, but...well, I did say we shouldn't go. Have you seen Mary?"

"Yes." She looked down.

"And?"

"She just stares straight ahead. But she eats when she's fed, drinks water. We'll get her home. The doctor said that she might snap out of it in a day or two or..."

"Or?"

"Never," Nancy said with a wince.

Jeremy's mind reeled in a new kind of agony. Mary. He had failed her. And yet...it was a miracle that they were all still alive.

He shook his head; it hurt, and he warned himself not to try that again. "If we could find the man in the trench coat.... It was black, like his hat. I never saw his face." He stared at Nancy. "He'll know. He's the one who brought me out."

There was a soft tapping at the door. They turned simultaneously.

Jessica Fraser was standing there, her soft blond hair rippling down her back, her immense blue eyes filled with concern. He felt a little flutter in his heart, a stir of appreciation. And he felt like a real kid again, glad an adult had come to help him.

"How are you?" she asked, entering.

Jeremy stared at her. "Grateful to be alive," he told her. "Mary…"

"I just saw her. We have to have faith."

She smiled at them, walking to the bedside, touching his forehead. "I was due to fly out today," Jessica said. "But the police said your parents wouldn't be here until tonight or tomorrow morning, so…I wanted to be sure you were all safe before I left."

Jeremy felt a pang. "You don't have to stay."

She laughed softly. "Maybe I do. You need looking after. You're very lucky, you know. There have been similar disturbances in several other places. The authorities believe there's a dangerous cult growing larger on a daily basis, well financed, with members who are adept at setting up in various countries and luring in victims. What on earth made you do something so stupid?" she asked.

He looked at Nancy. Nancy looked at him. *Mary*, they both thought. But Mary was barely alive, and he would never blame her.

"Stupidity," he told Jessica. Then his eyes widened. "You were the one who went to the police, who told them something was up."

"The minute I found your note," she told him.

Nancy let out a little sob. "Thank you."

"I was young once, too," Jessica said ruefully. "Jeremy," she asked, "how did you get away?"

Here I go again, he thought. Tell the truth and sound like an idiot? Or lie?

He took a deep breath and opted for the truth.

"There was a man," he said simply. He almost laughed. "There was a good man, and a bad man. Or a good man and a monster, a good man...and something that was pure evil. In the end, I'm pretty sure the good man won. Think the police will ever believe that as a story without insisting I'm the victim of mass hysteria?"

"You should rest now," Jessica told him, not pressing for more.

"Hard to do."

"Are you afraid?"

"You bet."

"I can stick around," she told Nancy, "if you want to go back to your hostel and sleep."

Nancy shook her head. "I can't go anywhere. I want to stay with Jeremy."

Jessica nodded her understanding. "I'll go sit with Mary for a while."

"Jessica," Jeremy said, then hesitated.

"Yes?"

"Don't leave. Please. Stay with her. Don't leave her alone. Stay with her all night. Please."

"I will. I promise. I'll be right down the hall, so call me if you need anything, if you feel uneasy...or just to talk."

Nancy fell asleep in the chair in his room, and he knew that Mary was just down the hall, and that she wasn't alone, that Jessica was with her. That seemed important, somehow.

Eventually he slept, but it was a restless sleep. It was as if he could hear the wind, and the wind was whispering a single word.

Vampyr.

But vampires weren't real.

Yes they were.

Panic seized him. He tried to awaken.

He thought that he opened his eyes. He was suddenly certain that a man was standing over him. A man wearing a low-brimmed hat and a railway frock coat.

Had the man come to check on him? Had he been to see Mary?

But Jessica was with her.

And this man wouldn't hurt Mary. He had saved their lives.

Hadn't he?

When Jeremy looked again, the man was gone and the panic left him. He felt a bizarre sense of safety.

He closed his eyes again, and this time he slept deeply.

4

"So, Mr. Peterson, if you don't mind, we need to start with the basics," Jessica said, smiling. She had her notebook open, her pen in hand, seated in a large, overstuffed leather recliner while Jacob Peterson, her last patient of the day, sprawled on the sofa in her New Orleans office. She never suggested that anyone lie down; she simply suggested they get comfortable. For Jacob Peterson, being comfortable apparently meant half sitting, scrunched down in the sofa, legs sprawled out and fingers laced as he scowled.

It was her first session with him, but over the years, she'd worked with many teenagers like Jake, as well as adults.

"The basics," he murmured. "The basics are that my folks are making me come here."

"Because they're worried about you. Tell me, do you believe you're a vampire?" She kept her tone serious, nonjudgmental.

"I should have known years ago," the boy told her. "I stay up all night."

"So I understand. And it makes it very difficult for you to get to school."

He waved a hand in the air. "School is for mortals."

"Mr. Peterson—"

"Jake. Just call me Jake."

"Jake, let's say you *are* a vampire. Even vampires have to make a living."

He frowned, startled. "Vampires…have to make a living?"

She leaned forward. "Jake, there are diseases that create a physiological desire to drink blood."

"I don't deserve blood, I *need* it."

"You need blood, or you've convinced yourself you need blood?" she asked.

"I'm not the only one," he said defensively. "Not the only one who needs blood."

"I'm not sure I'm the person you should be seeing. I'm a psychologist. If you really *need* blood, we should be looking at a number of physical tests."

He shook his head. "They—I—no."

"Why not?"

"They won't find anything." He scowled again. "Don't you understand? I'm a vampire."

She lowered her head, hiding her sigh. She had had this very conversation so often. Too many people came to this part of the country because they thought they were vampires, or because they wanted to rebel and become part of a cult. Some had even committed murders, so convinced were they of their own supernatural tendencies.

She thought back to the horror she had seen in Transylvania. Perpetuated by men, or by pure evil?

"I *am* a vampire," Jake said.

"When did you first realize you were a vampire?" she asked.

"You believe me?"

She put down her notebook and uncrossed her legs, leaning forward. "Jake, listen, you're in a lot of trouble. I just want to help you, but I can only do that if you'll tell what's really going on with you. Okay?"

He nodded and leaned back against the sofa, looking tired. Much better than before, when his attitude had reeked of sheer hostility.

Jake started to talk. As she had expected, he started off with esoteric words, trying to make her see a different world, one in which he *wanted* to exist. But once he started talking, his words flowed with very little encouragement from her. It became clear that Jake's case was very similar to several she had dealt with before. After all, this was New Orleans, city of voodoo and vampires.

Jake was a brilliant kid, nice-looking, if a little

thin. But he was shy and didn't speak to girls easily. He was great with a computer. He'd read extensively.

And everything he had read he had skewed in a certain direction.

"You said there are others like you," she said softly. "That you feel the urge for blood most often during nights when there's a full moon. And that you walk frequently during those nights. So...where do you walk? What do you do?"

He flushed a beet red suddenly. "Um, well, once...I paid for it."

Jessica frowned. "Paid for...it? Do you mean sex?"

"Yeah, well, that...and blood."

That was New Orleans, too. Most diversions could be found somewhere—if you had the money to pay for them.

"I see. You just wound up at a peep show, or... someone solicited you on the street, or...?"

She was startled when she saw that her question had left him seriously perplexed.

"Jake?" she prodded gently.

"I—I don't remember." He stared at her, still looking lost and confused. "I mean...I knew that I had drunk blood. But now that you ask..."

"Were you alone?" she asked him.

The confusion was gone. There was a hard mask in its place. "I can't tell you who I was with. I *won't* tell you who I was with. You can't make me."

"I'm not forcing you to do anything," she said with a shrug. "Tell me what you want, but I hope you'll learn to speak freely."

"There are others. Many others. And more are coming," he said.

"Oh?"

Once again he appeared confused. Her heartbeat quickened. This was worrying.

"I'm not the only one," he said.

"I'm concerned about you, Jake," she told him. "And since I can't make you tell me anything, I'll tell you what I think, and we'll leave it at that. You have friends who feel as you do, and you were out with one or more of them. I don't think you had a particular destination in mind, and you wandered into a bad area, where you were accosted. Don't take offense—you were easy prey. And when you left, you were probably minus every cent you had in your wallets, and maybe a nice watch or some jewelry, as well."

His hand instantly went to his throat, though he wasn't wearing any kind of medallion. His lips tightened, and she could tell that she had hit on the truth.

"Jake, I want you to do a couple of things for me. First, we'll rule nothing out, okay? So I'm going to have you go to your primary-care physician and get a complete physical, all right?"

"Look, I'm fine. I just—"

"Then, because it would be good for you, you're going to see a nutritionist and start on an exercise program." Before he could start complaining, she added, "Jake, I know you're extremely intelligent and can slide right through all your schoolwork, and that part of the reason you don't care if you make it to class is that you're way ahead of most of the work going on. That may mean you need to skip ahead, or start adding some university classes onto your schedule. We have a long way to go to get to the root of your unhappiness."

"I'm not unhappy."

"You're not?"

He flushed again, looking down. "I just don't belong."

"Then we'll find out where you *do* belong. And where you want to go."

"Games," he said.

"What?"

"I'd like to design computer games. I think I could do it. I think I'd be good at it."

"I'll bet you would be," she assured him. "Next week, same time. And I'll give your parents a call to—"

"I thought you couldn't repeat anything I said here," he demanded angrily.

"I'm not going to repeat anything. I just want them to get you set up with the right professionals. Now, if you want to say anything else, if you think we haven't covered anything, we still have a few minutes," she told him.

She was startled when he stood and took a step that brought him right in front of her chair. His eyes were alight; he was tense, excited. "I heard you were there," he told her. "In Transylvania. I read about it in the paper. I heard you blew the whistle on the vampires, that you were the one who called the police."

Oh, God, this again!

But she didn't intend to be secretive and feed into his fantasies. She stared at him levelly.

"I met some students over there. One of them left me a note, and I passed it on to the police," she said.

She was startled again when he set his hands on the arms of the chair. Leaned down and looked deeply into her eyes. "Aren't you afraid? Afraid the vampires will come after you—for revenge?"

She stared straight back into his eyes and let out a weary sigh. "From what I heard, Jake, someone freaked out way before the police got there, and the party was already over. Am I afraid the vampires will come after me? No. Feel free to stay if you have something important to discuss, Jake, but if you're just trying to turn the tables here, forget it. Okay?" Her voice was calm and steady. Bored. He had expected to get a rise out of her, but she knew better than to let him.

He shrugged, pushing away from the chair. "Sure sounded like a hell of a party," he murmured.

"Yeah, great party. A girl is still in the hospital," Jessica said, making a mental note to drop by the hospital over the weekend. She had left Romania soon after the students' parents had arrived, but she knew from the newspaper that Mary had been brought home to a New Orleans hospital. The papers had turned the event into a decadent costume party and little more, but anything that mentioned vampires intrigued the public, and even the national papers had picked up the story.

When Jake was gone, she walked to the front desk. Since they were expecting a lodger, she'd sent Stacey home early. Now she pulled out her appointment book, curious to see what her schedule was for the following Monday. When she opened the book, she sat back thoughtfully.

Jeremy had made an appointment for himself.

Bryan MacAllistair felt he'd arrived at the perfect time in New Orleans—not just the season, but the time of day, as well—when he first stood in front of the old Montresse place.

The dead heat of the day was gone, and night was just coming on. It came softly, perhaps deceptively, to this area of the French Quarter, just beyond reach of the neon lights, the blare of the music and the laughter of inebriated tourists. Here, only the faint sounds of a distant waltz could be heard, or perhaps they were only imagined as shadows fell over leafy trees. The Montresse house stood back beyond a brick wall and iron gate, gently cradled by the darkness. The night was kind, he thought. There was no aura of decay about the place. The grounds were slightly overgrown, and looked as if the paint were threatening to peel but hadn't quite reached the point where it was willing to abandon the splendor of the facade.

He stared at the house for a while. Then he found the hinge on the wrought-iron gate and entered, following the stone path from the sidewalk to the porch. Montresse House was old, built when there was still space to be had in the French Quarter. There was a graceful lawn, dotted with flowers and trees that dripped lazily with moss. The porch was more reminiscent of an old plantation house rather than a city dwelling.

As he walked, he was aware that, above him, from a window on the second floor, a curtain had been pulled back.

His arrival was being watched.

With a shrug, he stepped up on the porch and reached for the heavy door knocker, but before he could touch it, the door swung open.

The woman standing there appeared to be in her early twenties. She had a pretty face and a cheerful smile.

"Hi."

"Hi," he returned.

"You're the professor the travel agency booked?" she asked.

"Yes, that's me. Bryan MacAllistair."

"Cool. Come on in."

He stepped inside, and the woman shut the door behind him.

"I'm Stacey LeCroix, Ms. Fraser's assistant. Welcome."

"Thanks. This place sounded like heaven," he said. "It's a beautiful house. Is Ms. Fraser from New Orleans? Has she owned the house forever?"

"Oh, no, Jessica's from…actually, I'm not sure where she's from originally, but she was practicing in Jacksonville before she came here. She'd been here for a few years before I started working for her. I know about the house, though—a friend had been keeping an eye open for her and called her when it came up on the market. But, you're absolutely right. It's beautiful. Come on. I'll show you around."

A sweeping staircase was the central focus of the foyer, and he could well imagine being swept back through the decades to a time when cotton was king and Southern belles had whisked along the hallways in elegant ballgowns. There were broad double doors to both the right and left, closed now.

"The ladies' parlor was to your left and the men's

smoking room to the right. Of course, we prohibit smoking in the house, though your room has access to the wraparound balcony, just in case."

"A cigar here and there," he told her, shrugging. Her expression clearly displayed what she thought of cigar smoke, but he refused to back down. "However, I prefer my cigars with good brandy, right time, right place," he told her reassuringly.

"Humph," she murmured. "Well, in the morning, the doors to the right are open and it's a lovely dining room. The original dining room is Ms. Fraser's office. The bedrooms are upstairs. If you lose your key or have any maintenance problems, there's a grounds-keeper's cottage just to the rear of the main house— you can reach it through the yard. Ms. Fraser and I both work but Gareth Miller, our handyman, is just about always around."

"No problem," Bryan said.

She set one foot on the first step of the stairway, and turned, an uncertain look on her face. "You're a professor, right?" she asked. He had the feeling that she was uncertain, and irritated with herself because of it.

"Yes, just as the booking agency promised."

She nodded, still frowning. "Of course. Um… sorry. Follow me."

Up the stairs and to the left, she opened the first door on the right side of the hallway. "I'm sure you'll be very comfortable," she assured him. "The bath was added soon after the turn of the last century. Deco fixtures," she said proudly. "We do charge a bit more than most, but…"

"Worth every cent," he assured her, and he meant it. The room was huge, and the bath was really something. The room itself offered a queen-size bed, the usual modern entertainment center, a period dresser with a contemporary coffeemaker and micro-wave, a nineteenth-century desk with a printer and fax machine, and an ample closet. French doors opened out to the wraparound balcony. He strode out, inhaling the rich scent of new-grown foliage, and noting the attractive garden and small pool below. The backyard wasn't vast, but it was big enough to offer the swimming pool—blessed relief in the dead heat of summer, he was certain—and a small patio and garden. And from back here, the street might as well have been a million miles away. The house was a treasure and, he surmised, worth a small fortune.

He turned. Stacey LeCroix was waiting just inside the room, watching him, still looking uncertain.

"It's perfect," he told her.

She smiled. "Yes, isn't it? Sorry, I must be a little tired today. I…never mind. Ok, what else? Maid service only if you're out of the room by twelve. We only have two women who come in, and they both have school-age children. If you don't find anyone in the dining room in the morning, you'll find a *petit déjeuner* set up on the patio. And you're welcome downstairs anytime, except in the office or our private apartments."

"Naturally," he agreed.

"So that's all you have? That backpack?" she asked him.

"For now," he said simply.

"Well, then…I hope you'll be comfortable."

She smiled a little awkwardly. "Oh, your key." She dug into her skirt pocket and produced a key. "It opens both the front door and your room, and please try not to lose it. We're not set up with computer cards, so it's the real key thing."

"I seldom lose things," he assured her.

"Glad to hear it." She stared at him for a moment longer, then left.

He closed the door behind her and walked to the balcony.

It was perfect.

He closed his eyes. If he listened, he could hear the faint sounds of the city. To the rear, all was tranquil. And yet, out there, New Orleans teemed with life.

Night was falling, darkness sweeping down…with a hint of red.

"Oh, my God!"

Jessica stood in the doorway, staring at her wide-eyed assistant as Stacey caught hold of her arm and pulled her back out to the front porch, closing the door behind her.

"Oh, my God what?" Jessica demanded, amused to see Stacey lose her cool.

"He's gorgeous."

"Who?" Jessica asked.

"The professor. Wait till you see him. I just...I had to warn you."

"Warn me? Why? Is he dangerous?"

"Of course not. I'd have never opened the door to someone who looked as if he'd..."

"As if he'd what?"

"Be dangerous. He just wasn't what I expected," Stacey assured her.

"I don't think it's a prerequisite to be ugly to be a professor," Jessica said, still amused. And she was glad to be amused, she realized. Nothing had seemed right since she'd returned from Romania. The sky continued to bother her. And even her sessions with kids like Jake seemed disturbing, even though she'd worked with plenty of kids before who had been acting out fantasies, looking for attention. Looking to belong.

"Fine, laugh at me," Stacey said a little indignantly. "Wait until you see him."

Jessica stepped past her, entering the house, setting down her purse and briefcase. Stacey followed, hovering near her. Jessica shook her head, laughing. "This isn't a big corporation," she whispered. "You're welcome to have a crush on a guest."

Stacey flushed. "Don't be silly. I'm seeing Bobby Munro, and I wouldn't have a crush on a guest, anyway. He's just…oh, you'll see."

"I'm sure I will." She still felt a smile twitching her lips as she turned and walked back to the entry table to leaf through the mail.

"Oh, hey," Stacey said, "Big Jim wants to know if you're up for a game of Trivial Pursuit."

"Tonight?"

It was Stacey's turn to laugh. "Hey, Friday night, wild excitement, you know."

"Ha, ha."

"It'll do you good to have some fun."

"Well, I mean, your trip turned out to be… eventful," Stacey said. "I only know what was in the papers, but it sounded pretty awful."

"My heart bleeds for those kids, but I'm fine. Don't go tiptoeing around my feelings. Thank you for your concern, but it's not necessary. I'm not obsessed with it, so don't you be, okay?" What a crock. It was all still there in her mind, no matter whom she was working with or what she was doing.

She turned. "Trivial Pursuit will be fine. I want to take a shower and chill out first, though. Will you call Big Jim back for me? Tell him about eight. We'll play here. Who else is coming?"

"Sure. I'll call him. And Bobby and I will be there, too."

"We should invite Gareth, as well. And there's always Barry Larson. You know, the keyboard player."

"The one with the crush on you?"

"That's taken care of. He knows I'm not interested."

"Sure," Stacey said. "Strange guy. It's like he wants so badly to belong. He wants to be invited over here all the time. Maybe he has a crush on the house, not you."

"Maybe. But you know what? I don't think I will call him. Just Gareth."

Stacey shook her head. "Gareth isn't just reclusive these days—he doesn't even seem to want to come in for a cup of coffee. I bet he won't come"

Jessica frowned. Gareth had always been shy. He had come with her when she bought the house, and she had been surprised he was willing to leave the small town outside Jacksonville where he had taken care of her house. But he was wonderful at keeping the place running, a true jack-of-all-trades, polite, and sincere in his gratitude for not only getting to live in the cottage, but receiving a generous pay-check. He was loyal to a fault, Jessica thought, and she was equally grateful to have him.

Stacey grinned and looked up the stairs. "Maybe *he'll* come down and play. He's a professor—maybe he can beat you."

"Maybe he can. Or maybe he just wants to be left alone. I'm going to run up and shower."

"I'm going to call the Italian place and order in."

"Go for it."

Stacey headed for the office, and Jessica started upstairs. It was getting dark way too early. The time hadn't changed yet, though it would soon. Still, the last nights had seemed…

Dark. Dark, and far too…red.

Get a life, she told herself.

And a soft voice added, *A real one.*

She didn't head straight into her long, hot shower. She stayed out on the balcony, watching the evening come on with a strange, whispering, red malice. Ever since Romania…

She bit her lip, glad she would be seeing Jeremy again on Monday, but dreading the day, as well. It seemed to be gathering again….

What "it?" she demanded irritably of herself.

It.

The evil that had walked in that distant country, that seemed to come with the night and fill the air, whispering all around her, touching her….

She turned abruptly, certain someone else was on the balcony.

But she was alone. Had a door just closed? Had their guest been out there, watching her, as she had watched the night? She squared her shoulders. She was no easily intimidated child.

She could handle whatever came her way.

She wouldn't give way to whispers on the breeze that seemed to touch her with fingers of ice.

"A life," she said softly out loud.

Determined, she walked inside. No shower tonight. A bath. As hot as she could take it, long and sudsy and relaxing. And if she still had that old brandy decanter in her room somewhere, she would sip while she soaked.

She wouldn't think about what had happened.

Yes, she would.

Because she was obsessed.

"I think I want this man on my team all the time!" Stacey exclaimed.

"What can I say? I know my European history," Bryan said with a shrug. He had been wondering how to get to know both women better when Stacey had surprised him with a knock on his door and an invitation to play Trivial Pursuit.

The owner of the house, however, had yet to make it downstairs. But they had decided to play a few practice rounds, so he had pinched up with Stacey, while her boyfriend, a cop named Bobby, had teamed up with the massive sax player.

Big Jim gave a deep, rich laugh. "You do seem to be something of a walking encyclopedia, MacAllistair."

He offered the sax player a rueful smile. "Occupational hazard," he explained. He had liked the other man from the moment he met him. There was a serenity about him that seemed to come from wisdom rather than simply from knowledge. He had the ability to make a stranger feel as if they had been friends for life. Bryan thought he would be good to have around in an emergency.

"You're no slouch yourself," Bryan commented.

Big Jim's smile was vast. "I do all right." He laughed again. "Maybe, when the nights are too quiet, I just study all the cards and learn all the answers."

"Do you?" Stacey gasped.

Big Jim's deep laughter boomed again. "No, but maybe I should start."

"He comes from a long line of voodoo priestesses," Stacey said, as if that explained something about the man's abilities.

"Yeah, and I just come from a long line of cops," Bobby said with a sigh.

"But you have all the sports stuff down," Stacey said, patting his hand.

"Yeah, I've got all the answers," Bobby said, and rolled his eyes. "That's why you ditched me for the professor."

"Yes, and I'm sticking with him," Stacey said firmly.

"You're giving up on me?" a new voice, feminine, rich and melodic, chimed in.

Bryan turned to see who had spoken, and it was as if he had been struck by lightning.

She was a beautiful woman, but then again, the world was filled with beautiful women. She was about five six, slender but curved, with golden-blond hair that swept sensually down her back, and deep blue eyes. It wasn't just her appearance that was arresting; it was the way she moved, her casual ease.

It was the fact that she seemed to touch a distant, forgotten chord in his soul, the fact that she was so very much like...

Someone long gone. Someone who should have been entirely erased from his mind by time gone by. He had met women before who had touched a core of memory in him. Something about them the same, the way they looked, spoke, moved.

But nothing like this. Never like this.

He stood, ready to introduce himself.

"Hey, you made it down at last," Stacey said.

"Yeah, sorry, the hot-bath thing was more seductive than I'd imagined," Jessica Fraser mumbled, coming into the room.

Then she saw him.

She stopped. And stared.

"You two haven't met yet," Stacey said. She was clearly amused, enjoying her friend's hastily concealed reaction to him. There was an *I told you so* smirk on her face.

"Hi," Jessica murmured, stepping forward with a welcoming smile and extending a hand. "Welcome to the Montresse House. I must say, you don't look like…well, what I had imagined." She blushed, then added, "Sorry."

He took her hand. The feeling of being touched by lightning, shot through by a bolt of fire, hit him again. He stared back at her, forcing a casual smile and an apologetic shrug. "No apology necessary."

Jessica nodded and chose a chair at the other end of the table.

Big Jim smiled at her. "We've been practicing, getting into the groove while we waited," he said. "We can start for real now. I'll have you and Bobby."

"Three against two," Jessica said.

"Gareth turned us down," Stacey commented. "But that's okay. I've got the professor."

"Feeling confident, aren't you?" Jessica asked Stacey, but she was staring at Bryan, and he knew he was staring back.

There was something about her….

He shrugged and leaned back.

"Let the game begin," he said softly.

5

With Big Jim and Bobby gone home and their one lodger safely out of the way upstairs, Stacey closed the kitchen door, staring at Jessica, who was rinsing dishes at the sink before putting them in the dishwasher.

Jessica arched a brow.

Stacey burst into laughter.

"What?" Jessica demanded.

"And you were making fun of me."

"What does that mean?" Jessica asked.

"I was about to suggest that the two of you get a room," Stacey teased.

Jessica shook her head. "Stacey, I was at the other end of the table all night."

"Yes. And it was like an electrical storm was going on over the board. It was cool, and, hey—we won."

"And I'm so glad."

"No, you're not. You were dying to beat him."

"Stacey, it was a game."

"Yes, but I could see it in your eyes. He's a challenge to you. He interests you. I know you checked out his credentials."

"Yes, I did. I called the university. He's new there this semester, and they're thrilled to have him. He lectures all over the world. We should go hear him sometime. I wonder what his schedule's like."

"You didn't ask him?"

Jessica flushed. "Of course not."

Stacey laughed. "Fine. *I'll* ask him tomorrow. There's some excitement for you. An academic lecture. Except…I bet his lectures *are* exciting."

The two women finished cleaning up in silence, then headed upstairs.

At the landing, Jessica said good night, heading for her own room. She was aware of Stacey watching her until she closed and locked her door.

Inside, she hesitated, then walked out to the balcony. The nicest guest quarters were next to her own, and she was all too aware that *he* was there.

The French doors of his balcony were closed, the curtains drawn. The room was dark.

She looked at the sky.

There was still that flush of red that deepened the darkness of the night. A cool breeze swept by her. She sighed, closing her eyes, feeling the chill.

Yes, it was coming….

And he…

What did he have to do with it, if anything?

She walked back into her bedroom. As she lay down, she realized he made her think of the past, of a time when she had believed in life and love and commitment, a fight for right and all good things. When she had been young, she'd been such an idealist. And so naive.

She punched her pillow. Good Lord, that was ages ago.

Still, as she lay there, she was bizarrely disturbed by his nearness. He lay just beyond the wall. It almost seemed she could hear his heartbeat, feel the pulse of his vitality, as if he were nearer still.

She adjusted her pillow again. It didn't help. Sleep was a long time coming.

He watched.

From the shadows, from the darkness below, he watched

Anger and hatred raged through him as he cast his head back, relishing the feeling of power growing in him.

He'd waited so long.

Vengeance had been long in coming, but time, as they said, made it sweeter. All the charades, all the deceptions, revealed at last. And now, in an arena of pain and torture, it would all be over. Foolish creatures, so armored in righteousness. They did not see the truth blinded as they were by their own ignorance.

He moved, a shadow himself, a shadow that flowed like blood, and neared the house. How easy it would be to end it all now....

The temptation to move closer and prove that statement true filled him. He embodied the power of the ages, the greatest power ever known.

His will was far greater than their pathetic belief in themselves, he was certain.

And yet...

Rage exploded in him as he tried to enter the house. It was a bastion, fully secured against him. A complete bastion. In his raw fury, he attempted entry again and again, but it was fruitless.

He forced himself to remember that soon enough, he would walk right in. Soon enough, the invitation would come. He had taken care to grow close to one who was close to her, and he didn't need to be angry, he just needed to be patient. The time wasn't right, not quite yet. He had been very patient thus far, beginning his quest in distant places, knowing that soon enough, she would arrive, knowing that through the subtlety of his actions it would slowly dawn on her that she was being targeted, that he was touching those with a connection to her, no matter how slight. And she would begin to wonder....

Soon.

Soon enough, the last mocking lure would be cast,

havoc would reign, and then…in his realm, on a ground of his choosing…the end would come.

Bryan awoke with a jolt. Something disturbing had shattered his sleep, just as surely as a fire alarm clanging in the night.

He rose instantly and threw on a robe. He stepped onto the balcony but saw nothing that could have disturbed him so deeply. The window of the room next to his was open, the breeze blowing the curtains back so he could look inside Jessica's room. She was asleep, blond hair like a gleaming halo against the bedding, features as perfect as if they had been sculpted by Michelangelo. Excitement like lightning ripped through him, and he shook his head. He'd never seen anyone more angelic.

Nothing, he was certain, haunted her room.

He forced himself to retreat, back to his room, into the hallway, down the stairs. Nothing. Nothing at all.

He stepped out the back door.

The scent of something rotten filled the air. But was it real, or was he imagining it? Was he creating something wrong where nothing was amiss?

No.

There was just a hint, a whiff, of something lingering in the air like the remnants of a fire, long doused, but still not dissipated.

He approached the caretaker's cottage and looked through a window. He saw only the form of a man, sleeping soundly.

He returned to the house and up the stairs. Before retreating to his bed, he stepped onto the balcony and peered into her room again.

She slept. Again he thought of an angel. It was the color of her hair, the play of light and shadow, he thought.

She possessed not only beauty but vulnerability, evoking every protective instinct within his body.

He was tempted, beyond sanity and reason, to go to her.

In her sleep, a frown suddenly creased her brow; she tossed and turned. The temptation to go to her grew to sweeping proportions. He longed to ease whatever so furrowed her brow, to sweep her up, hold her safe against…

Against all evil.

The frown faded; she seemed to sleep in peace again.

He mentally gave himself a shake.

He had only met her that night, he reminded himself irritably. He hadn't come here to succumb to a sudden, startling—even overwhelming—attraction.

He was a professor; a scholar. A man who studied ancient fears and superstitions, human belief in an intangible battle between good and evil, older than time.

He had come for whatever it was that had created the fading miasma in the night.

He had followed it here.

He gritted his teeth. If it *was* here. If only there were something real and concrete, something palpable, some proof....

He forced himself to turn away and return to his room.

He had the sense that whatever had awakened him was only the beginning.

Dreams haunted her. Strange dreams of a different time and place.

In the bowels of a castle, she moved, certain of what she would find. And they were there, just as she had suspected, as she had known. They wore the elegant trappings that were a part of their lives; sweeping gowns of jeweled satin and velvet.

But the finery tonight was black.

Some wore masks, hiding their identities even from those who consorted with them.

Some played as if at a game, seeking love potions, powers to divert their enemies, strength to rise in life, to acquire greater riches.

The potions were often poison, and the game was deadly, for there were those who had died, those who would die in future. It had not been easy to find the root of these goings-on, for those who acted in this theater of the bizarre protected their sources.

That night, there was an altar. The game being played had nothing to do with the old pagan beliefs in the power of the earth and sky, the gods and goddesses of water or the harvest. The woman leading the pageant was referred to as a witch, but what she practiced was pure Satanism.

There was a babe on the altar, drugged into silence. As the witch murmured over it and cried out that she offered the greatest sacrifice to her dark lord, an alarm sounded.

It began with a clang of steel. The king's armed men had discovered the lair.

Those who had bowed down before the rite of darkness screamed and tried to flee, not so easy a task, for in their secret catacomb, they had set themselves up to be trapped. She backed away, hiding, watching....

Blood was spilled. There was a melee, a cacophony of shrieks, shouts, warnings, the sound of steel against steel.

There was the innocent babe, now screaming and crying upon the altar.

Did she dare?

Her discovery of this place deep in the earth, beneath ancient stone, had been perfect for all she needed. Perfect for escape.

But the child. She had not counted on the child!

There was no choice.

She ran toward the child, held it in her arms....

The nightmare scene that played out behind her eyes caused Jessica to twist and turn, to fight to awaken. The vision began to fade...

Then returned.

But now she was on horseback, racing across the country.

Her pursuers followed. It was as she had intended; it was what she had known she must do. And still...

What had come before had been worse. Far worse. And what she had done before had cast her into far greater danger.

"Die!" someone screamed from behind her.

No! She awoke completely, bolting up into a sitting position.

Jessica looked around, shaking. She rose, held still for a minute, listening. What had caused such a torment to come to her in the night, a horrible dream so real that it had seemed as if she could have reached out and touched the people in it?

The house was quiet.

She walked out on the balcony, deeply disturbed.

The sky remained red. Tense, she waited. And waited.

But there was nothing. Still, she felt as if something had been there....

At last she returned to her bed, where she lay

awake a long time. It was her lodger, she thought, suddenly irritated. The man talked about history as if he had been there. It was all his is fault. He had sent her dreams skidding back bizarrely in time.

He should have been a football player, not a scholar, she thought. A quarterback, calling the shots and knocking other players out of his way as he raced down the field to make the touchdown himself.

She groaned aloud.

He was right next door, such a short distance away. She closed her eyes, and she didn't dream, but in her mind's eye she saw herself simply walking out her door, opening his, rousing him from sleep.

Talk about nightmares. She groaned and buried her face in her pillow.

Bryan came down so early that he thought he would have to wander the streets to find coffee, but he found the kitchen already occupied and in full swing. Stacey was standing by the coffeemaker, waiting with her cup in hand. There was a man sitting on one of the stools by the center butcher-block table, reading the paper; he was almost skeletally thin, but he had a wiry strength. His face was weathered and brown, his hair a bit shaggy. He wore jeans and a T-shirt and looked up, an expression of alarm on his face, as Bryan walked in.

"Hello," Bryan said, casually stepping forward and offering a hand. "Bryan MacAllistair."

"Uh…" The man looked at Stacey, as if seeking her help, then turned to Bryan. "Hello. I'm Gareth."

Nodding, Bryan released the man's hand. He knew the other man was still watching him suspiciously as he walked over to the counter, helped himself to a mug and greeted Stacey. "Good morning. I wasn't actually expecting to find anyone up."

"Gareth and I are early birds. Jessica only wakes early on demand," she said lightly. "Ah, coffee's done." She picked up the pot and offered it to him.

"You first. We academics are good at pouring our own coffee."

She flushed slightly. "You're our only lodger at the moment. I can whip up breakfast whenever you want. Actually, I can whip up *whatever* you want."

"Now there's an invitation. Actually, I thought I'd take a walk—it's not often you get the streets to yourself here. And you don't have to hang around waiting to cook for me if you've got things to do."

"I'm just going to be hanging around the house for a while. Not a problem."

"Thanks, but don't worry about me." He finished his coffee and set down his cup. "That was great. The best I've had in New Orleans. Gareth, nice to meet you. I'll see you both later."

He knew they both watched him go.

And he knew they started talking about him the minute he was gone.

It was late afternoon by the time Jessica rose and got going for the day. Still, it disturbed her to notice how dark the sky had become by the time she reached the hospital. And that shade of red.

In the hospital parking lot, she just stood looking up for a moment and found herself growing angry with herself. Staring at the sky changed nothing.

She strode to the reception desk and asked for Mary's room. A friendly nurse gave her directions, and after buying a fresh bouquet of flowers in a pink vase, she made her way to the proper section of the hospital. She saw that Jeremy was there, head bowed, sprawled in a chair across from the foot of the bed. He had obviously been keeping watch for a long time. His exhaustion was evident.

"Hey," Jessica said softly.

He started and looked up. A smile crossed his weary features. "Hey."

"How's she doing?" Jessica asked.

He shook his head. "No change. But I think her color is a little bit better. Her dad just made her mom leave for a while. She opens her eyes sometimes. She's breathing. She doesn't talk, doesn't seem to hear…and doesn't react when someone touches her. I don't think she feels anything."

"Well," Jessica murmured, setting her vase of flowers on the bedside table and studying the girl. She looked like a fairy princess, doomed to sleep for a hundred years, beautiful, silent, pale. "What do the doctors say?" she asked Jeremy.

He shrugged, then indicated the IV. "She was scratched up some…I guess we all were, after that night. But they keep giving her blood. Her counts are all off, and they can't figure out why."

"How are her folks doing?"

"Better." Jeremy said. "Her brother and her two sisters come with her mom, and that seems to help keep her calm. Her father keeps everything low key." He looked directly at Jessica at last and offered a rueful smile. "No one believes me."

"About what?"

He laughed hollowly. "She was bitten by a vampire. A real one. Not some doped-out kid who thinks he's a vampire."

Jessica made a pretense of straightening Mary's covers, carefully moving the girl's head as she did so.

"You don't have to hide what you're doing from me," Jeremy said with a sigh. "There are puncture marks on her neck. The doctors insist they're stab wounds from the thorn bushes around the castle."

"I see," Jessica murmured.

And she did. There *were* puncture marks on Mary's neck.

"And she doesn't talk?" Jessica asked.

"Not yet, not that I know of."

"And what do the doctors say about that?"

"Shock."

Jessica straightened the girl's hair and saw a silver cross around her neck.

She took a seat beside Jeremy, reached over and squeezed his hand. "I saw you made an appointment with me."

He nodded. Then he looked at her, and a dry and weary grin twisted his mouth. "You may not believe me, but you'll listen to me. And if I talk to you and go over the entire story once again, maybe something—somewhere, somehow—will make sense to me."

"I'm very happy to see you, you know that."

"What if she dies?" he demanded suddenly, his voice a whisper.

And there was something more than just the dreaded pain for the loss of a friend that lurked behind the anguish in his question.

"Let's not think that way," Jessica said.

"I can't help it," he murmured.

She hesitated. "Jeremy, you haven't been contacted by anyone who had anything to do with the party at the castle, have you?"

He stared at her, confused. "Contacted? Hell, no. I wasn't the one who got the invitation in the first place. Mary got it from some girl on the street. Why?"

"No reason. I'm just hoping you can put everything that happened behind you. What about Nancy? Have you seen her? How is she?"

"All right. She's doing all right," Jeremy said, his eyes falling dully on Mary again. "She comes in and sits with Mary sometimes." He shook his head. "You don't understand. Mary could be…well, she could be careless of other people sometimes, but not out of malice. She just loved life. She wanted everything. She wanted to make a mark, I guess you'd say," he finished lamely. "But she wasn't mean. She wasn't…wasn't evil."

"No one's suggested that she is," Jessica said firmly.

"I'm so afraid." Jeremy said softly.

"Jeremy, you've got to believe the best will happen. If we spend our lives expecting the worst, we only add to our own anguish. As things happen, we deal with them. So let's believe in Mary right now. Let's give her a chance to get better."

Was she a liar? She asked herself. No. There was a chance.

Except that…

She found herself looking over her own shoulder. Far too often now, she had the feeling there was someone behind her. Someone…whispering her name.

"Jessica?"

When her name *was* actually spoken softly from the doorway, she nearly jumped from her seat.

But the speaker was real, and she knew the voice. Her eyes flew to the doorway, and she rose, surprised, but pleasantly so. Big Jim and Barry Larson were in the doorway.

"What are you two doing here?" she whispered.

"We play for the kids in the wards sometimes in the afternoons," Big Jim said. "Thought you knew that."

"You've probably mentioned it," she said.

"How's the girl?" Barry asked, concerned.

"She seems to be holding her own.

"Glad to hear it," Big Jim said, and nodded.

By then Jeremy had risen. He walked to the door, mouth tight. "Mary shouldn't be disturbed," he said, obviously not about to trust any visitors he didn't know.

"These are friends of mine, Jim and Barry. Musicians. They come to the hospital to play for the kids," she explained.

"Good to meet you," Jeremy said. "But she shouldn't be disturbed."

"We were just checking in," Big Jim said. "You come see us sometime, son."

Jeremy thanked him stiffly and waited pointedly for them to leave. As soon as they did, he resumed his seat.

Jessica did the same.

He reached for her hand, and she squeezed his in return.

Mary looked better. She should make it just fine. Or was she telling herself a pack of lies?

Sean Canady stared at his visitor, his years on the force allowing him to maintain a totally impassive expression, despite his surprise.

Admittedly, he'd expected some skinny guy with glasses who looked like he never left the university library, and he hadn't relished the job of talking to the man, even if the order had come straight down from the mayor's office.

Instead, the man sitting across from him wasn't huge, but he was still big; and he had...presence. The Indiana Jones type, Sean decided.

Had there been any recent rumors about vampire cults or activity? He wanted to know.

Hell, this was New Orleans. There were always rumors.

And that was exactly what he said. He stared at his visitor and indicated his computer. "If we spent the entire day here, I couldn't show you every report regarding some kook who thought he was a vampire, a 'vampire party' that had gone haywire, weird rites in a cemetery, or a drunk who bit another drunk on the street."

"I know," Bryan MacAllistair said, offering a rueful grin. "I know."

Sean glanced down at the notes on his desk, then

looked once again at the man before him. "So you were in Romania for that recent trouble?" Sean was careful when he spoke. He knew so much about the underworld. Information that, for the sake of his job and his family life, he was careful not to share too often.

"I was in Romania giving a series of lectures when the trouble occurred," MacAllistair corrected him. "I'd heard a few rumors in the street and mentioned the situation to the police. If they'd taken the matter a little more seriously…." He shrugged. "Who knows? Apparently whoever was behind the trouble got away."

"But no one was killed?" Sean asked. Then he leaned back, shaking his head. "I guess the girl in the hospital…well, I've heard she might not make it. The doctors can't find a reason, but she seems to be slipping away." He shook his head, tired. "I know kids from here were there," he said, "but no crime took place here, and there must have been people from all over the world at that party. I'm not sure why you think something might happen in New Orleans."

The sky, he thought, unbidden. Even Maggie had mentioned the sky.

"I'm not saying anything is going to happen here," MacAllistair told him. "It's just that three kids from here were involved in the mess. And there's often trouble in places that celebrate some of the grislier aspects of history, or where you tend to get people who think they're vampires or whatever. A young woman was found dead in Edinburgh after an illegal party in the vaults beneath the city. They do ghost tours there the same way they do here, and the vaults are supposed to be haunted. Paris, three months ago, after an illegal party in the catacombs several people were found dead—beheaded. In Italy, a party in an old castle left four dead. From what the police in each city gathered, the victims were sucked in by thinking they were going to a wild, sensual, ever so slightly illicit vampire-themed party."

"Has an international task force been set up?" Sean asked.

MacAllistair shook his head in disgust. "Most of the authorities seem to think it's a sign of the times, that there's no connection from one party to another. I can't really blame them, not completely. The whole vampire thing makes it pretty far-fetched."

Sean glanced at his notes again. "You warned the police in both Edinburgh and Paris?"

MacAllistair nodded.

"A suspicious man might think these parties are following you around," Sean said, eyes hard.

Bryan reached into the briefcase on the floor beside him and produced a folder full of newspaper clippings. "The first is about a small town in Switzerland where five people went missing. The accepted theory is that they disappeared skiing, but the bodies were never found. And there was a party there that weekend."

Sean looked up sharply. "I take it you weren't in Switzerland."

"No, I wasn't."

Sean studied the man.

"Were you ever a cop?" he asked, following a hunch.

For the first time, Bryan hesitated. Then he shrugged. "Officially a police officer? No. I've just aided a lot of investigations because of my expertise."

"In vampires?" Sean asked skeptically.

"In old legends, ancient societies, that kind of thing."

Sean eased back in his chair. "Do you believe in vampires, Mr. MacAllistair?"

If the man thought he was being baited, he took no offense. "I believe there's evil out there, that's for certain. I believe there are people who believe they're vampires or the Devil's disciples or what have you. And here's one of my important beliefs—some of these people have money. They can pay for whatever debauchery or fantasy they want. They can travel around the globe. They can get the word out. They can pay for all the right stuff to pull in the unwary. That's one of the reasons I stopped by today, hoping I could at least warn you that if you hear about promoters pushing something that's a little hush-hush, you'll be on the lookout."

Sean nodded. "Right. Well, if you discover you *know* anything about anything going on here, I'm sure you'll be right back in."

It wasn't a question; it was a command.

Red skies at night...

MacAllistair stared straight back at him, bemused. He seemed like a man who held his temper, who knew how to show respect—and demand it in return as well. "I'll be in now and then. And I'm sure, if you decide you need my help, you'll let me know immediately."

Sean felt a grin twisting his lips. He liked the guy.

"I've got a cell number here for you, compliments of the mayor's office. Where are you staying in New Orleans?"

"At Montresse House."

Sean couldn't help it; his eyebrows shot up. "With Jessica?"

"You know my hostess?" MacAllistair was clearly surprised.

Sean nodded carefully. "Yes, she's a friend."

"Are you from here, Detective?"

"I am."

"But Jessica Fraser isn't."

"No, we were introduced by mutual friends."

Sean didn't know why he had offered that much information; he didn't owe this man any explanations.

He felt a warning chill at the back of his neck, like hackles rising. He was as suspicious as all hell, and yet...

He still liked the guy. He hesitated and let out a sigh. "I'll take help in any form that I can get it. We were devastated by the storms, you know. This place was like a war zone. I love this city, and there are areas where it will be years before things get back to anything like normal. We don't need anything to set us back further. Don't worry. If I think you can help, if I think I have information that can help you to help me, you can bet I'll call you. This is a tough town to know the simply bizarre from the bizarre and dangerous. So when will you be lecturing, Professor?" Sean asked, consciously changing the subject.

MacAllistair looked at his watch. "Actually, in about three hours. You're more than welcome to attend. It's in the main auditorium at seven."

With a wave, he rose and left. Sean watched him go, then kept staring at the door, deep in thought.

"Hey, Lieutenant?"

He started. Bobby Munro was standing in the doorway.

"Yeah, Bobby. What is it?"

"I've got those McCardle case files you asked for."

"Oh, yeah. Thanks."

"Why was the professor here? The guy who just left."

"You know him?"

"Yeah. I met him over at Montresse House the other night. What, he thinks he's a cop or something, just because he's smart?"

"He thinks we may have some cult activity around here. You know, wackos who think they're vampires."

Bobby laughed. "Oh, like that would be weird—in New Orleans."

Sean smiled. "You have a point. Anyway, let me see the records, and thanks. I think McCardle is at it again. I think the woman we found dead in a Dumpster last week was one of his victims. I want to be ready when we go to the D.A. with this."

"Right, Lieutenant."

Bobby left. Sean stared at the files until his eyes swam. McCardle was dangerous. A big-time dealer. He needed to be in prison. Beyond a doubt, the man was evil.

Yeah, but he was an evil Sean could do something about. He knew he would get the perp locked away for good. *Knew it.*

But the kind of evil MacAllistair was talking about…

He swore, wishing to hell the man had never walked into his office.

6

Jessica had barely left, but it had seemed to Jeremy that he had been exhausted forever. He felt himself drifting off, then started, a sense of panic filling him as he realized he was not alone with Mary. There was a man in the room.

The man turned toward him, and Jeremy let out a breath of relief and stood. It was the professor, Bryan MacAllistair. He'd heard the guy was teaching in New Orleans, and any other time, he would have been at every lecture.

He'd heard him speak in Transylvania and been impressed. He'd even talked to him briefly before...before the night of evil, as he thought of it now.

And he knew that MacAllistair had talked to the police; during his own final interview with Florenscu, just before he'd headed home, the Romanian detective had been far more willing to listen. The policeman had never believed in real vampires, but something MacAllistair had said to him had made him pay more attention to Jeremy's assertions.

"Professor. Or doctor. What should I call you?"

"How about Bryan?" the man suggested, greeting Jeremy with a firm handshake.

"How are you doing?" Bryan asked him.

"Okay," Jeremy said. What a crock. He wasn't okay. He was going crazy.

"And Mary?"

"I'm feeling pretty good about her today," Jeremy said. "The doctor said earlier that her blood levels were stabilizing."

"Good."

Bryan walked over to the bed, touching Mary's forehead. Did he—like Jessica—move her hair around to get a good look at her neck?

"You stay here all the time?" Bryan asked.

"Mostly. Her folks come, and so do Nancy and some of the other kids. I don't know why, but I never leave her alone," Jeremy said.

"Because you're a good friend to her, that's why," Bryan said softly. Jeremy nodded and smiled, lowering his head and blushing a little. "I try to be."

"I'm going to stop by the nurses' station, but I'll be back." Jeremy was surprised by the way, despite his words, the professor stood by Mary's bed, looking deeply concerned.

"What is it?"

"There were some real crazies in Transylvania. I think you could use some help. I'll spell you later. I have to give a lecture tonight, but you need a little time away, too, so I'll come back after."

"That would be great," Jeremy said.

MacAllistair started to leave, then hesitated. "Hey, Jeremy."

"Yeah?"

"Has anyone been around who...well, who seems a bit strange?"

"Strange?"

"Anyone you feel...doesn't belong."

Jeremy frowned, but he gave the question careful thought. At last, he shook his head. "No. Not that I can think of. Hospital people. Family. Friends." He hesitated. "Why? Have you seen someone who seems strange?"

"I'm not sure," MacAllistair said. "Last night... never mind. I'm honestly not sure." MacAllistair glanced at his watch and swore softly. "I need to get going, but I'll be back. You take care. And if I can help, let me know."

"You bet."

MacAllistair left, and Jeremy sat down again.

Strange people?

In a way, Professor MacAllistair was strange, what with his questions and weird knowledge. Still, Jeremy liked him. Trusted him. Maybe he shouldn't.

He was more disturbed now than he had been before the man's visit. He felt the need to stay awake, to figure it all out.

He was just so damned tired.

It was impossible not to doze off....

He blinked, trying to stay awake, but his chin fell to his chest. His eyes closed.

He tried hard not to sleep, because sleep brought dreams.

No.

Nightmares.

But even knowing they would come, he couldn't help himself.

He began to doze, a strange red mist entering his mind.

Darkness again.

Red darkness.

As she walked through the parking lot, Jessica felt irritated. She normally loved the night, loved the darkness and the strange shadows the clouds made in the sky. But it felt far too early to be so dark. And the color...

Impatiently, she strode forward, anxious to reach her car. She didn't like the way she was feeling, though, and she made a mental note to ask Sean if they could get an officer to watch over Mary. She hadn't imagined the girl would be in danger here, but...

Why not? With such a red sky, with a feeling of evil haunting her constantly now.

She was deep in thought, paying no attention to her surroundings. As she reached her car door, there was a flurry of action.

There was a split second when panic seized her. There had been so many times lately when she had been certain she was being followed. *Stalked*.

Times when she had felt darkness and shadows and the deep red, fetid breath of evil.

She knew instantly that this was something else when she felt metal against her back even as she heard the words "Drop the keys and your purse. And stand still. Be good, and we'll let you live."

Despite the warning, perhaps because she felt so on edge, she turned angrily to face them.

Her impatience worked. The man who had pressed the blade against her ribs backed away a step, next to his buddy.

She stared at them in disbelief. They were in black jeans and shirts—and capes. The one with the knife was gaping in shock at her boldness.

He had vampire teeth. Fake ones. *Bad* fake ones.

"Stupid bitch!" he said, glancing at his friend, and Jessica knew he was thinking that she'd seen their faces. A strange discomfort settled over her then, and she frowned. There was something oddly familiar about him, though she couldn't place him. He had long, greasy dark hair and more than five o'clock shadow, though his facial hair couldn't be described as an actual beard.

"Too bad," the second attacker said softly. "She's a pretty one."

Jessica inhaled, trying for calm. The teeth were fake, but the blade was plenty real.

"You're going to give vampires everywhere a bad name," she said dryly.

"We are what we are, we do what we have to do," the first one said.

"Oh, please," Jessica protested.

"Shut up. Just shut up," the second one said. He was lighter, and nowhere near as hairy. "We need your purse and just a taste of blood, lady. But if you don't shut up…well, things could get really nasty."

"Look, please. Right now you can drop the knife and walk away. Just walk away. Think about what you really are, who you really are, and save yourselves from a life in prison. Or worse," Jessica said softly. "If you leave now, I won't even report you to the police."

"What?" the first one said. He stepped closer to her. "You don't understand. Can't you feel it? Our time is coming. We will rule."

"You're never going to rule anything." she said firmly.

The second boy suddenly gasped. "She's that psychologist! I saw her picture in the paper. And you—remember, you—"

The one who had first accosted her looked uneasy. "Let's go," he said.

"Not on your life. She owes us some blood. A lot of blood." He grabbed the knife from his friend and pressed his body against her, the knife raised threateningly. Jessica controlled herself, remaining dead still. "You can still walk away," she whispered.

Before he had a chance to respond, he was suddenly ripped away from her, violently and in a flash. First he was there, and then he wasn't—he was sailing across the parking lot as if he'd been tossed by a giant. She gaped in shock, unable even to scream.

The attacker crashed hard into a car and slid down to the pavement.

The second boy, like Jessica, just stood there gaping.

Then she saw the source of her salvation. To her amazement, it was none other than Bryan MacAllistair. He was just straightening the sleeves on his tweed jacket.

The remaining attacker reached beneath his cape, producing another blade—a very respectable bowie knife. Jessica almost cried out, certain that MacAllistair couldn't respond fast enough to save her.

Casually, but with a look of annoyance, he shot a

hand out, his fingers forming a vise around the boy's wrist, causing him to scream in pain. The knife dropped to the pavement.

"Call the cops, Jessica, please," MacAllistair said.

"I think you've handled the situation—"

"Call the cops."

She fumbled in her purse for her phone and dialed 911. The second would-be vampire wasn't concerned about his buddy on the ground. He started to back away, ready to turn and run. Jessica barely saw MacAllistair's arm shoot out, nabbing him by the back of the cape. He pulled him close, whispering into his ear, "Sit down, hands behind your head, and keep them that way until the cops show, or I'll break every bone in your body. One warning, and that's it."

The boy scrambled to do as he was told. MacAllistair stared at Jessica. "Are you all right?"

She nodded.

"Sure? You're not going to pass out or anything, are you?"

She knew she should be grateful he had shown up. But there was something so condescending, so patronizing, in his voice that she couldn't help a flare of temper.

"I'm fine. I never pass out, and I could have handled the situation on my own."

His brows drew together in a deep, surprised frown.

"You were going to talk your way out of this?"

"I was handling the situation," she repeated.

The sound of sirens split the air. As she stared at him, they heard the screech of tires and then the pounding of footsteps. Officers rushed up, weapons drawn.

"Here's one," MacAllistair announced. "The other one is by that car. They attacked this lady."

A man in uniform approached Jessica. "Are you hurt?"

"No. I'm absolutely fine, thank you."

"And you, sir?"

"Fine," MacAllistair said, his eyes still on Jessica.

And there they remained while the officers cuffed the toughs, asking Jessica and MacAllistair if they could come to the station to give statements. Another car drove up then, an unmarked police vehicle. Sean Canady stepped out with an air of authority, staring at the scene, looking sharply at Jessica.

"What happened?" he asked, running his fingers through his ink-dark hair.

"Two kids with knives," she said wearily.

Sean glanced sharply at MacAllistair. "Strange to see you here."

MacAllistair shrugged. "It's not strange at all. I came to check on the girl who got hurt in Romania."

Jessica's eyes widened. "Mary?"

"Yes."

"Why?" she demanded.

"That can wait. I need to know what happened here," Sean said, staring them down very effectively.

"I was attacked," Jessica explained. "Mr. MacAllistair happened to walk up at just the right moment."

Sean stared at Bryan MacAllistair. "Convenient," he murmured.

MacAllistair shrugged. "You know my interest in Mary. I had a few hours before my lecture. I thought I'd stop by and ask about her condition. Convenient? I suppose it was, though apparently my help wasn't necessary. It seems that Jessica intended to talk her way out of the situation." He glared at her sternly. "And let them go."

"What?" Sean demanded.

"Why are you working on a Saturday?" Jessica asked him, ignoring his question.

"Long story, and never mind. You were going to let the guys go?"

"I was hoping this was a stupid stunt, and they didn't need to have a criminal record," Jessica explained. She sighed. "Okay, sorry. I was wrong."

She looked past Sean, realizing suddenly just how stupid it would have been to let them go. It had been the very cheap vampire teeth, she decided, that had kept her from taking them seriously. She felt a chill. They might have gone on to really hurt someone else.

"Sean," she said suddenly and softly, not wanting Bryan MacAllistair to hear her. "Make sure...I need to know their names, their addresses, all that."

"Jessica, they're being arrested." Sean said. "We'll get all that. And you have to come in, too, because you're the victim."

"I'm not a victim."

"You were the attempted victim. And Professor MacAllistair was involved, too. You both need to make statements," Sean said, staring at her.

"You two know each other?" she asked, surprised.

"We just met," Sean said.

"I see." But she didn't see at all. She stared at her lodger with naked curiosity.

"I stopped by the station," he explained.

"Why?"

"Because I'm afraid you may have a dangerous cult at work here in New Orleans," MacAllistair explained.

She almost laughed out loud. "This is New Orleans. We have tons of voodoo practitioners, would-be vampires...you name it."

"I don't mean to cut this conversation short," MacAllistair said, "but I'm due at the university soon. If there's paperwork..."

"Yes, let's move," Sean said. He indicated his car.

"I have my own car," Jessica said quickly.

"I don't, but I'm sure my hostess will be happy to drive me," MacAllistair said.

Sean arched a brow; Jessica shrugged. She opened her car door. MacAllistair walked around to take the passenger seat.

As she followed Sean's car to the station, Jessica glanced in the askew rearview mirror at the man beside her. "I'm still confused. What do you have to do with Mary? Why were you visiting Sean?"

He stared straight at her, frowning. "What were you doing at the hospital?"

"Visiting Mary."

"Are you a relative?"

"No. I met her in Transylvania."

"You what?"

She exhaled impatiently. "I was at an international meeting. I happened to meet Mary and some of her friends. So what were you really doing visiting Sean?"

He was still staring at her. Suspiciously. She returned the glare. "Well?"

He lifted his hands. "It's what I do."

"What do you mean?"

"I know a great deal about pagan beliefs, cults and so on. The problem with anything like that is when people become fanatics. I'm sure you surely know that yourself. Mix up a few voodoo love spells and it's fun. Become convinced you're the servant of some devil or demon, and God knows what you'll get. Since my field is ancient beliefs, I've been involved in a few investigations where fanatics have taken something to the extreme and someone has gotten hurt. Since I'm afraid something similar may be happening here, I went and visited Sean."

She felt as if a frown had become permanently furrowed into her forehead.

"The road," he warned.

She realized she had been staring at him for too long and turned her attention back to her driving.

She felt her pulse pounding at her temples, felt the magnetism, and the sheer strength and size, of the man at her side.

She felt as if she would be happy if there were a ten-foot wall of concrete between them. And at the same time, there was a hint of...

She winced. He was frighteningly attractive. Entirely sensually, sexually attractive. He could walk into a room and make her forget all sense of respectability and just wonder what it would be like if...

There was a whisper of something about him. Something in the way he moved, in the way he looked at her. Something that compelled and seduced like...

She gave herself a shake. He was dangerous, she decided, if only to her peace of mind. The concrete wall was exactly what she needed.

At the station, they had to wait an uncomfortable

amount of time. The two assailants had to be booked before she and Bryan could give their statements.

As soon as he was finished, Bryan MacAllistair hurried out.

Sean Canady stood with Jessica at the door as he left. MacAllistair didn't look back, but Jessica was certain he knew they were watching him.

"He was in Romania," she said.

"And all over Europe when parties like that one took place," Sean said.

"And he was there tonight, when I was attacked," Jessica went on.

"Right."

"It's awfully coincidental," she pressed.

Sean turned and studied her. Then he said softly, "The same could be said about you, Jessica."

She frowned, staring at him, but before she could speak, she was startled by someone hurrying up behind her. She whirled, instantly alarmed, then let out a breath of relief.

It was just Bobby Munro.

"Jessica, word got around. You were attacked? Are you all right?" he asked anxiously, taking her into his arms for a quick hug.

"I'm fine." she assured him.

He backed away, looking a little abashed. "Sorry, Lieutenant Canady. I just heard what happened."

"It's all right, Bobby," Sean assured him.

Bobby looked at Jessica worriedly again. "You're sure?"

"Bobby, I'm fine."

"Professor MacAllistair made an appearance, and I think the toughs are pretty damned sorry," Sean explained. "Not, mind you," he said, grinning as he caught Jessica's glance, "that our Ms. Fraser is not a most capable woman."

"Yeah, but those two...they were detained just a few days ago," Bobby said.

"Oh?" Jessica said, startled.

"Cal Hodges and Niles Goolighan. We couldn't hold them, couldn't prove anything. But we brought them in for questioning. One of the nurses at the hospital thought they might have been prowling around."

"That was these two?" Sean said frowning.

"Yes. They were in a lineup, but the nurse couldn't make a positive identification, so we had to let them go. They had a lawyer in here screaming about their rights."

"They won't be getting out this time," Sean said firmly.

"Anyway, my shift's over and I gotta get going. I have a side job tonight." He flushed. "I've been taking a bunch of them lately. Trying to save up some money. It's all right, isn't it?" he asked Sean.

"Yeah. Sure."

"Well, Jessica, I just wanted to make sure you were really all right," Bobby said. "So…night."

"Night," Sean and Jessica chorused.

When he was gone, Sean murmured. "Great. Those two were prowling around the hospital before."

"Could they have been…after Mary?" Jessica wondered aloud. "That can't be. They're just a pair of idiots."

"You need to be careful," he said simply.

"Sean, I am careful."

"I mean *really* careful."

She gasped suddenly.

"What?" Sean asked.

"I think…how stupid of me," she murmured, irritated with herself.

"What?" Sean asked again in exasperation.

"I've seen one of them before. In fact, I've more than seen him."

"Which one? Where? And what do you mean?"

"At the college…about a year ago. There was a symposium going on. I didn't recognize him at first because he's grown his hair…but I wound up talking to him at one point."

"What was the symposium about?"

"Occultism in New Orleans. Cal was there. I'm sure of it. I can't believe it's took me so long to realize why he looked familiar."

"You meet tons of people."

She shook her head. "No, you don't understand. I did more than just talk to him. He made it clear he didn't want to talk to a woman about what was bothering him, so I set him up with a male colleague, Dr. Darnell. But in our conversation, he told me that his folks were dead, and he was saddled with a little sister. Sean, I called social services about the situation. They took the sister away."

"You think he attacked you because of that?"

"No, that's the weird thing. He was grateful she was taken away. She went to live in the Midwest with an aunt, and I guess she's much happier, too. Sean, this is disturbing."

"You were attacked. Of course it's disturbing."

"Look, in Transylvania, I knew the kids involved. Now I've been attacked and I know one of my attackers. I would have sworn he was a basically good kid, so this...doesn't make any sense."

"Jessica, you can't save the entire world. Cal and Niles are punks. Sometimes people are bad and there's nothing you can do. I don't think you should be worried that every bad thing that happens centers around you."

"I don't think that."

"The fact that you knew one of the kids who attacked you is probably just a coincidence."

"Probably. But...what if there *is* a connection? Sean, do you have some men you can assign to the hospital? Men to watch over Mary?"

"You mean you really think those two might have been after Mary? That's a little far-fetched, don't you think?"

"Nothing is too far-fetched."

"These two will go to jail and stay there," Sean assured her.

"What if they get out on bail?"

"I'll get the D.A.'s office to see that they don't," he promised.

"Sean, even having been there in Romania, I didn't imagine that anything this bad would happen here. It never occurred to me that something like that would follow us back here to New Orleans. But now, as bizarre as it seems, I do think that New Orleans is slated for…."

"For what? Jessica, what's going on here? What are you thinking?"

"I'm really frightened for Mary. I should have been from the start. But I thought she'd be okay, that it was over, that we'd come home, that…evil had moved on. I didn't realize it might have moved on to my own home. I should have been concerned from the second I returned."

"You sound as if you're blaming yourself."

"Well…."

"Okay, we need to see to it that Mary is guarded. Help me out here. What, precisely, do you suggest I tell my men they're watching out for?" He shook his head. "I'll definitely have to hire off-duty guys. I won't be able to explain this one to the city. I take it you want someone there right away?"

"Yes."

"Too bad Bobby already has a gig tonight," Sean muttered.

"There are other good cops."

"Yeah, I know. Give me a few minutes."

Sean went back inside. Jessica waited.

When he returned he said, "I'll have a guy over there within the half hour."

"That long?"

"To drive over, park, get to the floor?" he said, staring at her. "Twenty to thirty minutes. My guys are only human."

"Maybe I should head back over myself?"

"An officer will be there just as quickly as you can get there."

She sighed. "I guess you're right."

"So what's wrong?"

"I just should have thought of it before," she murmured. Then she grimaced at Sean. "So…should we head over to his lecture?"

Jeremy had been awakened several times. The nurses had been in and out.

Mary's folks had been and gone, her father insisting her mother had to spend time with the rest of the family, too.

The doctor had been in, and the news had been encouraging.

Mary was holding her own. Even though the doctors couldn't understand why her blood platelet count wasn't completely stabilized, it was getting there.

Jeremy had decided he wasn't leaving that night, even though everyone seemed to think she was out of the woods. His mind was in such turmoil that he knew he wouldn't be able to sleep, anyway.

He would just keep waking up, thinking he should be here.

So he watched reruns on TNT. He talked to Mary now and then, and made himself comfortable on the visitor's chair. He'd already drifted in and out of sleep several times. He didn't want to sleep, but he couldn't fight it.

Sleeping brought on dreams.

And the dreams were always the same.

He was back in the old ruined castle in Transylvania. Watching, paralyzed, forced to see the scene replay over and over again, except in his dream, he was watching the film again, but it was playing on the hospital television set.

Mary was there, but not in the bed, on the screen. She was awake and smiling, at the mirror and unafraid. She was brushing her hair, her movements sensual. She turned, knowing that someone…something…was in the room.

Jeremy felt the leaden darkness, like something that sat on his chest, stealing his breath, stealing his resolve, his thoughts…his humanity. Whatever had entered the room was *evil*.

But Mary welcomed the presence. She turned, as sensual as a cat, eyes hooded, wicked, waiting. She longed for the touch of darkness. The breeze came, lifting her hair, baring her throat, her breast. The gossamer gown drifted low.

She ripped the cross from her neck.

He struggled to awaken, to stop her.

The shadow moved closer, enveloping her. She lifted her chin, rapture in her eyes. She waited….

No, no, no, it was a dream.

"No!" He cried the word aloud, startling himself awake.

The television had gone to static.

He jerked his head around. Mary was still in her hospital bed. He looked across the room, feeling a cool breeze, as if the windows had been opened.

A chill had entered the room. Not from the too-efficient air-conditioning.

This was a different kind of chill.

But no windows were open. They were sealed shut, he reminded himself, probably to keep patients from jumping.

He realized then that the door to the hallway was ajar.

He looked at Mary. Her eyes were opened, but she was staring straight ahead, as she always seemed to do now.

But something was different.

His blood turned to ice as he realized what had changed.

Mary was smiling.

He stood, walking to her side, taking her hand. She didn't protest; she just kept smiling.

"It's all right," he assured her.

It was then that he noticed her silver cross, the chain broken, lying on the floor. A tap at the door made him jump.

A police officer was standing there. "Hey, son, I just wanted you to know I'm out here, if you need anything," the man said.

He was a big guy.

With a heavy silver cross only half-hidden beneath his uniform.

Jeremy nodded. "Thanks, but why are you here?"

"Lieutenant said his friend, some psychologist, was worried about you all. So I'm here. And everything is going to be okay."

"Sure."

Jeremy wondered why he was so certain that everything *wasn't* going to be okay, that in fact it had already gone straight to hell.

And Mary just kept smiling.

7

Bryan MacAllistair was an excellent lecturer. Not only did he know his subject, but he could be grave, then allow laughter, then drive home the seriousness of a point in a way that a straight diatribe could not.

He was also strikingly handsome, Jessica thought, not for the first time.

She felt a stir of something in her heart; a glimpse of a long-gone memory she couldn't touch. She shook her head.

The rest of his charm was in his voice, in the grin he offered now and then, even the absent way he pushed back a lock of stray hair falling over his forehead now and then. Watching the man speak, Jessica realized he literally seduced his audience.

Whatever they were paying him, he was worth it.

"He came straight to see you, and you were given orders from the mayor's office to speak to him?" Jessica whispered to Sean.

"He's apparently been instrumental in solving

occult murders all over the world," Sean said. "You really are suspicious of this guy. Why can't he be just what he seems?"

Jessica stared at MacAllistair again.

"Because."

"Because why?"

She shook her head. "He's after something. He's dangerous. I can feel it."

Sean sighed, shook his head and looked at the stage again. "We'll put him to the test," he said after a moment, his voice deep and teasingly dramatic. "We'll gather all our friends and put him in a room with them. If there's something…not right about him, he'll give himself away and we'll know it. And then we'll see."

"That's a brilliant idea," Jessica said.

When the lecture was over, the room burst into applause. To her genuine annoyance, he even received a standing ovation.

Standing and clapping, Sean looked at her with amusement. "It's not like he crept into town anonymously," he said with a laugh. "We'll put him to the test tonight. How's that?"

"What? You're going to throw an instant party?"

"A small one. Let's invite him to my house. Nothing big—just the four of us. I'll call Maggie. We'll have coffee and beignets or something."

"Okay." Jessica agreed.

"He might say no," Sean warned.

But the man of the hour didn't refuse the invitation. It seemed as if they had to wait forever for his throng of admirers to dissipate, but when they were finally able to reach him, Sean did the talking, issuing the invitation.

Bryan MacAllistair smiled slowly and looked at Jessica. "Sure."

She felt as if they'd thrown down a gauntlet—and he'd picked it up with tremendous amusement.

The house was beautiful, a true old Southern plantation. Maggie was equally beautiful, Bryan thought, the perfect mistress of such a place, with a regal stance, thick hair of vibrant auburn and mystical hazel eyes. She and Sean had three children, two boys and a girl, who were quick to throw their arms around their father and Jessica, and just a shade reticent when they saw him. Then they gravely shook his hand before being sent off to bed.

Maggie Canady seemed pleased to have him in her home; she was friendly and gracious, but Bryan knew that she was studying him as curiously as her husband and Jessica did. As suspiciously.

Not a problem. They were welcome to be just as suspicious as they chose.

He could wear a smile, and he knew how to be on guard.

"This is quite a house," he told Sean, after being shown the downstairs. It was the kind of place that might have been a stop on a tour of historic New Orleans, antebellum, with a graceful staircase, massive foyer and comfortably proportioned side rooms meant for entertainment.

"And you're wondering how I can afford it on a cop's salary?" Sean inquired dryly.

"Actually, I was just admiring it at the moment."

"The house has been in Maggie's family for a couple of centuries," Sean told him.

"The house, the kids…your wife is really something."

The look on Canady's face as he smiled was something Bryan envied. Here was a man who didn't just love his wife but was still *in love* with her, as well. "She's a miracle worker. She has a shop in the Quarter, too. All back in full gear now, after the storms. We have help around the house, though."

"Hey, guys, coffee is on, unless you prefer tea," Jessica said, appearing from the kitchen.

She held her head at an angle, smiling as she spoke. Her beauty was delicate and fine, the structure of her face perfect, her blond hair a captivating frame for it. He felt something stirring deep within himself. A memory, a nostalgic longing. But that was the past. Long over and dead. He knew that.

Still, she aroused him in a way he hadn't felt in ages.

"Coffee," he said. "And thanks."

He and Sean followed her back into the kitchen. There was a formal dining room, but they gathered around the large table that sat not far from the giant hearth, once used to cook meals for both family and servants. "I hear the house has been in your family for years," he said, addressing Maggie as he took the chair she indicated. "That's a gorgeous painting at the top of the stairs. You really resemble your ancestor."

"Thank you," she murmured. "Pecan pie? Brownies?"

He waved a hand. "Thanks. Just coffee is fine."

"It's the best pecan pie in the world," Jessica commented, a subtle smile still curving her lips.

"You made it?" he asked Maggie.

"I made it," Sean announced. "I can't tell you how many cops actually watch the cooking channel."

Bryan laughed and accepted a piece of pecan pie.

"How are you doing with my new bathing suit?" Maggie asked Jessica. "She's got a great eye for fashion," she went on, turning to Bryan.

"I've done some sketches. Sorry, I've been slow," Jessica said.

"No problem, but you should know that I'm thinking of carrying as many as you can make in my shop."

"Sounds good," Jessica said.

Then Maggie suddenly looked sharply at Bryan.

"So you're a professor?"

He nodded. "Yes, I'm lecturing at the university for a few months."

"But you went to the station to see Sean. And you're staying at Jessica's place. What a coincidence," Maggie said, staring at him.

He shrugged, leaning forward slightly, not letting his gaze slip from hers. "I believe there's going to be trouble here," he said flatly.

"Trouble?" she arched a brow. "Are you bringing the trouble?"

Hardly a discreet question. He leaned back, grinning. "No, ma'am. I don't bring trouble."

"But you do follow it?" Jessica asked softly.

He turned to her. "I haven't come here hiding anything," he said, as if he knew they all suspected him of having done just that. "I've explained several times—"

"Not to me," Maggie said politely.

"No, nor to me, not really," Jessica agreed.

He glanced apologetically at Sean. "Because of my expertise in ancient beliefs, and the way they're often twisted in the present, I've been able to help the police solve cult-related murders in several countries. A number of them have been associated with parties like the one several local students attended in Romania recently. Rumor has it that New Orleans is the next city on the circuit, that celebrities will show up, that it's going to be very wild and sexy."

"There's a sex party coming to New Orleans?" Jessica asked. She looked at Maggie, shrugged and turned to him, speaking dryly. "What a shock."

"It's a little more than that," Bryan said. "There's talk of something dangerous. Vampires. Latex and leather."

Jessica stood suddenly. "More coffee, anyone?"

"I'm fine, thanks," Maggie murmured.

"So? Such a party is hardly uncommon," Sean said.

"There's a big party this fall at one of the big hotel chains," Maggie said. "I heard some women talking about it the other day in the shop. It's got a bondage theme. That kind of thing goes on all the time."

"There's something called the Voodoo Ball this Friday night," Jessica added. "One of my patients is a dancer. She's part of the entertainment."

"You can buy just about any kind of entertainment on Bourbon Street," Sean said.

"What went down in Transylvania was hardly your usual party," Bryan told them bluntly.

Silence.

"These parties are all about the *vampyr*," he said.

Jessica's cup clinked against her saucer.

"Well, people who *think* they're vampires," Maggie said after a minute, but her voice sounded strange.

"I think Jessica might be of some help on that subject," Bryan said.

"What?" Jessica demanded, shocked, staring at him.

He smiled. "Sorry. I meant you talk with young people all the time. And then there are the two who went after you this afternoon."

She waved a hand in the air. "Hey, this is New Orleans. There are flocks of Anne Rice fans all over town. There are—"

"There are those who play at the fantasy," Bryan said.

"Yes, of course," Jessica agreed. She seemed annoyed. "I understand what you're saying, and it's true that people's beliefs, however misguided, can make them dangerous."

"You have talked to some of them, right?"

"Them…?"

"People who think they're vampires. The ones who literally practice blood rituals, and the ones who think they're spiritual vampires, sucking the life force from others."

She nodded.

"Then I would think, if something was stirring on the breeze, you'd know."

Jessica shook her head. "Like I said, there's always something like that going on around here."

"Wouldn't you know if it was something more serious? Like the situation in Transylvania."

"Actually, I think Transylvania might have been some kind of mass hysteria—" Jessica began.

"A girl almost died. May still be dying," Bryan said.

Maggie rose abruptly, going for the coffeepot. "That poor girl isn't doing any better?"

"She's holding her own," Jessica said. "A friend of hers, Jeremy, stays with her constantly."

"People were meant to die at that party," Bryan said. "I'm sure of it."

Sean leaned forward. "Okay, so someone is throwing parties where the guests are invited to be the entrée by people who are either rich, perverted and sick, and believe that they're carrying out some ancient ritual, or people who are simply perverted sexual killers, or..."

"Or?" Bryan said.

Sean shrugged. "Or vampires."

"Why would they come here?" Jessica demanded.

Bryan stared at her. "It's a good place to hide in plain sight. You just said so yourself," he told her.

"I didn't say that," Jessica protested.

"Yes, you did. Who would really notice another weirdo walking around in a cape?"

"He's got you there," Sean pointed out.

Bryan realized both he and Sean were staring at Jessica thoughtfully. And she knew it.

"You're both making me really uneasy. You know I have a professional obligation, both legal and moral, to keep my sessions confidential."

"Yes, but…if you know about something danger-ous, you have to let us know," Sean said.

Bryan tried not to show his appreciation for the fact that Sean had used the word *us*. At least in this, the cop had accepted him, even if only on a subconscious level.

"I'd never let anything bad happen, not if I could stop it," Jessica said. She picked up her cup and a few of the plates on the table. "It's getting late. Thanks, Maggie, this was great, especially on the spur of the moment and all."

"My pleasure," Maggie said. She stood, setting a hand on Jessica's arm. "Hey, leave it. I'll get it."

"But—"

"Tomorrow's Sunday. A lazy day."

"You'll still wake up with three kids," Jessica said.

"It's a few dishes. I'll whip them into the dish-washer while Sean drives you back into the city."

"I brought my car. Sean doesn't have to go anywhere."

"In that case, between the two of us, I think we can pick up a few plates."

"All right, then…thanks again."

Bryan stood, reaching out a hand to Maggie. "A pleasure to meet you. And thanks for the pecan pie."

Maggie thanked him, carefully freeing her hand. "My pleasure. I look forward to seeing you again."

Though the last was said very pleasantly, he

wondered if there wasn't a little bit of a warning in the words, as well.

As he followed Sean, who escorted them to the door, he could hear Maggie and Jessica whispering. He knew damned well they were talking about him, but he pretended not to hear anything.

As they drove, Jessica asked him, "Do you know New Orleans, then?"

"Yes," he said.

"So you've been here before?"

"Yes."

"Before Hurricane Katrina, I take it?"

"Yes, before Katrina."

He looked at her, trying to see her face in the shadows that intermingled with the neon lights of the city.

She looked out the window. "It's an incredible place, and it's doing well now," she said, almost angrily.

Doing well. Just what did she mean by that? Stores were open, people were working and music was flowing?

Or that it was filled with the customary good and bad of humanity, but not something that was…pure evil?

Again he felt the stirring of memory, of a longing that lingered like pain. There was something about her that seemed to arouse not just his senses, but a darkened place deep in his soul.

Without talking, they drove slowly along the streets of the French Quarter, then into her driveway, where they exited the car.

Her fingers seemed to have lost coordination as she turned the key in the lock. "I loved your lecture," she said into the silence. "Not just your material but your delivery."

"Thanks. I've had a lot of practice," he told her.

She nodded. She'd gotten the door open at last.

The house was filled with silence and shadows when they entered. Another awkward moment followed, neither are knowing quite what to say.

"Thanks for the invitation to Sean's house. It was nice getting to know your friends, and I appreciate Sean's trust in me."

She tipped her head at an angle. "You *are* worthy of trust, I hope?"

"I swear I am."

She faked a yawn. "Well, good night, then."

"Good night."

They started up the stairs together. Stopped. "I'm sorry," he said. "After you."

"No, no, you're the guest here. After you."

He laughed then, and caught her hand. "It is a wide staircase."

Her lashes fell, and then she looked up at him. Eyes were supposedly the window to the soul, he thought, and she had beautiful eyes. They were filled with passion and strength, and with a strange vulnerability, as well. Where he touched her, his hand seemed to burn, his blood to boil. He felt the strangest longing to tell her, "I would die for you."

Ridiculous.

His laughter faded. "Plenty of room for both of us," he said, seeking nonchalance, but the words were husky with passion instead.

"Of course," she said, easing her hand from his.

Their footfalls matched. They reached the hallway.

"Good night," she murmured, but she didn't move.

"Good night," he replied.

She was the one who finally managed to step away.

"Tomorrow," he managed lightly, and went into his room.

"Tomorrow," she said, and walked past.

In his room, he stripped and headed for the shower, thinking that the old wisdom was right, the flesh *was* weak!

He stayed under the water for a long time, waiting for his skin to prune and his sex to shrivel. He thought about Mary, about Jeremy sitting sentinel in her room. The kid had seemed so haunted.

Of course he was. If the girl wasn't getting any better…

It had been a good night. The lecture had gone

well, and the aftermath had been better. He needed the cops to trust him, needed Jessica's insights.

It was closer than he could have imagined just a few days ago. His next steps had to be measured and careful. They required careful thought and planning.

But he couldn't keep his mind on the days ahead. Instead, he kept seeing her so clearly in his mind's eye.

Those eyes...

He turned off the water. The bathroom was supplied with a terry robe that boasted the words Montresse House on the pocket. He slipped into it and went back into his bedroom.

He tried the television.

No good. He felt as if he were caged. Tense, a rampant pulse beating through his veins. Swearing, he walked to the French doors, opened them.

There was a breeze. That was good. The night was filled with the scent of blooming flowers. Soft. Away from the street, the sounds of the city were muted, the earth seemed still.

The night sky remained red. He walked to the balcony and caught something out of the corner of his eye. He turned.

She was on the balcony, as well. She knew he was there, knew he had come. She was watching him, as still as the darkness.

Long moments passed as they stood silently,

watching each other in the red light of the strange moon and the bloody shadows it cast. He felt the thunder of his own heart growing louder. Felt the heat of her, as if he moved closer ever when he did not. A dozen inane things to say swept through the periphery of his mind; none came to his lips.

In the end, he was never sure if he walked to her or she to him, but the distance was gone.

8

He took her into his arms, and felt as if life and fire swept through him. He lifted her chin and felt the fierce trembling in his own limbs, and in hers.

Then his mouth was on hers. The taste of her lips was achingly sweet. He reveled in the quivering length of her, from the infinite seduction of her mouth to the curved pressure of her body, so compellingly pressed to his own. She was slender; she was strong. There were seconds when it seemed she did no more than accept his lips, the yearning pressure of his mouth, as if she tested, determined and then gave. Her lips parted to his, and the return of his touch was filled with an exotic invitation and quest. She returned his hunger, his passion, the length of her tongue hot, liquid, erotic, against his own. He felt unleashed. His hand slid down the endless grace of her back, his fingers curved over the delicate sculpture of her face, teased over the soft texture of her flesh, brushed over the back of her neck. He felt her fingers playing at his own nape, molding his shoulders, seducing the nerve endings along his back. His thumb and forefinger found her chin, lifting her head, his lips parting from hers at last. His breath was ragged, but his eyes searched hers, asking in silence what had been left unsaid before.

She touched his face in return, as if she, too, in turn needed more than what her eyes could take in, needed to feel, to know, the rising pulse between them giving answer to his unspoken question. Mistrust there might be, but it was nothing against their passion and the rising red tide of the night.

He lifted her against him. There was nothing soft, timid or weak about her, and yet her weight seemed as nothing.

No question of where to go: her room. He walked with her through the door. The queen-size bed waited, pale sheets steeped in the red moonlight. They were dressed alike in Montresse House robes, robes that fell open easily, baring flesh that seemed to burn with the color of the night.

Her hands were on him, each stroke of her fingers eliciting more than desire, more than hunger. He was anxious to know every part of her, insane to feel the explosion of release that racked his body. The agony was unbearable, the temptation greater. He found her mouth again, drowned in the sweetness of it, burned to ever greater heights with the wicked return of desire. His hands fell upon her flesh, stroked and teased. His lips found the length of her, lingered, aroused, burned, trailed to her waist, followed the curve of her hips. With every inch of his flesh, he felt her slightest movement, the rise and fall of her breasts with every breath she took, the arch of her hips against him, the brush of her fingers against him, tempting and taunting. Her lips were against his shoulders, his collarbone, his throat....

He moved against her, growing more heedless with urgency and desperation. Her hands slipped between them, creating a line of wanton flames down his chest, to his waist, back again, circling around him. He groaned, moved against her, lips, tongue, body, hands, knowing her, exploring her. Down. Finding the heart of life and fire and desire. Teasing at first, then losing himself in the honeyed sweetness of desperate arousal and desire, his hands on her hips, her fingers digging into his shoulders, her body writhing wildly, words escaping her at last, sounds making no sense, saying all...

And then they rolled and she rose above him, straddling him. The red light cast an eerie glow over the lithe grace and angelic perfection of her. Her eyes were in shadow, yet he saw them still, filled with both strength and vulnerability. He had never wanted anyone so much in all his years, never needed anyone so much. She hovered for a split second of red-swept time; then he caught her hips, drawing her down on him, thrust deeply into her at last, felt the fierce rocking that ripped through them both. He couldn't stop touching her, hands finding her face again, drawing her down, locking his mouth to hers, feeling the maddened rush of pure pleasure through his veins, the wet frenzy of the kiss, the wildfire of their bodies, one and not one, every movement goading him higher. He rolled her beneath him, and sank, drowned, died inside.

God, yes, he would die for her. If only...

His climax shot through him with something far more than the usual pleasure and release. Sex, something so natural, a human need, an instinct, could be beautiful or basic, motivated by love or simple lust.

But never had it been like this.

Her body tensed like a bowstring beneath his, her breath expelled with a soft cry that seemed to echo through him. He eased himself to her side, loathe to part in any way. He held her against him, feeling the thunder of his own heart, the pulsing in his veins, begin to slow. In the aftermath, he drifted on a sea of warm pleasure, and visions shot through his mind, visions of years gone by, of affairs that came and went in the flicker of a night, of love known, love lost, and the crucial distinction between having sex and making love.

At his side, she was silent and unmoving.

As sanity returned to him, he wondered what thoughts filled her mind now, certain she, too, had drifted into introspection after the explosion that had raged between them.

Time passed, their bodies cooled.

The red moon bathed the room.

At last she sighed, inched every so slightly closer to him.

Time to speak. He moistened his lips, then lost himself in the feel of her against him, flesh against flesh.

The hell with it.

He didn't speak, just took her into his arms again. Felt the flicker of her tongue against his lips, against his chest, against...

Hunger rose again in a rapid burst of flame. The night faded to the intimacy of nothing more than the two of them together. Once again the world trembled and rocked and exploded.

Once more she lay against him, silent.

In that red splendor, the night passed. Somewhere along the line, near dawn, he knew she slept. He allowed himself to rest, to sleep, as well.

Visions haunted his dreams. Visions of time long past. Visions...of time to come. Visions so vibrant he woke with a start. She was still asleep at his side, curled so sweetly against him. He rose carefully, planning a quick escape, since she probably didn't want anyone else to know what had passed between them.

He didn't move quickly.

He watched her as she slept.

Then, angry with himself, he forced himself to turn away. It was impossible to become so infatuated in an evening, he told himself, that he could just stand there, savoring the experience of watching her sleep.

He forced himself to move, leaving by the balcony door, slipping back into his room. He was tired, but too restless to sleep. After showering again and dressing casually, he slipped downstairs. He could hear soft music and a quiet drone of conversation from the kitchen.

He evaded human contact, though, letting himself out and heading for the street.

New Orleans was the same and yet not the same. Some areas had been so devastated that they would never be the same. Other blocks had hardly changed at all.

The city was a lot like him.

Jessica awoke in a slow daze, swimming in a strange comfort as the day began to seep into her consciousness. She didn't want to rise. She wanted to bask in the sensations that still filled her, not so

much erotic now as just…satisfying. A sense of…
warmth, being held, belonging, security…

Warmth, comfort, pleasure, pure happiness in the
presence of another.

Then she started up.

She was alone.

She exhaled. It was so much easier to think when
he wasn't with her. Had she lost her mind?

She jumped out of bed, looking at the time. She
was known for sleeping late, so that didn't mean
much. But…

Where was Bryan MacAllistair?

Discreetly gone, she knew, and she inhaled deeply.
Did it matter? Did she care? She was certainly well
over twenty-one, she mused dryly. She could make
love to anyone she chose.

Still…

What the hell was he doing here? What was he
really after?

And just who the hell was he really?

With that question ringing in her mind, she
headed for the shower. Was he sleeping now? What
should she do? Where should she go from here?

She needed to stop worrying about their relationship and the erotic turn it had taken. She had far
more important things to worry about. Mary, certainly. The toughs in the parking lot. The color of the
sky, the things that had happened in Transylvania.

Bryan MacAllistair.

It all kept coming back to him.

Sean observed Cal Hodges, the taller and skinnier of the two youths arrested the night before. Usually, when seated alone in an interrogation room, a suspect was restless. This one was just sitting.

Almost as if he were in a trance.

Sean had watched one of his detectives question the man a few minutes earlier, but so far he'd gotten nothing but a few shrugs, followed by a sly smile and a warning that they'd better not touch him or he would claim police brutality.

The detective now stood behind the one-way mirror with Sean, and lifted his hands helplessly. "He doesn't deny anything, he doesn't admit anything. Even when I tell him his friend is turning on him—that Niles will cut a deal with the D.A.—he just shrugs."

"When is his lawyer due?"

"Any minute."

"Has he actually said he won't talk without his lawyer?" Sean asked.

"Nope."

"I'll take a stab at him," Sean said.

He walked in and took a seat across from the man. Barely into his twenties, Sean thought. Cal gave him a sly look. He had hazel eyes that seemed almost yellow and snakelike. They were ordinary eyes, Sean thought grimly. It was the man's attitude that made his eyes seem so alien.

"Why were you prowling around the hospital?" Sean demanded.

"Who said I was?"

"A nurse who saw you."

Cal smiled in self-satisfaction and shook his head. "She couldn't identify me."

Sean leaned very close to him. He'd seen to it there were no recorders in the room. "Are you working for someone, Cal?"

The man's smile deepened. "I was working for me. Pretty broad, that psychologist, huh, Lieutenant? Great tits." He leaned closer to Sean. "What I could have done to her with just a few minutes more."

Sean controlled the urge to slug the man. He knew that was what the perp wanted. He leaned back, smiling himself, speaking softly. "You're no vampire, kid. You're just a punk. And you're being used."

Something in his words seemed to have gotten to the guy. Cal blinked; his mouth worked. Then, angrily, he shook his head. "The time of power is coming," he said.

"Too bad you won't be around for it," Sean said casually.

"Oh? You going to shoot me, cop?"

"Hell, no. I wouldn't waste the bullet. You're too stupid to be trusted by anyone with any real power."

"Fuck you."

Sean rose. There was a tap on the door. He was sure the defense attorney had arrived. "Good luck, punk," Sean said pleasantly. He paused before exiting. "You get scared and want to talk, tell the guards to call me. I think that, eventually, you will, and when you do…"

He opened the door. The attorney handling the case was a terribly thin young woman who always made Sean think of a rat run ragged on a treadmill, at a loss as how to get off.

"Morning, Counselor," he said.

"Lieutenant, if you've—"

"Trust me. I haven't violated your client's rights in any way. Good day."

He let her enter the room and started back to his office, thoughful. There was something…lacking about the young man. Intelligence? No, the guy wasn't the sharpest tool in the shed, but what he seemed to lack was…

Substance.

He reached his office and sat wearily, then was immediately distracted by Bobby Munro, who walked in on him, shaking his head.

"You're not going to like this, Lieutenant. Not one bit."

Sean started to rise. Another visitor was standing behind Bobby. Inwardly, he groaned, ready to chew Bobby out for having left the door open. Too late now.

Bryan MacAllistair heard the news as he did.

"Morning," Jessica said, showered and dressed, ready to face the day.

Gareth, pouring himself a cup of coffee, grunted. He looked at her worriedly, then offered her the cup.

She smiled and accepted it. "You," he said, pointing at her, shaking his head.

"What?"

"You've got to learn to be careful, missy, that's all I've got to say."

He stared at her firmly for a long moment, got another cup and filled it with coffee for himself. "Stuff to do to this house," he said, shaking his head. "As if time and nature weren't enough." Tsking, he turned away. "Now I have to worry about you more and more."

"Hey, I can take care of myself."

"Don't care what you say. I'll be watching your back." He started out determinedly.

"Gareth," she called.

He looked back.

"Thank you."

He smiled.

Stacey had been reading the morning paper. Now she stared at Jessica, a question in her eyes.

Jessica's fingers trembled slightly. She wondered if she looked different. "Good morning, Stace," she said. She noticed there were plates on the counter, covered with plastic wrap; Stacey had made pancakes and bacon.

"Good morning," Stacey said, still staring at her. "Well?"

"Well?"

"You were attacked last night," Stacey said. "How are you feeling?"

"Oh," Jessica said. After the night she had spent, she hadn't been thinking about the attack at all. So that was why Gareth had acted so strangely. They both knew what had happened in the hospital parking lot.

"It wasn't anything, really. Just a pair of idiots wearing really bad vampire fangs."

Stacey shook her head. "Gareth is all kinds of worried. He's going to spend the day prowling around making sure this place is tight."

"They were a pair of idiots. Seriously. It was nothing."

Stacey pointed a finger at her. "Don't try to tell me that. I've known you awhile now, and when I heard about the attack on the radio, I recognized one of the names. You tried to help that Cal kid."

Jessica shook her head. "He didn't attack me because of who I am—I just happened to be in the wrong place at the wrong time."

"But I heard they were prowling around the hospital. Were they after Mary?"

Jessica was uneasy that Stacey's thoughts seemed to follow her own. "Who knows?"

Stacey leaned forward, whispering, "Are you being targeted? Does it have something to do with that party?"

"Don't be ridiculous. Those parties go on all over the place. Let's drop it, okay? So—our guest is out?" Jessica asked.

"Yes. And I'm rather insulted. He doesn't seem interested in tasting our delicious breakfasts," she said, grinning quickly to show it didn't really bother her. "I get the impression he loves to roam the streets when it's early—before everyone else is out."

Jessica shrugged, then yawned and stretched.

"What are your plans for the day?" Stacey asked.

"I'm going to finish up Maggie's bathing suit," Jessica said. "I promised I'd have it done as soon as I came back from Romania. Then, I don't know. I might drive out to Sean and Maggie's again."

"Again?"

"I went there last night for coffee." She hesitated. "With Bryan."

"Oh?" Stacey dropped the paper. "After he rescued you? But...he had a lecture last night."

Jessica shrugged. "Sean and I went to hear him."

"And you didn't invite me?"

"It was a spur-of-the-moment thing."

"And?"

Jessica sipped her coffee. "He's good. He really knows his stuff."

"Did you see Bobby there?"

"Bobby—your Bobby?"

"Well, I don't think he's actually *my* Bobby," Stacey said with a smile. "But, yeah, Bobby Munro."

"I saw him at the station, but he said he was working an off-duty job. I didn't see him at the lecture. Did he go?"

"Yeah, he said he happened to be in the area when he was done working. He's been doing a lot of parties and weddings, even funerals, lately. I hope he's saving up for a ring—or at least a fast trip to Vegas."

"Hey, he loves you. It's obvious. Still, it's strange that he wound up at the lecture and didn't call you to join him. Plus he must not have had to work more than about an hour."

"That's about it. Can you believe it? You wind up going, my boyfriend goes—and no one invites me."

"I would have invited you if there had been time."

"Never mind, I'll get there on my own one of these days, and I won't invite any of you."

"He's here for the semester," Jessica said. "So you'll have plenty of chances. The hall was absolutely overflowing—that's probably why we didn't see Bobby and he didn't see us. There were tons of students, of course, but plenty of other people were there, too. It's such a cool topic, and I guess the word that he's an incredible speaker has gotten around."

"You think some of your crazies were there?"

"Don't call them crazies. And I don't know. I'm just musing aloud. They would have been interested, though. He talks about the differences between deep-rooted beliefs and the way something becomes trendy at a certain point in time, like these vampire parties."

Stacey leaned toward her. "What do you think he knows that he doesn't say?"

"I don't know," Jessica murmured, sitting back. She hesitated. "He wants my help, though."

"Your help? Doing what?" Stacey asked.

"He thinks there's going to be a party here, like the one in Transylvania. He thinks I might hear about the details through my practice."

"Well?" Stacey said.

Jessica lifted a hand evasively. "It's against the law for me to reveal anything a patient tells me in confidence."

"You're nervous, aren't you?"

Jessica nodded. "It's like knowing something is going to happen, *knowing* it, but being powerless to stop it."

"Yeah," Stacey muttered. "I've been wondering what's going on with all this—with Bryan MacAl-listair. Bobby saw him when he was there before, at the police station, leaving Sean's office."

"What does Bobby think?"

Stacey opened her mouth to speak, but Jessica frowned in warning, suddenly aware that they were not alone.

Bryan MacAllistair was back.

She stared at him, at first thinking of nothing but the night just past. How could she explain her behavior? In today's society, she knew she needed no explanation, but in her heart, she did. That thought raced through her mind, along with the fear that he hadn't felt what she had, that for him it hadn't been unique, something once in a lifetime, not just sex.

Because she'd felt as if they'd been made to be together, something neither heaven nor hell could stop.

She felt an awkward moment coming up.

But it wasn't awkward. It was worse. Far worse.

She saw the darkness, the gravity, in his rugged features, in his eyes.

"Mary is dead," he said.

9

Jeremy was beyond distraught. Jessica wondered if Mary had ever known just what a friend she'd had.

By the time she reached the hospital, Mary's parents were long gone, her mother apparently sedated, her father taking what comfort he could from his other children.

Students hovered in the waiting room, though there was nothing to wait for. Except for Nancy and Jeremy, they began to drift away, muttering words, knowing they weren't the right ones.

Jessica sat with the Jeremy and Nancy for several minutes in near silence. She had voiced her sorrow and had nothing left to say. She felt stunned, though she knew she shouldn't have been. How could she have been so blind? But Sean had sent an officer, who had been on duty all night.

Then Jeremy started talking and told her that no one had been there but him, that he'd had horrible dreams every time he dozed, but no one else had been in the room.

He was holding something, though. Something he kept a tight grip on. She pried his fingers open, then gasped when she saw what it was.

Mary's little silver cross.

Again she damned herself.

Then, forcing herself to speak, she asked, "Do you know what the arrangements will be?"

His eyes were red, his face damp with tears. "They wanted to take her home right away, but…it may be several days before the hospital releases the body."

"Oh?" Jessica murmured.

He looked at her. Numb. "There's going to be an autopsy."

"I see."

"She's in the hospital morgue now."

Nancy looked at her helplessly. "She died because of Transylvania. I'm so…"

"Scared?" Jessica suggested softly.

"Yes."

"Come on. Let's get out of here. Let me take you both for something to eat."

"I couldn't. I couldn't swallow," Jeremy said.

"You need to."

He looked at her blankly. "Why?"

"Because you're alive," she said softly. "Whether you want to be right now or not. And you have to do the things people do when they're alive." She stood, pulling him to his feet, not giving him a chance to protest further.

Nancy, seemingly glad to have a leader, stood, as well. Jeremy rose at last. "Where are we going?"

"My office. We'll order something."

Twenty minutes later, the two students were on her couch, waiting for pizza. Jeremy had muttered that he'd like a beer, and though Jessica was afraid the alcohol might enhance his misery, she knew he deserved a drink if that was what he wanted, so she ran down to the street and bought a six-pack.

He looked a lot like Mary had, just staring ahead, occasionally sipping his beer.

Suddenly he looked at Jessica.

"They were vampires. Not people who thought they were vampires, not nut jobs who like to drink blood. Vampires."

Jessica exhaled softly, her expression skeptical.

"You weren't there. You didn't see," Nancy said, glaring at her. She looked at Jeremy in misery. "Now *we're* going to die." She turned to face Jessica again. "They'll come after us, too."

Jessica felt a chill snake along her spine, but she hesitated, knowing she needed to speak carefully. "All right," she said at last. "Say that such creatures do exist. Was either of you actually bitten?"

Jeremy and Nancy stared at each other.

"No," Nancy said.

"No," Jeremy echoed.

Another silent moment passed.

"Good God!" Jeremy said sickly.

"What?" Jessica asked.

"She'll become a vampire."

"Oh, God!" Nancy agreed. "Mary will be...one of the undead." Her words were so dramatic that they would have been funny, if the situation hadn't been so tragic.

"It's the truth," Jeremy said firmly.

"All right, listen. Often truth is simply what we believe it to be," Jessica said.

"Don't start with the psychobabble," Jeremy said angrily.

"I'm not. The point is, if you see something as true—and I'm not going to try to tell either of you that you're mistaken or it's all in your minds—then, in your life, at the very least, it *is* true. So let's say vampires do exist. Make a list of ways to deal with them."

Nancy and Jeremy stared at each other in confusion.

"Like...garlic?" Nancy asked.

Jessica smiled. "Like garlic. Is either of you religious?"

"I was raised Catholic," Jeremy said.

"Methodist," Nancy said. "Like Mary."

"Great big silver crosses would be good, then," Jessica said.

"What if Mary was Jewish?" Nancy asked suspiciously.

"Then I would suggest a great big Star of David," Jessica told her.

"I see. Because what's important is that I believe that would stop a Jewish vampire?" Nancy asked.

Again, Jessica answered carefully. "Here's one way to look at it. There is a supreme being, and for the sake of argument, we'll make it a 'he.' And he's the ultimate good. But there's evil in the world, and good or evil are in a constant battle for supremacy. We'll assume that the two of you are good, and that whatever killed Mary is evil. So as representatives of good, you have to combat the evil."

"With garlic?" Nancy asked.

"With whatever you believe will work," Jessica said.

They needed to believe they could fight. She was pretty sure she had accomplished that, at the least.

"So what should we do now?" Nancy asked.

"Go back to your dorms and get what you need, then come back here. I'll have everything set up for you. No one will know you're here." She paused, then offered a rueful smile. "We'll go by all the old legends, so don't invite anyone in. Anyone at all."

"Right. A vampire can't come in unless invited," Nancy said.

"That's the traditional thought," Jessica agreed.

"We need holy water and crosses," Jeremy said.

"Right. And I'll see you have everything you need for a good night's sleep," Jessica assured them.

"I don't know if I'll ever sleep again," Jeremy said.

Jessica placed a hand on his. "I wish I could make this not hurt so badly for you," she told him. "But grief…it's something you have to go through. All the stages, but you have to live, too. You have people who love you. Think of how badly you're hurting. You wouldn't want to make anyone else hurt like that, right?"

He sighed deeply. "Of course I want to live, of course. It's instinct, isn't it?"

Oh, yes, he was right about that.

She acknowledged his words with a slight smile and a nod. Just then the pizza arrived, and both Nancy and Jeremy found themselves able to eat.

In the middle of a bite, Jeremy started crying.

Nancy held him. Jessica sat silently.

Her heart seemed to bleed. He was truly in misery.

And he was truly afraid.

There was little he could do.

Little but be frustrated.

Bryan chafed irritably through the rest of the morning and the early hours of the afternoon. Jessica had befriended Jeremy and his fellow students, but he barely knew them. He had nothing to offer them after their loss.

Jessica, pale and shaken, had been out of the house as soon as he finished telling them what had happened. He simply bided his time, watching the sky all the while.

At last the afternoon waned. He had checked the times when the nurses' shifts changed, and, thanks to modern technology, he had found the blueprints for the hospital online, as well as the current delegation of space.

He arrived with time to spare, making his way first to the cafeteria.

It was busy, which was good. He took his time, pretending to read the newspaper, watching, ready to grab his opportunity when it came. When it did, it was easy enough to snag a key card from a young orderly who neglected to realize he had left it on his tray.

After that, a supply room afforded him a choice of lab coats complete with name tags. Again, he took his time, deciding he looked more like a MacDonald than a DeVries, Garcia or Gustafson. Hell, maybe it didn't matter. This was America.

After that, he walked down the halls with complete confidence, found the right staircase and then reached the morgue.

Cold and sad. Technology had done little to alter the character of the place.

There was a lone attendant, a young man sitting at the desk outside the door. An ID tag offered up his name: David Hayes. He was engrossed in a sci-fi novel. When Bryan entered, he glanced up looking guilty as his eyes fell back to the pages. Then he dragged them up again.

"Sorry," he murmured quickly.

"No problem."

"Thanks. Evening, Doctor...MacDonald."

"Evening. I need one of the bodies that came in today."

"The gunshot victim?"

"No, the girl who was over in Europe."

"Second cubicle on the left. They're all clearly tagged."

"Thanks."

Bryan started into the room. He had barely made it to the second doorway when the lights suddenly went out, pitching the morgue into a cold sea of blackness.

An autopsy meant Mary would be in the hospital morgue. Jessica hoped and prayed that Mary might not have become...what she was about to become, but the truth was, she *knew*.

The very fact that Bryan MacAllistair was here was a warning.

But Mary hadn't been alone at night. That was the puzzle.

In the end, it didn't matter. Jessica was certain she needed to find the poor girl's corpse. That night.

By day, there were so many people milling around, by night, so few.

She had thought about calling Sean, but she decided she didn't want him involved. He was on his way up the cop ladder, and he didn't need any questions being asked about his integrity. Or his sanity. No, this was something she had to take care of on her own.

In a supply room, she chose a green cleaning-crew jacket. She already had a fake identification. She also took a bucket and a mop, which gave off the strong odor of antibacterial cleaning solution. She put on a head scarf and a mask against the fumes, and mumbled a few words with a French accent to the attendant on duty at the morgue.

She could hardly ask for the location of the body she was interested in; she would just have to find it.

She moved down the hall and entered the first room.

Six gurneys. Five held the earthly remains of patients who had died. She noted with a sinking heart that the sixth was draped with a sheet but otherwise empty.

Then the lights went out.

David Hayes swore softly in amazement. Was it a flipping blackout? And if so, why hadn't the emergency lights kicked on?

Was it the whole hospital? Or just the morgue?

He started to stand, then felt a hand on his shoulder.

"Hey, handsome."

The whisper was soft, feminine and totally sexual. He froze, even as her voice awakened his libido.

Who the hell did he know who would seduce him in the morgue during a blackout?

At last purple emergency lights flickered on to illuminate the room.

His eyes widened. His jaw dropped. Lord...

The most beautiful creature he'd seen in his whole life was standing in front of him.

Totally naked.

Blond and beautiful, with enormous breasts and a tiny waist. Not an ounce of cellulite on her. Her complexion was pale and perfect. Her eyes were enormous and...carnal.

She smiled, a finger touching his lips. "I've been waiting. We're alone, aren't we?"

They weren't alone, he thought. There was a cleaning lady somewhere. And a doctor. And the lights would come back on any minute, and...he didn't care.

"I've been watching you," she said softly. Her fingers trailed down his face. He needed to tell her that they weren't alone, but he couldn't.

He needed this job. It was his way of making it through school. He liked it. He sat at the desk, and he read. It was quiet, and it paid well, and it beat the hell out of sweating to death in a coffee house or a burger joint. If he got caught, he could kiss it goodbye.

He needed to tell her.

But his lips wouldn't work.

He could only stare at her.

Her hands were cold.

This was a morgue, for God's sake. The whole place was cold.

At last he managed to open his mouth, but no sound came.

She smiled deeply, watching his face. "Silly boy…"

It sounded as if she were hissing. Like a snake.

Her tongue teased his lips. Cold, so cold…

Something was wrong.

She started to kiss him. She might be cold, and this might be a morgue, but he was suddenly on fire. He reached out, acting on instinct. Lord, she was built. And her cold lips on his, then against his throat…

Oh, Lord…

Bryan stood perfectly still, listening. The door behind him had closed. For a moment, it seemed the world was totally silent in the stygian darkness.

Then…something. Just a rustle of movement.

And he knew, in the darkness, he was not the only stalker.

He was being stalked in turn.

He moved as silently as he could. There was a gurney before him. He touched it carefully. There was a corpse on it, cold and still. Unmoving.

He remained cautious as he felt his way around it. Things could change. Lucky for him, they didn't.

He found the next gurney. Again, he felt its occupant carefully. A woman, he thought. But she didn't move.

The next table offered a very big man.

The next...was empty.

The total darkness unnerved her.

Jessica's heart caught in her throat. She sensed movement, and she knew. Someone else was there, near her in the darkness.

Hospital personnel, she told herself, unconvincingly. There was the attendant on duty in the hallway. And, of course, with a blackout, someone from Maintenance would be down soon.

There were rolling blackouts from time to time, she reminded herself, but she knew—somehow— that this wasn't one of them.

This one had been planned.

She moved across the room very carefully, abandoning her mop and pail. She paused at each gurney.

She found the empty one.

She sensed movement again, felt a sense of

someone near. Time stood still as she fought a rising wave of panic. As she listened, her skin began to crawl.

Where the hell were the emergency lights?

It seemed like eons since the power had gone out.

Logic prevailed. It had been seconds, maybe a minute.

She was tempted to slip onto the empty gurney, hide beneath the sheet. Pretend to be among the dead.

She refrained, afraid that in the pitch dark, she would be putting herself in even greater danger.

She sensed it again. Someone near. She reached into the pocket of her smock and her fingers felt the cold cross she'd hidden there and closed around it.

Bryan's heart sank. He had expected the worst when the darkness came so suddenly. Had known he was too late. And yet…he should have been in plenty of time. It didn't matter. He knew he wasn't alone in the room.

Something shifted every so slightly in the darkness just across the gurney. He reached into the lab coat and closed his fingers around the shaft of wood. He shifted his position. There was the slightest rustle in the air as he moved.

He had been heard.

The creature across from him moved.

He drew his weapon.

Purple lights suddenly came on, dim, but nearly blinding after the pitch darkness.

He barely stopped his attack in time.

She fell across the empty gurney, a cross gripped tightly in her hands.

"You!" she cried.

"You!" he returned.

Then they heard the scream from the hallway.

They both raced across the room and burst through the door that led to the desk and the attendant, Dave, who had so recently been reading his book.

Dave was still there.

Slumped down on the floor.

Bryan raced to the boy, reaching for his throat, seeking a pulse. There was one. "Hit the code button!" he cried to Jessica.

She already had. An alarm was already sounding.

What the hell was Jessica doing here?

He'd nearly killed her.

No time to think about that now. He'd would talk to her later.

There were puncture marks on Dave's neck, just as he had expected. He ripped off the lab coat and used it to put pressure against the wounds, though there was no flow of blood on his throat. Mary! She hadn't finished her task, but she hadn't let a drop go to waste, he thought. That meant she had awakened alone—if she'd had an experienced vampire to tutor her, Dave would be dead.

He damned himself a thousand times over. But something was off about this! She shouldn't have awakened so quickly. At least this kid was still alive.

But for how long?

The boy's pulse was growing stronger. He was young, and he had a good chance of survival, especially since help would arrive any minute. No better place to suffer severe blood loss than a hospital.

"He has to make it," he said aloud.

No reply. He looked up.

Jessica was no longer there.

He'd never planned on having to explain he wasn't Dr. MacDonald, and he really couldn't afford the scrutiny that would result. He sat the boy up against the desk, opening his shirt, checking his breathing. He heard the elevator clanking. Only then did he rise and hurry down the hall. There was a fire emergency door at the end of it.

Another alarm would go off, but he would be gone.

He sprinted toward the exit, certain help had come, leaving himself just time enough to disappear before all hell broke loose.

"Wow!" Nancy said when they returned to Jessica's office on Royal Street.

Silently, Jeremy repeated the same sentiment.

He had been convinced, despite what he'd said

that she hadn't believed a word he and Nancy had said. Even in Transylvania, no one had taken them seriously. Detective Florenscu had all but waved a hand dismissively every time they had spoken.

Had he really known the truth? Maybe he had just thought he was safe, that the terror in his own country had ended, that he just needed to get them out and finish up the paperwork. Or maybe he had believed there was nothing he could do. He might even believe that Mary was going to survive, that evil couldn't track her down across an ocean.

"Wow," Nancy repeated.

Jessica had adorned the windows and both the inner and outer doors with garlic. The window sills were lined with vases filled with water. Holy water, he was certain. There were cuttings in the water. More garlic, he presumed.

There were crosses everywhere. For good measure, she'd added a handsome Star of David in a frame, a small statue of Buddha and a picture of Confucius.

Everything had been arranged to look like decorations, homage to different religious teachings around the world.

He even found a voodoo doll in a chair, and there were other artifacts about the room that seemed to be religious symbols he just didn't recognize.

She wasn't there when they arrived; no problem, since she'd given him a key. A note on her desk was weighted down with two silver chains bearing large silver crosses. They were to wear the crosses and remember not to open the doors or the windows, no matter who tried to gain entry.

They gravely put on the crosses. As they did so, Jeremy noted one last provision she had made for them.

Stakes.

"Do you feel safe?" Nancy asked.

"I feel better," he said, managing a smile.

They found a deck of cards and played war for a while, but neither one of them could manage to pay attention.

At last they figured they could at least rest. She'd provided the couch and recliner with pillows and blankets, so they drifted off as afternoon became evening and evening segued into night.

That was when Mary came.

At first Jessica didn't leave the hospital.

She shed her disguise and circled around to the emergency room, then the main entrance, and made a meticulous search of the place, floor by floor. She was seized with a greater and greater sense of desperation as she searched; somehow, Mary had made her escape.

As she conducted her search, trying to appear as if she were looking for a friend's room, her mind seethed.

Bryan MacAllistair had been there, wielding a stake.

Who the hell was he? *What* the hell was he?

And he had seen her, too. What was going through his mind? The same questions she was asking? She felt a deep chill run through her, something far more disturbing than anything she had known in years.

At last she gave up searching. Wherever Mary was, it wasn't the hospital.

Outside, she dialed Sean's number. When he answered, she gave him the news tersely. "Mary is up—and gone."

"What?" Sean said sharply.

She inhaled. "You heard me. Don't ask questions, just believe what I'm saying and get me some help."

"Lord God," he muttered. "All right."

She winced slightly. Sunday. She could imagine the man home with his wife and children. But this was far more important than anyone's leisure time and Maggie, through experience and more than any other woman, would understand completely.

"Jeremy and Nancy are in my office," she said. "I think she'll sense Jeremy and go after him."

"Most likely. I'll head there right—"

"No, Sean. You've got the credentials to find out what's going on at the hospital. I'll go to my office."

"Makes sense."

"Sean, it's all my fault."

"Jessica, none of us could have foreseen this."

"I think—" She broke off and winced. "I think she might have been targeted specifically to…taunt me."

Bryan seethed with anger, but this was no time to forget everything and lose sight of the business at hand. He roamed the streets, searching for Mary. Alone, it was an almost impossible task, no matter how good his senses were.

Mary knew the area.

Where would a quite possibly naked woman head?

A strip club on Bourbon Street.

"Jeremy."

He heard her voice. She was there in his dream. Her smile sweet, a little lost.

"Jeremy…"

He opened his eyes. The sound was coming from the window.

Don't go, an inner voice warned him, but he couldn't help himself. And anyway, this was just a dream, right? Not really happening. All he had left of her was a dream.

He glanced over at Nancy. She was sound asleep. He was sure he was asleep, as imagining that he was only hearing the girl who had meant so much to him in life.

He rose and headed for the window. It was framed in garlic, guarded by holy water. But there were no bars, and when he opened the drapes, he could see her.

They were on the second floor of a nineteenth-century building, but Mary appeared to be standing, floating in the air, just beyond the pane.

"Mary!" His heart caught in his throat. She looked so pure and perfect, naked as the day she was born, but somehow innocent, nonetheless.

"Jeremy, I need you. I always need you, don't I? Help me, Jeremy. I'm so cold, so desperate. So hungry."

"Oh, Mary…"

"You have to let me in. You have to get rid of all that stuff blocking me, and you have to let me in."

"Mary, I can't let you in. Don't you know? You're a vampire now."

"I'm cold, Jeremy. I'm hungry. I'm so hungry that it's agony. Please, Jeremy."

The sound of her voice tore at his heart. He couldn't bear to see her in pain.

And it was only a dream.

In a dream it wouldn't matter if he opened the window. Removed all that stuff Jessica had put there to humor him, to ease his fear.

In a dream, he could let her in. Hold her as he had always longed to do…

"Jeremy…"

Her voice seemed to reach inside him. Wrap around his very soul. How could he bear to witness such agony?

He reached for the window….

10

Sean Canady stood by the uniformed officer at the door, George Mendez, looking in on the young man who had been attacked in the morgue.

So far, David hadn't woken up, so he hadn't been able to tell anyone anything. But he was stabilizing, and he appeared to be in better shape than Mary had been.

"Don't leave him; not for a minute," Sean ordered his officer.

"No, sir."

"Not even to take a leak, I mean it. I've got Howlett down the hallway. Call him if you need a break."

"Yes, sir," George Mendez promised. He was new to the force and a quietly practicing Catholic. Sean had chosen him for exactly that reason. He'd seemed to take it in stride, no questions asked, when Sean had hung a crucifix around David's neck.

In fact, he'd seen Mendez fingering the large silver cross he wore himself, usually beneath his uniform.

"Sir?" Mendez asked.

"Yeah?"

"Did they make a mistake? Was the girl alive?"

"Mendez, right now, we don't know what went down. A body is missing, and a young man has suffered serious blood loss. For all I know, it could be a sick fraternity prank. Anyway, until we know more, we say nothing. Howlett will be keeping away the press and the just plain curious. But I want one of you with this young man at all times. I've informed the staff that not even the doctors are to draw a curtain against you, got it? If he needs a bedpan, you're still right here."

"Yes, sir. I won't let you down, sir."

Sean nodded and started down the hall. Howlett stopped him. "The press is outside," he warned.

"Thanks."

Sean straightened his spine and headed out to meet the enemy.

Praying that she had made an impression on Jeremy and Nancy earlier, and that she wasn't too late if she hadn't, Jessica raced to her office.

She banged on the door. "Jeremy, let me in."

She waited, somehow sensing that he was in terrible danger. She winced as she stood there, fearful his good heart would be his downfall.

She fumbled for her key, finally got it into the

lock, then rushed through the door and ran to the inner office.

As she burst in, Jeremy, who had been facing the window, turned at last. He blinked, staring at her stupidly.

"I was...sleeping," he said, sounding confused.

Jessica went to him and grabbed him by the shoulders trying to shake him into awareness.

"You can never—never—let her in."

"But...it was Mary."

Nancy began to stir at last. "I thought I heard banging. It was so strange. I thought I heard—"

She broke off, staring from Jeremy to Jessica.

Jeremy continued to face Jessica, his features drawn and taut, his eyes filled with sorrow.

"It was Mary," he repeated.

Jessica lowered her lashes, shaking her head. Then she looked up at him.

"I know," she said softly.

Going from strip club to strip club was probably not something that most men would consider an onerous task, but the tension gripping Bryan was so tight that he couldn't even summon a pretense of normal courtesy.

No, he didn't want a lap dance.

No, it wasn't the price.

No, he wasn't gay.

It was just that there was only one woman who interested him, and comparing her to anyone else was like comparing the elegance of silk, the electricity of a lightning storm, to raw linen and a pale dawn. Last night...

But right now, he had to find Mary. He wondered if he was wasting his time.

Then, at last, he found her.

It was one of the tawdrier places, off the beaten track. The bouncers were big, but flabby. The shine was worn off the poles, the runway carpets threadbare. The girls looked to be older than the usual and, like the bouncers, less than perfectly fit.

Until Mary made her appearance.

She'd picked up some kind of apparel—if it could be called that—backstage. Bryan gritted his teeth, wondering how she'd acquired it, but he had a feeling she hadn't made any further attacks. There were no private dressing rooms in this establishment.

No, she was waiting to take a customer into one of the little curtained alcoves.

She strutted down the runway as if she'd been born to it. She had the naughty schoolgirl look that was such a come-on to some men. She had a smile that was a sheer tease, full of forbidden promises.

She posed, teased, tempted. She practically had sex with the pole.

Money was flying; men were roaring. She began

to offer her services for lap dances. One man offered a thousand dollars. Hoots and jeers filled the air.

Mary assessed the double-chinned businessman, and a smile of disdain touched her lips before she wetted them with her tongue.

"Why not?" she whispered, and beckoned to him, starting backstage.

The man nearly tripped over himself running after ‾her. Discreetly, Bryan followed.

There was darkness. A very strange darkness. Not like ebony, not like a blackout. Officer Mendez couldn't have said exactly when he began to notice it, because it was subtle. It was as if a shadow had descended. Not a real shadow, nothing with a shape or definable edges, just a strange, new sense and *feel* of darkness.

And then cold.

Officer Mendez knew his duty. Pure terror began to rip through him, but he had vowed he wouldn't leave, and he wouldn't. He fought his fear and approached the young man on the bed. He touched the boy's crucifix, then noticed that the pillow was oddly damp.

Holy water? Had the lieutenant actually sprinkled the young man's pillow with holy water?

Please, yes.

Mendez curled his fingers around the silver cross that protected his own throat. He began to pray aloud. "Yea, though I walk through the valley of the shadow of death…"

It felt as if he were being strangled. As if the shadow had taken on a physical form and was attacking him, reaching for him….

"I will fear no evil," he continued.

He closed his eyes for a minute, afraid he was about to lose it completely and go tearing out of the room.

He thought he heard laughter, it was gone as quickly as it had come. With it went the shadow, the sensation of cold. Gone as if it had never been.

He had broken out into a cold sweat, and he was shaking, but now he began to breathe more easily.

Then it came again. The laughter. He placed his hands over his ears, never thinking for a second to reach for his firearm. He knew it would be useless.

"I will fear no evil."

Again the laughter drifted away.

This time it stayed gone.

Mendez sank into the visitor's chair at the foot of the bed and looked around nervously. Nothing appeared to have changed. He thanked God he hadn't given in to his fear, thanked God he hadn't run screaming down the hall.

He sank to his knees and humbly begged God never to be given this assignment again. He was newly married, with a baby on the way. He had to live.

He stayed on his knees as the night progressed, wondering if he dared try to explain to Detective Canady that there had been a shadow in the room.

And that he was afraid it would come back.

The curtain drew closed behind the businessman. Bryan took a quick look around; there were other curtains, providing privacy for whatever went on in the alcoves. There was nothing he could do. She had to be stopped.

He wrenched aside the curtain just in time to see the overeager fat man kneeling on the floor, blubbering like a two-year-old. His eyes were wide, his toupee askew.

Mary stood over him, telling him to shut up and bare his throat, and though he shook and gasped for breath, he didn't have the will to deny her. He was like a bleeding diver in a chummed sea, watching the approach of a great white, knowing he was about to be bitten in half. He could see his life—and his death—all at once.

Mary hissed as the drapery opened and stared at Bryan. For a moment he could see the sudden sharp growth of her canines, could see what the fat man could see, the promise of death, as surely as if the fangs belonged to a deadly asp.

He drew out a vial of holy water, thrice blessed, and doused her.

She screamed. A terrible scream, like a banshee crying out, and there was the terrible smell of burning flesh.

The fat man cried out, ducking.

Mary doubled over.

Bryan moved, ready to deliver the coup de grâce. But the fat man suddenly screamed again, leaping to his feet.

And in those seconds Mary found the will to survive. She whirled with the speed of light and burst away from the alcove and the curtain. Someone screamed in her path, and people went flying, landing hard against the runway, where a nearly naked woman was doing a come-on with a bull whip.

Everyone in the place was suddenly standing, and fists were flying wildly. It had all happened in just seconds.

Swearing, Bryan leapt over the still screaming and blubbering fat man. He thrust out an arm, pushing his way through the crowd.

Mary had escaped into a back alley. He did the same.

Jessica stayed with Nancy and Jeremy until the sun began to rise. By then Jeremy seemed to have made a major change. He grew calm, no longer so shattered. He was quiet and pensive.

"It's safe to leave by day, isn't it?" he asked Jessica.

She hesitated. "I don't really—"

She broke off; he was staring at her with something close to contempt.

"You do know," he said quietly. "I don't know how you know, but you know."

She stared back at him. "You're probably safe by daylight," she said at last. Then she shrugged and started across the room, taking a seat at her desk and staring at them. "Don't believe the legend that vampires can't move about by day. They can, and they need only sleep near or with a few granules of their native soil. They don't like sunlight, but it won't kill them, and too much saltwater, not just holy water, can kill them. What else? A really powerful vampire can make you forget just about anything. And a really powerful vampire can twist most people to his or her will without even looking them in the eyes." She paused again. The kids had worried that everyone would think they were crazy. Now they probably thought *she* was totally insane.

"I wouldn't talk about this, if I were you. If you try to convince other people that vampires are real, they'll probably find a way to lock you up. Maybe we all deny what we're afraid to believe, I don't know. The point is…" She gritted her teeth and leaned forward. "The point is, there is a particularly powerful vampire known as the Master. He's just about as evil as sin itself. He has appeared many times throughout history. He was dormant for many years, and I actually believed he might have been destroyed, but…anyway, I believe he followed Mary here. So it's not just Mary walking the streets of New Orleans. There's far worse out there," she finished softly.

"Are you a slayer, then? Are there really such things?" Jeremy asked.

She lowered her lashes, shaking her head. "No. I'm not a slayer. I simply try to stop them from killing, from making more of their kind. Sadly, I failed to save Mary."

"How do you know about this…Master?" Jeremy asked.

"He's been around before," she said simply. "I went to the conference in Romania hoping to hear rumors of vampire activity. As usual, there was lots of talk about cults and people who think they need to suck blood, but in all that hot air, you can usually find some glimmer of truth or catch wind of one of the parties the Master has started hosting as his personal feast. He likes to pick and choose. Mary was quite beautiful," she added softly.

"This is insane," Nancy said.

Of course it sounded insane. They'd insisted they'd seen vampires without having any idea of what that really meant.

"You wanted the truth. I've given it to you. You'll need to protect yourselves at all times. Especially if I'm right and the Master is here, planning one of his parties."

She was surprised when Nancy said, "The sad thing is, I believe you." Her voice turned to a whisper. "I was there. And I know that you're telling the truth. I just want it to be insane."

Suddenly Jeremy sprang to life and shook his head. "But…the whole city needs to be warned. The entire state. Hell, the world!"

Jessica sighed. "Don't you understand? You can't go creating panic, or a situation in which you condemn those who can fight the evil to being stuck in a mental ward."

Nancy looked at Jeremy. "We need to go. We can help our friends, at the very least. We can hand out crosses to our friends. We can ask them to wear them in memory of Mary."

"I'm going to suggest you come back here tonight," Jessica said.

"But our friends—"

"You two are the ones he wants. He'll be angry with Mary, because she wasn't able to seduce you into letting her in."

"If he hurts her—" Jeremy began angrily.

"Jeremy," Nancy said, taking his arm, "she's dead. The Mary we know is dead. Isn't that true?"

Again Jessica looked down, wondering what to say. She lifted her head and stared up at the two of them. "The Master is evil—excessively cruel. I'm afraid that Mary, who is now his creature, isn't at all the person you once knew. She'll sound like the woman you knew and loved, but she is his to command. Jeremy, you have to be strong. Strong for her."

"You mean, so I can kill her," he said bitterly.

"If need be."

"Maybe I can—"

"You have no idea what you're up against. You have to keep yourself safe and let me know any time she comes. Do you understand?" She hesitated. "Jeremy, the Master hates me, and he will try especially hard to hurt the two of you, because he knows we've grown close. He'll target some people for his amusement, but others..." She trailed off, not certain how much to say. "I believe the Master is intent on ruining my life, hurting those I care about. You have to be strong, Jeremy. You have to resist Mary, no matter how hard that is. Do you understand? She intends to kill you."

Nancy was frowning, but she clearly comprehended that they were in serious danger. "He understands." Nancy said firmly. "I'll see to it."

"Let's go," Jeremy said dully.

"Be back before dark," Jessica warned them firmly.

Jeremy looked at her, troubled. "Why does he want to hurt you so badly?"

"It's a very long story."

He waited. She remained quiet.

"All right," he said softly. "I'm going to assume you had something to do with the fact that he was…gone for so long. So you need to be careful, too."

"I will be," she vowed.

Then the two of them were gone.

She leaned back and folded her hands in her lap. After a moment, she murmured aloud, "That didn't go too badly."

She took a deep breath. Then she started to cancel her appointments for the week.

Except for one.

Sean leaned his head wearily against the back of his chair, momentarily closing his eyes. Maybe the aspirin would kick in soon.

What a night, and what a horrendous beginning to the day.

He'd already had to make the call to Mary's parents to tell them that their daughter's body had disappeared. At the hospital, there were two rumors going around. One claimed that a psychotic necrophiliac had stolen the body. Then there was the suggestion—taken more seriously by most—that the girl had never been dead, that the doctor on call had made a horrible mistake, and she had simply awakened, perhaps suffering some memory loss, and had grabbed some clothes from somewhere and headed out to the streets.

He'd also had to arrange for constant surveillance of Dave where he lay in the hospital, and he had to make sure he chose the right men for the job. The days were easy enough, but the nights were murder.

Now he was being told that Bryan MacAllistair was waiting to see him.

"Send him in," Sean told the desk clerk.

MacAllistair entered the room and just stood there imposingly, waiting.

"What can I do for you?" Sean demanded.

MacAllistair looked worn, exhausted. "Come clean," he said, taking a seat at least.

Sean groaned. "Come clean? You're a fine one to insist on honesty."

"I almost had her," MacAllistair said softly.

"Oh?"

MacAllistair shook his head. "The way I see it, you know damned well I was in the morgue. Jessica must have called you by now."

Sean leaned forward. "So, what the hell were you doing in the morgue?"

A humorless smile curved the man's lips. "Trying to stop a vampire," he said quietly.

Sean was shocked into silence, though he shouldn't have been, he thought.

"She's a vampire now. I tracked her down in one of the strip clubs. I almost had her, but she got away."

Sean blinked.

MacAllistair's grim smile deepened as he leaned forward. "I don't know what the hell is going on here, but I will find out. I think you know as well as I do that there's a vampire loose in the city. I intend to stop it. I can help you, you can help me."

MacAllistair rose. Sean fought to control his temper as MacAllistair spoke again.

"Call me if you need me. I promise I'll call you. Thanks for your time. I thought I should let you know I almost had her. I'd be watching my back tonight, if I were you."

With that, he nodded a goodbye and left.

"Son of a bitch!" Sean swore. "I should have arrested him."

For what? He asked himself. Knowing the truth?

Stacey was at the house, along with Gareth. She seemed relieved to see Jessica.

As Jessica walked up the steps, she surveyed the work being done.

Strings of garlic, dressed up with flowers, were hanging everywhere. There were containers of holy water and other religious symbols as if they had gotten their holidays confused.

"Nice job," she said dryly.

"You all right?" Gareth asked tensely.

She offered him a weary smile. "Just fine."

"We've heard all the news," Stacey said.

"I imagine."

"So, she's...gone?" Stacey asked.

Jessica nodded. "I'm going to lie down for a while. Get a little rest. If everything is all right here?"

"We've got it covered," Gareth assured her.

She hesitated, about to head inside. "Have you seen Bryan MacAllistair?" she asked.

"No," Stacey said, frowning and looking at Gareth. He shook his head solemnly.

Jessica lowered her head, letting out a sigh of exhaustion. "I've got to catch a few minutes of sleep. We'll talk later."

"No problem," Stacey replied.

Jessica walked through the front door and up the stairs to her room. In the hallway, she stopped, tempted to slip into his room and go through his things.

She was so tired, but it suddenly felt necessary.

She glanced around, though she knew she was alone in the house, then took out her master key and slipped into his room, locking the door behind her.

She stared around the room. Neat and tidy. His computer was on the desk. There were no papers beside it. In the closet, there were two dress jackets, shoes, a windbreaker and a few good shirts. She walked quickly to the dresser. T-shirts, boxers and flannel pajama bottoms.

Frustrated, she closed the drawer and moved

back to the computer. She turned it on and scanned his files. Nothing of interest. The computer was either brand-new, or everything was encrypted in someway she didn't have time to figure out. She connected to the Internet, anxious to view his past searches.

Startled, she swallowed and stepped back.

Then she gritted her teeth, telling herself she was a fool to be nervous. Of course he had looked up everything to do with vampires. Naturally some of the sites he had found discussed interesting cases revolving around vampirism. Naturally some of those cases involved her.

She thought she heard a sound in the hall. She turned off the computer, stepped back, froze and listened. Nothing. She was just so tired that she was hearing things.

She stepped out of his room, locking the door in her wake. Down the hall, she entered her own room. Good Lord, but she was exhausted. She kicked off her shoes, pulled her shirt over her head and shed her skirt, letting everything fall on the floor as she headed into the bathroom. She let the shower pour down on her long and hard.

Just two nights ago she had been in heaven. And now...

Who the hell was he and what the hell had he been doing there? He'd had a stake!

And where the hell was he now?

He had stirred such deep emotions in her. Awakened feelings she hadn't known in forever. He had reminded her so much of…

What was gone. Dead. What could never be again.

Wrapped in her robe, she strode back out to the bedroom, threw herself down on the bed and staring up at the ceiling.

Only then did she realize she wasn't alone in the room.

"At last." came the deep voice, barely a whisper on the breeze. "At last. I've been waiting for you, you know."

11

For an instant, terror filled her. It couldn't be…

There had been so many years when she had run, when she had spent her days and nights in hiding. There had been years when she had thought she had managed a real escape. Then she had finally realized that she would never live in peace if she didn't face the truth, and become a hunter. And still, no matter what pretense of confidence and assurance she had cultivated, there had still been the awful and absolute fear, the horror ….

She bolted up to a sitting position, all thoughts of exhaustion gone, ready to defend herself. But she wasn't being attacked. Not physically, at least.

Bryan MacAllistair was seated in the huge wing chair that flanked her bed. She had no idea how long he had been there. He could have been there when she entered the room; she had never so much as glanced around.

She hadn't seen him. Worse, she hadn't even sensed his presence!

She fought for control.

Swinging back a lock of hair, she clasped her arms around her knees and stared at him, slowly arching a brow. "What the hell are you doing in my room?"

He smiled grimly and queried, "What were you doing in mine?"

"Trying to find out who you are," she said flatly.

He lifted his hands. "My credentials speak for themselves."

"Your credentials are bullshit."

"I beg to differ. I'm not entirely sure about yours, however."

"My diploma is at my office," she informed him dryly.

"And I imagine it's completely in order," he said pleasantly, then stood, walked over and sat on the foot of her bed.

"What were you doing at the hospital?" he demanded.

"I knew the girl," she said indignantly.

"So you dressed up like the cleaning woman to visit her corpse?"

"What were *you* doing at the hospital?" she demanded.

"I went to kill a vampire," he said bluntly.

She swallowed, staring at him. No, gaping. "You've

been listening to your own lectures too long, Professor."

"Get off it."

"What?"

"Don't try to turn your psychology on me. You know what's out there."

"I…" *Who the hell was he?*

"You know that's what the girl has become," he said. It wasn't a question; it was a statement. "You know it, and your buddy the cop knows it. *How* you know it would make an entertaining story, I'm sure, but the truth is, you both know exactly what's going on."

She let her lashes fall. Then she sighed. "There has been vampire activity in the area before," she told him. She felt a chill. She forced herself to think, rather than feel. "So how do *you* know the truth of what's going on? Who the hell are you? Where did you come across a situation like this before?"

"All over the world," he said curtly. "We're dealing with the here and now, though, and that's what matters."

"I see. So…have you taken it on yourself to rid the world of vampires?" she asked, genuinely curious despite all her suspicions about him.

"I don't think any one person can rid the world of vampires. Like all other creatures, they have an instinct for survival. These days some of them hide as suburban housewives and stockbrokers. But I've been following one in particular."

"Oh?"

"The creature in Transylvania. The one who took Mary, and is apparently in New Orleans now. The one known as the Master."

"The Master?" He even knew her enemy's name. "The Master," she repeated, then could have slapped herself. She was starting to sound like a parrot. She was unnerved, and she needed to keep it together. Repeating his words would get her nowhere.

And of course the Master was in New Orleans. Had Romania been a tease? Had he known that she would be there? She had felt the evil before she had gone, no matter how hard she had tried to deny it. She knew it now. Knew it every waking moment. Knew it from the color of the sky.

There had been times when it had almost been possible to believe it was over, that the Master had been killed, that the darkness might never come again. But he had always been out there. And that was why she had to hunt.

But there was no way to explain any of that, especially to a man who needed to be explained himself.

"You were going to stake Mary!" she said.

"You bet. She's a creature of the Master's now. There's no choice."

She stared at him. "I believe, then, that we're on the same side."

"Are we?" he asked. "I don't really know you."

"And I don't know you."

"Those kids trusted you," he said quietly. "And look what happened to them."

Dear God, that hurt. But it was true.

"I knew nothing about that party until I received Jeremy's note," she said, and that, too, was true. "What were you doing in the area—without lifting a finger to help?"

He didn't reply but let out a soft groan of exasperation. "What matters now is this—you should stay out of it," he told her.

"What?" she demanded.

"I don't know what *you* know about the Master, but trust me, you're up against something you haven't encountered before."

"Oh?"

"There have been times through the years when vampire hunters, warriors, even kings, tried to kill him. They all failed. He has learned skills throughout the centuries that allow him to evade those who would stop him, and he's constantly on the move." He stood suddenly, pacing, and she was stunned by the ardor in his voice. "I have dedicated my life to finding this creature, to stopping him. There is no greater evil that walks the earth." He turned to her. "You need to take a step back. You *and* your friends. Whatever strength you think you have, whatever you think you know, you are facing a danger with a greater strength than you can begin to imagine."

She frowned, taken aback by his fury.

She answered slowly. "Trust me, it's not like I want to make contact," she said softly. "But I don't really have any choice. Because of what happened in Transylvania, I'm involved whether I want to be or not."

"You need to step back. I can't watch your back and defeat this creature."

"I can watch my own back," she snapped in return. "And who do you think you are, anyway? Some kind of great vampire slayer?"

"No, but as I told you, the Master has been my quest for some time now."

"But you'd kill all vampires if you could?"

"Of course."

"But…"

He laughed bitterly. "Are you going to suggest that some of them are actually good? If so, you're in greater danger than I had begun to imagine. Trust me, there is no such thing as a good vampire."

She looked down quickly. "I beg to differ. I've heard of some."

He hesitated, taking a long, deep breath. Then, rather than argue with her again, he startled her by walking to her side. "There's just something about you…you remind me so much of someone I knew once."

The tone of his voice seemed to stir an old

emotion, deep in her heart. "Maybe," she murmured huskily, "we've crossed paths before."

He shook his head. "No," he said, the pad of his thumb caressing her cheek. "She was…evil. And she is dead. Dead and gone. And if she were not…then I would have to kill her myself. As far as the Master goes, I have been close, so close that I could smell the fetid stench of his breath. I will see this through, and I will prevail. But to do so, I have to know you'll be stay out of it, stay safe."

Her heart seemed to take a little leap. How could this be?

How could she feel such a shattering depth of passion for a man who had just walked into her life? How could she feel—as insane as it sounded—that she had known him before?

The great love of her life was so long gone.

"You underestimate me," she told him.

He sat beside her. "Trust me," he said.

"If you'll believe in me," she told him. "So what do you know about the Master?"

"I can't tell you how long I've been tracking him. Long enough to know his strength. I know the dominatrix who works with him is rumored to be the newest incarnation of his creature Katherine, a British countess believed destroyed in the reign of Louis XIV. She didn't begin her existence in that guise, of course. She was an evil created long before.

It was easy then for such creatures to disappear from one place and reappear elsewhere. Some say she moved on to China, to Cairo...to countries in turmoil, where murder is not so easily noticed. And if so, then she, too, must die before this can be over. You simply don't know what you're up against with the two of them. I beg you, listen to me on this."

Jessica turned away from him, shaking her head. "Maybe we're both asking the impossible."

"What is it about you?" he asked very softly. "I just can't walk away."

She turned her head lowered, then slowly raised her eyes to his. "So what do we do?" she asked.

"You could listen to me. You see, I...failed once. I let someone down. I lost her. That same steel and resolve, courage, confidence, are part of you, too. And the way that I felt then..." He took a deep breath. "I touch you, and I'm paralyzed with the fear of losing you as I did her.

"Don't be afraid for me. Please."

She spoke in a whisper. He was so close, and suddenly a yearning filled her that was stronger than any fear for what the future might bring. Once upon a time, so long ago, there had been hope, no matter how bitter the reality of life. And then...

But now, when he touched her, hope and belief stirred in her heart again, along with a yearning, poignant, sad and agonizing, yet beautiful, as well.

Turmoil raged around and within her, but it didn't matter, not at this moment.

Perhaps similar thoughts rode through his mind, because he didn't speak again. He simply kissed her. And this time there was no almost-maddened desperation as there had been before. This time his lips spoke of whatever was real and fine within the soul and the very heart. She kissed him in return, seeking the answers neither spoke, an end to the war of need raging within her, expressing her own yearning to touch something long gone, to experience the spiral of erotic fantasy and raw rapture he could create.

In seconds, questions were forgotten, answers were no longer needed.

Her fingers found wanton pleasure in moving delicately over his face, his body, finding the obstruction of clothing, slipping beneath it. His flesh heated beneath her touch as her hands softly moved down the line of his back, curved over the tautness of his muscled form. She reveled in the pressure of his body against her own as her lips traced seductive patterns down the length of his throat; she stroked and teased with her tongue, with the sinuous movement of her own body against his.

She cherished the madness, the oblivion, she found in his arms. Desire rose higher, and she lost all thought, all fear, all sense of the future. There was only the here and now, nothing more, the thunder of her pulse against the clamor of his, lips, tongues, fingertips. His lips against her breasts. The liquid tender touch of his tongue, urgently insane. Her fingers, stroking against the aroused length of him. The two of them twisting and rolling, finding new positions in which to touch each other. His caress against her inner thighs, the flicker of her tongue upon the hardness of him, his arms wrapped around her, drawing her against him again, mouths meshing again. And then, at last, the streak of molten steel inside her. Pleasure burst through her in a shower of relief, and she felt his fierce tremor and release at the same time. She lay there, dazed, the room becoming real again, savoring the feel of slick flesh against slick flesh and the feeling of succoring arms, something she had never thought to feel again. She felt a sense of amazement and security, and yet she found herself fighting against the desire to lose herself so completely.

Sex was one thing, truth was another. And now, more than ever, she needed distance.

"Jessica?"

The sound of his voice, rich, husky and deep, seemed to stroke her soul.

"I'm so tired," she whispered, and that was the truth.

With a sigh, he held her. She feigned sleep, and in a few minutes, it became real.

* * *

Nightmares again.

She was alone, a different person, in a different place, a different time.

Born to war, born in sin, a bastard, she learned to wield a sword, learned to fight.

Learned to kill.

Learned the hardest lesson of all. Courage.

Remnants of memory, faded and torn, remained of a time when her fight had been just, when lives had been at stake, an entire nation at risk.

And then...

Death but no peace. Waking in an agony far beyond that of death and with a hunger that seemed to rake inside her like a thousand daggers. Awaking to the maddened laughter of a hated enemy, who commanded her to serve, mocked her, swore that all she had loved were dead and he had won, so she was now a prize of war.

To the victor went the spoils.

The Master—for that was what he called himself—was the power, but from the beginning she defied him. She endured the pain of unnatural hunger, determined that though her soul might be damned, she would not allow her will to be twisted. The focus of her existence became to fight his power. And she escaped. For years, she managed a strange kind of life beyond death....

She escaped him at last, dined upon the rightfully condemned, found it a blessed bounty to be able to release the innocent, but despite her efforts, she became known as a creature of evil.

Then the Master found her again.

But years had passed; she had gained strength. They met upon a tor in the Highlands. He thought to take her with his will and his bare hands. He was not expecting her to be prepared with sharp wooden stakes.

But he wasn't killed, only injured, and he retreated.

They met next in the dark fog of the Carpathian Mountains, where ancient legend and fear ran deep, where the horrors of life were sometimes far greater than the horrors of death.

It was there that she slew the thirteen guardsmen stationed outside his castle to destroy her before she could reach him. Could she have bested him if she had not caught him unaware? She didn't know. He had been at his great table, eagerly reading an ancient text. She entered like a soft silver mist, seducing first, and then when he was unaware, staking him....

But the stake was not enough, and so the battle was begun. He taunted her, reminding her that he had destroyed Ioin, the mighty knight who had been her love.

Perhaps he hadn't realized how much power she could access from her pain, because he underestimated her strength. She fought with renewed vigor. His head was attached by little more than bone and a few shreds of cartilage, his limbs and torso gashed. She chased him through deep underground crypts, and there she lost him. Exhausted, still she forced herself to turn the crypt into a prison that would hold forever—silver crossbars everywhere, holy relics— knowing he was there, hidden, unseen. As she finished, she knew her nightmare was not over, for she heard his whispered vow. He would survive. He would find her.

She awoke in a cold sweat. Damn Bryan MacAllistair. Being with him was a sweet ecstasy she had never dared dream of knowing yet being near him also evoked nightmares of the past.

She was cold, she realized. Horribly cold. Of course. He was gone; she was alone.

Glancing outside, she saw that the day was waning.

She bolted out of bed and sped back into the shower, then dressed with an ever-growing sense of urgency. Running downstairs, she nearly ran over Stacey.

"Jess—"

"Where's our lodger?"

"Bryan?"

"He's the only one we've got," she said curtly. "Where is he?"

"He's gone. And he told me not to let you leave."

"What?"

"He said I needed to keep you here. That it was crucial you stay home tonight."

"My God! He knows something. Something is happening tonight."

"Jessica, honest to God, he scared me. I think you really should stay home tonight."

"I can't. You know that."

"Yes, you can. You can let someone else—"

"Stacey, he could get himself killed. I've got to go. You stay here. You know the drill. Call Jeremy, make sure he and Nancy either come here—which might be the best idea—or go to my office. Before dark. No, don't call him, find them both—even if you and Gareth have to comb the streets—and bring them back here. I've got to go."

"Jessica, wait. At least—"

"I have to go."

She ran out of the house and was in the driver's seat of her car before Stacey even made it out the door. A growing sense of urgency filled her, and though Stacey's intentions were good, talking to her was costing too much time, and none of her words could change anything. Jessica waved, taking advantage of an immediate chance to slide out of the driveway.

At Maggie's house, she banged on the door impatiently. Maggie let her in, finger to her lips. "Kids napping," she whispered.

Jessica nodded, taking a deep gulp of air. "I think I'm in severe trouble."

"That poor girl…dead. And the corpse disappearing. The mayor's office is screaming, and Sean is…in a vise," Maggie responded.

"Maggie, he's after the vampire."

"Of course he is. It's his job," Maggie said, frowning.

"Not Sean. Bryan MacAllistair. I can't figure it out. Who the hell is he? What is he? How does he know…what he knows?"

"Let's go in the kitchen," Maggie suggested. "I don't want to wake the children."

Jessica followed her to the other room, where Maggie, ever practical, poured coffee for them.

Maggie sat down at the breakfast table. The daily paper was open on the table, as if she'd been reading it when Jessica arrived.

Jessica paced in agitation. "Maggie, he was there, in the morgue, ready to stake Mary. Except she came back so fast, it was amazing. She should have needed hours of darkness."

"It was still light?" Maggie asked.

"Barely dusk."

Maggie drummed her fingers on the table. "It has to be the Master at work. We should have known it. You never should have gone to Transylvania."

"Oh, come on, Maggie. I can't spend my life hiding."

"We should have known," Maggie repeated softly. "I haven't seen anything like this sky in years. I think you were being conned, lured."

"To Transylvania?"

"Yes."

"How could the Master have been luring me? He doesn't—didn't—even know I'm here, living in New Orleans."

"Maybe he did know."

Jessica shook her head. "No, to him, I'm dead."

"Think about it. I could be right. I wish the others were here. You should have waited. We should have had help. There's no way you should have gone alone. I think you walked into a trap."

"We're getting off track. Bryan MacAllistair...I can't figure him out."

"He's definitely not a vampire?" Maggie asked, then answered her own question. "No, I would have known."

"But what is he, then? He knows there are vampires out there. I'm sure he's killed them before. But he's obsessed with the Master."

"Well, if he *is* a vampire hunter, that's not a surprise, considering the Master is pretty much evil incarnate," Maggie said.

"He scares me," Jessica murmured.

"Bryan MacAllistair?" Maggie arched a brow, delicately sipping her coffee. "I thought he affected you in quite a different way."

Jessica flushed. "That too," she whispered. "And that's what's wrong! I haven't felt like this... haven't wanted..."

"Haven't given in?" Maggie suggested.

Jessica shook her head. "It's as if I've known him forever. As if we somehow belong together."

"But?"

"Maggie, what if he were to discover just who I am? No, that's impossible," she said, trying to assure herself as much as her friend.

She waited for a reply, but Maggie was silent for a long time. Finally she said, "I think it would be a good idea to find out as much as we can about him." She tapped the paper meaningfully.

"What is it?"

"His lecture series is listed here. The next one is on villains in history and legend."

"And?"

"He'll be speaking about Katherine, Countess Valor."

"Katherine Valor…" Jessica shook her head. "She died. Thousands of witnesses said so. It's in all the history books."

"Maybe your vampire hunter doesn't think so," Maggie offered.

Jessica shook her head again, as if dismissing the possibility. Then she whispered, "How can he be so familiar to me?"

"Maybe you *did* know him before," Maggie suggested.

"Impossible. He reminds me…but I saw him die, Maggie. *I saw him die.*"

"Forget that for now. You have to get out there

and find Mary. That's a priority. Sean has a really good man watching over the morgue attendant who was bitten. So you shouldn't bother with the hospital at all. Focus on the big stuff. The Master will know you, now he's here. And Mary's friends will be vulnerable. You need to protect them. As to the professor, we can do some research," Maggie said. "In fact, I can start on that right now."

"Maggie, you can't go running around out there. You have a family to take care of."

"I'm not running around anywhere," Maggie told her. "I'm heading straight to the Internet."

Bryan hadn't slept. He hadn't dared let himself relax.

Lying beside Jessica, he'd felt a rush of emotion that had been all but paralyzing.

The need to fight, to protect this woman.

And sheer dread. A pounding in his mind, as if something dark, heavy and oppressive had settled over him. A feeling like the one he had experienced in Transylvania.

There had been long moments when he had stayed at her side and held her, savoring the sensation of warmth in his soul, of completeness. He couldn't remember ever feeling such a sense of being where he should be as he'd felt then, his arms around her, her body so intimate and trusting against his own.

He yearned to remain.

And because of that, he was at last spurred to action.

He left the house after delivering something that was both a plea and a threat, hoping Stacey would have some influence with Jessica. But whether she did or did not, he knew he had to move.

When he arrived at Jessica's office, receiving no answer to his persistent knocking, he simply picked the lock. No sign of Jeremy and Nancy.

He had to admit, the place was impressively protected. Still, it wasn't Mary's ability to get in that worried him—it was the fact that Jeremy might be all too willing and eager to welcome her.

As he stood there, there was a tentative knock at the door.

He opened it.

An attractive but worn-looking woman in her thirties was standing there, along with a sullen boy of perhaps seventeen. The kid was all in black. Bryan was certain he had been dragged here.

"Hello. Can I help you?" he asked.

"We were looking for Miss Fraser," the woman said.

"I'm afraid she's not in today."

"Oh." The woman looked distressed.

"Is there anything that I can do?" he asked.

To his surprise, the sullen teenager suddenly spoke up. "Hey, you're him!"

Bryan arched a brow.

"You're that professor." He turned to his mother, a look of enthusiasm on his face. "He was in the newspaper. He talks about vampires."

The mother appeared to be horrified, ready to back away and run.

"I really am a professor," Bryan explained. Assessing the situation, he added quickly, "I warn people about cults, along with talking about legends and beliefs."

For a moment she just stared at him. Then she flushed. "Maybe you can convince my son to stay out of the cemetery."

Bryan looked politely at the boy, hiding the fact that he had felt his pulse quicken. "Oh?"

The kid shrugged, looking unhappy. "Hey, it's New Orleans, you know?"

"As if we haven't been through enough," his mother muttered.

"Do you meet friends in the cemetery?" Bryan asked. "The thing is, dark, isolated places create an atmosphere where criminals...evil...are present."

The woman stretched out her hand, looking as if she'd crossed an inner Rubicon. "Myra Peterson. My son, Jacob."

"Perhaps I could speak with Jacob alone for a minute," Bryan said.

Myra Peterson looked uncertain for a minute. "I...well, I..."

"I think I might be able to help," he said.

She nodded. "You're a friend of Jessica's? Have you worked with her? But you're a teacher, not a psychologist."

He stared at her. "I can help," he repeated.

"I…." she murmured, staring back at him. "Yes, of course. Thank you."

He nodded, a grim smile on his face. "Jacob?"

The boy looked a little surprised, a little intrigued—and suddenly frightened, but he walked ahead of Bryan into the inner office, looking over his shoulder.

Bryan shut the door behind him.

"What the hell were you doing in the cemetery, Jacob?" he asked.

"What?" Startled by the tone of Bryan's voice, the boy spun and looked at him.

"You heard me. What the fuck were you doing in the cemetery?"

The kid's jaw dropped. "You can't talk to me like that. I'll tell my mom."

"Go right ahead. But first, you'll tell me what you were doing in the cemetery."

"Some people I know, they're talking about something cool coming here, to New Orleans. A leader, like a master vampire or something. And we'll find everything our hearts desire."

"So a vampire is going to be hanging out in a cemetery?"

Jacob reddened and flushed. "Yeah. I guess skeletons don't offer much blood, but the thing was... there were other people there."

"People who think they're vampires?"

Jacob stared back at him, then nodded.

"You're being taken, kid," Bryan said flatly.

"Hey, I just—"

"You want a place where you can belong? Fine. Everyone wants that. But this ain't it, believe me. Think about it. What would a real vampire want? Blood—and slaves. You need to stay the hell away from these people."

The kid's eyes flickered away from his. "But...what if...I mean...it sounds cool to be a vampire."

"Kid, vampires just want to suck you dry. Yeah, you may come back. In agony. Then you go after every-one you love. Then a bigger, stronger, tougher, older vampire uses you, letting someone catch you instead of him, and you're toast."

Jacob was staring at him eyes wide and full of fear.

"What?" Bryan said harshly. "Did you think some vicious creature out there wanted a few more pals?"

"You...you're acting as if...as if they're real."

Bryan shrugged. "One way or the other, getting involved with anything to do with vampires can only lead to disaster. So what did you find out in the cemetery?"

"Nothing."

"You're a shitty liar, kid."

Jacob moistened his lips, unable to meet Bryan's eyes.

"Where were you told to go?" Bryan persisted.

The kid kept silent, shuffling uneasily.

Bryan strode to him, taking him by the shoulders, grabbing his chin and forcing him to look up. "The girl in the hospital is dead, Jacob. Dead. Was she killed by a vampire? You'll never see that written in the papers. Will she come back as a bloodsucker? Hey, who knows? If so, will she have her heart staked and her throat slashed? You bet. Don't go to any party, kid. Save yourself. Where the hell is it going to be?"

"I don't know. Honest! There were whispers about going to the graveyard. Not the St. Louie. The nice one."

"Lambs to the slaughter," Bryan murmured.

12

Leaving Maggie, Jessica moved as quickly as possible. Darkness was coming far too quickly.

Despite Maggie's assurances, she felt she had to personally check on the situation at the hospital. She went to David's room and saw that there was indeed a cop on duty.

Yeah, well, there had been a cop on duty with Mary, too. Discreetly, pretending she was looking for another room, she tried to get a good look at the officer. She should have faith in Sean, of course, but...

The officer was huge, a big, handsome man of mixed heritage. She saw the chain around his neck. It held a crucifix, she was certain.

She tarried until she heard the officer speaking to a nurse leaving the room. "How's he doing?"

"Good, good. He's talking. Doesn't remember a thing, though." She lowered her voice to a near whisper. "Spooky, if you ask me. I tell you, we never lost a patient here before. I mean a dead patient. You know. We've never lost a corpse from the morgue."

"College kids. Pranks," the cop said, his voice reassuring.

"I don't know. I just get the willies around here these days." she said, and then she smiled, gave a little wave and started down the hall.

Jessica left the hospital and went on to her office, hoping to find Jeremy and Nancy there. No luck.

Looking around, she had a strange feeling, as if someone had been there, as if they'd just left. She told herself that she'd let the kids use the office, and that was all it was.

Still, a sense of unease plagued her. Something unnerving had happened here. She paused, looking around, then closing her eyes. Had the Master been here?

No. It was a different sense of...violation that plagued her. But she didn't have time to dwell on it.

She started out, then nearly screamed aloud when she ran straight into Big Jim.

He immediately looked sheepish. "Sorry. Didn't mean to scare you."

"My fault. But what the heck are you doing here? I can't imagine you've come for my services."

He shook his head. "I read the newspaper," he said softly. "And I'm worried."

"I'm okay."

"You've got to be careful. I can feel it in my old bones when things are going wrong. You know me. And you know I can feel it when the, er, other-worldly is going down. Comes from all the voodoo in my life, I suppose."

"Your bones aren't all that old, Jim."

"I don't like this. I don't like this one bit. And too many good folks are still out of town."

"I know. I think Maggie is going to make some calls."

"I saw the sky turn red. This evil is after you."

Jessica looked around quickly. "You're alone, right?"

"Yeah, I'm alone. Barry Larson is a good old boy, but don't worry, we never do anything but tease about my old voodoo-queen granny."

"Big Jim, you need to be careful. The whole city needs to be careful. If I had my way, I'd ask Sean to impose a curfew."

"And he'd be locked up in an insane asylum."

"I know. That's all that stops me."

"You call me when you need me."

"You be careful. You could be in danger, too."

He gave her a huge smile. "Not me. I know what I'm up against."

"No. No one really understands what they're up against."

"When you need me, I'm here."

"I know." She gave him a fierce hug. "Thank you."

He stepped back, studying her. "You know what I

think? I think there's got to be someone close to you who isn't what he seems."

She froze, frowning, and asked sharply, "What do you mean?"

"If *he's* here, he's got help."

"You mean...the Master?"

"Honey, think about it. He must have someone working for him, right here."

She exhaled softly, staring at him. *He was right.* Even so, she shook her head in denial. "The only people who were in Romania were the kids and Bryan MacAllistair. But it can't be him. He's hunting the Master himself. He wants to destroy him."

"Yeah? How do you know that? Only because he says so, right? And think about it. Where is he staying? Your place."

"No. I can't believe..."

"Watch your back. He doesn't need an invitation to come in."

"Look, it could be anyone. The Master didn't need any help in Transylvania." She didn't allow her voice to falter.

Big Jim wouldn't be swayed. "There's someone, and it's someone close to you," he warned.

"I've get to get moving," she said, putting an end to the uncomfortable topic. "You listen to what people are saying in the bar, okay?"

"You know it," he promised.

Her cell started to ring. She answered it, still meeting his grave stare. "Hello?"

"Jessica, its Maggie. Get over here. Now."

"But I haven't found—"

"I think you should come. Seriously. There's still time before dark."

Jessica nodded and hung up. "Big Jim, if you see those kids, tell them to go to my place. To Montresse House. Okay?"

Maggie was at the door when she parked in the drive. Jessica frowned. "What's going on?"

"Ancient texts," Maggie told her.

"You got ancient texts off the computer?" Jessica asked incredulously.

"With patience, you can find anything you want on the computer," Maggie assured her. "Come in. Sit down."

They returned to the kitchen. There were papers from Maggie's printer spread out all over the breakfast table.

"Here, this one is Babylonian. The translation is, 'He rises when the time is right, when the succubi ride rampant over the land. Neither god nor man nor beast, he rises to wage war against the miasma that reigns.'"

"Ancient Babylonian?" Jessica murmured doubtfully.

"Yes. And this is a release from the Vatican, twelfth century."

"This is in Latin," Jessica said.

"Translation to the left," Maggie warned.

"'As there shall be demons, so there shall be angels. And as the war within the world is not the war within the soul, there are those whose demonic strength shall cast terror into the innocents. Yet so there shall be warriors, those granted life and breath, to do battle. Therefore, have ye faith, have ye strength, have ye courage. Ever and eternally, such a battle will rage, for if there is darkness, there is light, if there is love, there is hatred. So shall they rise, by the strength and goodness of His love and mercy, those who were warriors, and where there is despair, they will bring hope. Thus may they fight the eternal battle.'"

Jessica set down the printed sheet, staring at Maggie. "How did you find this?"

"I've been at it since you've left. I've found a dozen other references to these beings known as warriors. I had heard about them before. I remember a time in Europe when there was a great fear of them. I never came across any such beings, but…I should have remembered. Come on, think about it—you must have heard something, too."

"Now that you mention it, I had heard of them, but…that was a long time ago. I thought that they were men sent out by the Church in a time when people believed that an old woman with healing powers was a witch, a bride of Satan—that people signed away their souls to the devil and danced naked in the moonlight. So...you think Bryan Mac-Allistair is one of them?" Jessica asked.

"I don't think he's just any warrior," Maggie said softly. "I think he is—or was—the champion who fought for Robert Bruce. The great warrior who strode onto the field at Hay Glen and allowed the fledgling king to escape when Edward III first took the throne and decided to battle the Scots."

Jessica sank into a chair and stared at Maggie. "That's not possible."

"It is."

"He'd be more than a thousand years old."

"I didn't find a life span noted in any of the references to the warriors," Maggie said.

"It's impossible," Jessica repeated.

"Why?"

"He died. I've studied history. He died."

"Things aren't always what they seem," Maggie said grimly. "You need to go back to your house and stay there."

"I can't, and you know it. Thank you, Maggie. I don't believe what you're telling me, but I promise to be careful."

"Just keep your distance from him."

"He's living in my house."

"Perhaps you should ask him to leave."

Jessica couldn't help the guilty look that came over her face, followed by a hot blush.

"Oh, no," Maggie groaned. "You're not going to ask him to leave. You're *sleeping* with him."

"Yes," Jessica answered at last. "And yes, there's something about him, but..." Unable to put her feelings into words, she let her voice trail off.

"Just be careful. That's all I ask."

Jessica gave her friend a hug and headed for the door. Then she turned around. "I saw Big Jim. He thinks the Master has help here. Someone close to me."

"Who?"

"Someone who might have been in Romania, as well."

"The kids?" Maggie said dubiously.

"No, Bryan MacAllistair. Your warrior."

"I still say I'm right," Maggie said.

"There was someone else there. Someone who got there before me and went up against the Master. That was when panic set in. I had to wait before I could make my move. His power over his followers is so great that if he's threatened, they'd die like lemmings tossing themselves into the sea in their single-minded willingness to protect him. He has to be taken by surprise. I had to see how the stage was set before I did anything, but before I could, the battle began. But the Master knew I was there, and…he'll be out to kill me."

"My point, exactly," Maggie said. "You need to keep the hell away from him."

Jessica nodded. "No, I need to make sure that I'm ahead of the game this time. But it's happening fast. The time is right…I can *feel* it."

"Maybe you should back out—let MacAllistair face the battle. That's the whole point of his existence."

"I can't. From the beginning, this has been my battle."

"Let it go," Maggie begged. "But you won't, will you?" she asked, meeting Jessica's determined gaze.

At the door, Jessica gave her friend another fierce hug.

When she stepped outside, her unease grew. Dusk had not yet come, and yet, even by day, the sky was turning colors, streaks of red curling across it.

She held very still, afraid.

Something was happening.

Tonight.

To his own astonishment, Bryan was able to find Jeremy and Nancy. They were just a block down Bourbon Street, sipping green drinks in glasses that lit up and listening to a mellow rock group.

He slid into the booth next to Jeremy.

"Hey, Prof," Jeremy said dully.

"Hey," Nancy said, forcing a note of cheerfulness into her voice.

"You two doing okay?"

"Yeah, great," Jeremy said morosely. "My best friend is dead, and you all think she's a vampire who wants to kill me, so you want to stake her. Her mom has been calling me, and I haven't got the guts to call her back. On top of that, I'm thinking I'm going to have to spend the rest of my life hiding. I'm afraid, and I want to see her. And if I said this to anyone else, I'd be committed."

"I think you captured the situation fairly accurately in the first few sentences," Bryan said flatly. "Meanwhile, it's getting late."

"Yeah, right, late," Jeremy murmured.

"I'm going to take you to Montresse House. Now," Bryan said firmly.

"Jessica has us all set up at her office," Nancy reminded him.

Bryan shook his head. "Montresse House will be safer," he assured her. "You'll have more company."

"Like hell." Jeremy turned accusing eyes on him. "You're hoping Mary will come, and then you can kill her."

Nancy put a hand on his. "Jeremy, Mary is already dead."

"But she looks the same. And when she calls to me…"

"She's hungry, nothing more," Bryan told him and rose. "Now let's go," he said curtly.

Montresse House was beautiful, and there was certainly plenty of room. Stacey, who apparently ran the inn, along with whatever else she could get away with, was nice, if bossy, Jeremy decided. The handyman, Gareth, wasn't bossy, just quiet and a little bit creepy. You didn't know he was there, he was so silent, and then you'd get an eerie feeling down your spine, turn around and see him standing there.

But the house did seem safe, and it was good to be around Stacey, because she seemed calm and relaxed, as if nothing could scare her. When she showed Jeremy to his room, he asked her, "You believe in all this, then? I mean, I haven't missed a big news story or something, have I? This is crazy, right?"

Stacey smiled. "Most of the time, there's an order to things in life, a balance, but sometimes, that balance gets shifted a bit."

"So you believe in vampires?" he persisted.

"Yes."

"But…how?"

"There are different planes of existence. Mostly, they all co-exist. Sometimes the world we know and what we call the netherworld collide. How's that?"

"It's more bullshit."

"It's all I'm going to give you," she said. "I'll check on Nancy. You make yourself comfortable, okay?"

"Where's Jessica?" he asked. "If I could just see Jessica…"

"I'm not sure," Stacey said. "But I know she wants you here. And I know she wants you to be careful."

"I have to tell her about Mary. That Mary can't be evil."

Stacey took his hand. "What Mary is now…she was created by evil. You have to accept that. I'll be back in a little while. You shouldn't be alone. Settle in. Then we'll all be together, all right?"

She left him.

He walked over to the French doors that led to the wraparound balcony. The drapes were open and he drew them shut. There were fresh vines and flowers draped around the windows and the doors—and they all had garlic artfully entwined in them. He fingered the cross around his neck, then held it very tightly.

And remembered the way Mary had torn the cross she wore from around hers.

Stacey walked down the hall, hesitating outside Jessica's room. She tapped; Jessica didn't answer. She hadn't expected she would. She moved on and tried Bryan MacAllistair's door. He should have been there, having just come in with Jeremy and Nancy.

"Bryan?"

Still no answer. His door was locked. She had a passkey, and even though she knew she shouldn't, she opened his door. The room was empty.

Frowning, she shut and relocked the door, then hurried downstairs. "Bryan? Professor MacAllistair?"

There was no reply.

Swearing, she went to the front and looked outside. She could see no one. She went to the back, running across to Gareth's cottage. She banged on his door. "Gareth!"

He didn't answer, either, which concerned her even more than Bryan's absence.

Her cell phone rang. She dug it from her pocket.

"Stacey, it's Jessica."

"Jessica! Thank God. I think you should get back here right now."

"I can't. But you've got to make sure Bryan Mac-Allistair stays there."

"Jessica, the kids are here, he brought them. But I can't find him." And even if I did, I couldn't keep him here, anyway, she thought.

On the other end of the line, Jessica swore softly. "If you see him again, tell him you think he's needed there, that you're sure Mary is nearby. Tell him...I don't know. If you see him again, just convince him that he's got to stay there."

"I'll do my best. Jessica..."

"What?"

"Mary really will come, won't she?"

Jessica lowered her head, knowing the truth.

"Yes, Mary really will come."

"Jeremy..."

Jeremy had been doing nothing but sitting dully in a chair in his room, staring into space, since Stacey had left him.

"Jeremy..."

He groaned. "I'm not hearing this," he said aloud.

But he was hearing it.

Mary's voice came again.

"Please!"

He knew he shouldn't do it.

He rose, anyway. Her voice was coming from the window. He walked to it and drew back the heavy drapes.

And she was there.

She was no longer naked, but that didn't help any. She had found a beautiful white dress.

Almost like a wedding dress.

It bared her arms, and emphasized the perfection of her breasts, the slimness of her waist. She didn't look evil. She looked...angelic, floating outside the window, elegant in drifting, filmy white.

He tried to tell himself that he had seen this scene before in a thousand movies, the seductive beauty staring hungrily at...

A meal.

"Oh, Mary," he said miserably.

"Jeremy, I'm so scared."

"You're dead, Mary," he forced himself to say dully.

"No, I'm here, and I need your help. Please, Jeremy. I won't hurt you, I swear. I'm just afraid. I can't go, Jeremy. If I go, I'll die. You have to let me in, keep me with you, keep me safe."

She was a vampire, he told himself. She had always used him, and now she wanted to do it again, only this time she wanted his blood. She wanted his life.

"Jeremy?"

She said his name, then nothing more. Could vampires cry? Evidently. Huge tears appeared in her eyes, trailed down the pale contours of her still beautiful face.

"Don't cry, Mary."

"I'm so afraid. I'm being called…I've been ordered…. Help me, Jeremy. Keep me with you. Keep me here, with you."

He didn't know if her whisper created his insanity or if he actually believed her, but he opened the French doors. He reached out, and she joined him on the balcony. She should have felt cold, he thought, but she didn't.

He took her tightly into his arms. She hugged him in return, then leaned against him and kissed his lips. She was shaking. He felt the pressure of her lips against his throat. Felt them quivering.

His heart slammed. This was it. He had never been able to resist her. And now he was going to die for it.

13

Night had fallen, and the moon rode high. Crimson.

Bleeding.

A strange instinct made Jessica hurry for her own home, certain she should have been there already. She had to get there, and quickly—and be on her way out again even more quickly.

Night had come. *The* night. And she rued the fact she hadn't realized before that it would happen so quickly. She should have known. She should have believed the sky, known that a bad moon was rising.

Hurry, hurry, hurry, her senses warned her.

Hurry where?

The question throbbed in her mind. Why wasn't instinct giving her an answer? Logic told her it might be a cemetery, but which one?

She glanced at the sky as she drove. Bad moon, yes, and yet not quite the Demon Moon. Not quite that full moon that rode the sky in pure, brilliant red, bathing the entire night with blood. She would have thought that when it came, it would be under the Demon Moon, but it was bad enough even without that.

As she pulled into the driveway, she felt a shock, like an electrical jolt. Just as she had known that her office had been invaded, she knew that the sanctity of her home had been breached, as well.

She exited the car, staring at the house, then closed her eyes and felt the chill of warning.

She burst through the front door. Stacey was there, staunch and prepared. She was dripping wet, and Jessica knew she had doused herself with holy water. She held a gun, and Jessica knew the bullets were specially crafted with wood mixed into the silver.

She cried out when she saw Jessica. "I could have shot you!"

"But you didn't," Jessica said. "I taught you, and I trust you."

"Honestly, Jess, I've never been so afraid. I keep thinking someone's here."

"Someone *is* here," Jessica said, then added instantly, "Where's Jeremy?"

"Upstairs in his room. It's completely protected. I checked."

Jessica was already bounding up the stairs. "Yeah, protected against everything—but Jeremy himself."

She tore down the hall past Bryan's room and her own. She threw open the first guest room. Nancy, half asleep, began to rise. "What is it?" she asked.

"Nothing, go back to sleep," Jessica told her.

She burst through the door of the next room.

And there they were. Jeremy and Mary. Embracing on the balcony.

In a fury, Jessica rushed forward. She seemed to glide like an avenging mist across the floor. Before she could reach Mary, Jeremy thrust the vampire behind him.

"No! She didn't do anything to me, I swear! And I didn't let her in. If you're going to kill her, you'll have to kill me first."

From behind him, Mary said, "Please. He's telling the truth. I didn't hurt him."

"Look." Jeremy bared his throat, tipped his head from side to side. His skin was unmarked.

Jessica knew she shouldn't be hesitating. There was no time.

Stacey burst into the room behind her and let out a horrified gasp. Hand shaking, she raised her gun.

Jessica set a hand on her arm, stopping her from shooting.

"Your veins, Jeremy. Show me your arms."

He rolled up his sleeves and did so.

There were still ways, she reminded herself. But she knew Jeremy wasn't lying, that he would die for the girl. And maybe, just maybe, they could use her, even—somehow—save her.

"Stacey, get her something," Jessica said.

"What?"

"You heard me," she said softly.

"How can you trust—"

"Because I have to believe in something," Jessica said. "Please…hurry."

With that, Stacey disappeared, racing down the stairs.

"You're not going to stake her, are you?" Jeremy said, his voice a whispered prayer.

"I haven't killed anyone, I swear," Mary said. "Almost, but…I was stopped. And then…well, then I stumbled on a cat…and there were a few birds. I tried for a Rottweiler, but it was too ferocious. I'm… I'm really hungry, but I didn't hurt Jeremy, and I won't hurt Jeremy. I swear I only came so he could stop me," she said in a whisper.

"Stop you from what?"

Mary hesitated, pale, beautiful and wide-eyed.

"From what?" Jessica repeated with harsh authority.

"The feast. The feast that's supposed to take place tonight. I've been called to be there, but I'm afraid," Mary said.

"Where?"

"The cemetery," Mary whispered.

"Which cemetery?"

"We are called there first," Mary said, as if distracted, trying to put thoughts together in her own mind. She set her hands to her skull, pressing it. "It will be my first, the Master says. He says I'm his, and once I'm there, I'll know…the truth of what I am, the truth of what I can have and the truth of his law. From the cemetery, we'll be taken to a haven on the river."

"Which cemetery?" Jessica demanded again.

Stacey burst back into the room, a plastic soda bottle in her hands. Jessica took it, holding it out to Mary. The girl's face puckered into a frown, and at last she dared to step out from behind Jeremy.

"What…what is it?" she asked.

"O-positive," Jessica snapped. "Now, which cemetery?"

When Mary finally offered the information, Jessica gave a few orders—the most important being that Mary was to be confined to one area.

Then, she was gone.

Bryan made it a point not to make an appearance, not at first.

He stayed at a distance after arriving. Oaks dripping Spanish moss lined the sidewalks along the streets that bordered the cemetery. The city always made an attempt to illuminate the places where danger might skulk, where the dregs of society too often sought to prey upon the unwary. But even as he stood across the street, just watching, one of the streetlights burned for a moment of brightness, sputtered, then died.

He waited, very still, eyes adjusting to the shadows. He could already sense movement inside the cemetery. Shadows moved furtively. Grew large, faded.

He heard the sound of laughter, quickly suppressed, and he shook his head, damning the foolishness of those who were so easily seduced by the raw edge of a little sex or a little danger. Frustration filled him. Time and again, he'd been so close.

And time and again, he had lost the battle in the attempt to salvage the innocent.

Or, he thought wryly, those who were innocent of that particular brand of evil.

The gates loomed tall, wrought iron with Victorian arches and the sense of elegant and faded decay so common in the area, both beautiful and sad. The wall was stone, crumbling in too many places.

With a deft leap, he scaled the wall. He was instantly struck by the miasma in the place, something unusual even for a city of the dead, where the elegant above-ground mausoleums housed their burden of humanity long gone. He followed a narrow, overgrown trail past the grandiose memorials, slipping from the shadows of one to the next, deep into the growing darkness. It was one of the largest cemeteries in the area, filled with dark alleys between tombs forgotten over time and trees that had all but grown through stone and slab as their roots crushed and cracked it. Here, broken angels seemed to weep.

Against one of the tombs, he saw a shadow, already lurking, waiting.

It was a girl. She had dressed to look like the infamous dominatrix; her boots were high, her skirt short. There was something a little off about her clothing, though. It was a good imitation of the contemporary but held traces of a not so distant past. Her hair was dyed many colors, cut short and styled in the fashion of the heavy-duty punk era.

"Hey," she whispered from the darkness. She grinned, stepping from the shadows to accost him. "I like that outfit. It suits you. You're here for the gathering, huh? You'll have fun. It will be the wildest thing you've ever done." As she spoke, she glided closer and closer to him. He smiled in welcome. She came close, reaching out a hand, sidling up to him.

"Want to get started right away?" she whispered huskily. "Here, now…no waiting? I'm ready. I've been waiting for someone like you. Hey. What's the matter?" She giggled. "I can make you want me in a matter of seconds. In fact, believe me, I'm the wildest dream of men—and women, for that matter." Her giggle rang out again. "I've made them all die for me. Come on, just give me a chance, one little kiss…."

"Not in this lifetime or any other," he assured her.

"Trust me," she whispered, and this time, there was a sibilance in her words that hadn't been there before. Her tongue flicked out and she rose on her toes.

He knew her intent. He had seen it time and time again. He smiled, watching her move closer.

She nuzzled against him, then opened her mouth.

A shred of the red moonlight touched her fangs. They dripped with anticipation.

As she leaned in for his throat, he drew the stake from beneath his coat. He had thrust it deep into her chest before she even knew what had happened.

She let out a little cry and stared at him in fury, then disintegrated right before his eyes. Pieces of bone and ash lay at his feet. "Sure. The wildest dream. Or nightmare." he murmured softly. He wondered how many more were here, and decided it was going to be a bad night. He had a sixth sense that warned him when vampires were near, and it told him that there would be plenty here tonight, emboldened by the Master, many drawn from their lives deep in hiding. There were so many kinds. Those who had adapted well to the modern world of instant communication and technology, those who dined on the blood of beasts, as most men dined on their meat. Those who wanted nothing more than to survive, pretend to lead normal lives…

But tonight all were here, heeding the call of the

Master. He was a ruler reminding them of what they were, convincing them of their power, that the word was there, that human beings were their cattle.

There was no such thing as a good vampire.

He lowered the brim of his hat, ready to move on.

Jessica strode among them, bold, her cape and leather cowl making her one with the shadows to any outside observer. She eavesdropped as she went.

A young group of literary fanatics who had taken the tales of New Orleans far too seriously were dressed as if they had returned to the 1700s. There was a little group of tittering girls, pierced and tattooed, all in black, some with sweeping skirts and others with little more than kerchiefs covering their butts. There were a few drunks, growing too loud, giggling.

And then there were those moving among them. Those who seemed to be calculating, choosing their positions. Those who were not from New Orleans… those who had come only for this night, for the easily led, the misled, those looking for something in their lives…those upon whom they could feast. She could feel the leashed hunger in them and knew they were savoring the anticipation, grateful to the power of the Master that allowed them that pleasure.

"He will come," someone said, stopping Jessica. It was a tall, slender, dark-haired man. He wasn't old, but his eyes held both knowledge and weariness.

And sweet licentious patience.

"But then, you know that. You are his beloved servant. The world knows about the dominatrix." He bowed, as if she were royalty.

She had done well, starting rumors in Transylvania, she thought dryly. In Transylvania, the Master had not known he had a dominatrix, but everyone else had. When she arrived at the castle in the woods, she had been easily accepted. Those who had heard, who had felt the summons, had heard about the dominatrix, as well. They had welcomed her; they had looked up to her. Of course. She was what she was. And she knew how to play a part.

Now the Master knew, too. He would be waiting. Before, perhaps he *had* been baiting her. Tonight…

She should have recruited help. She should at least have told Sean what she was doing.

No, she couldn't have risked his life.

In Transylvania, she'd had faith in herself. She'd had the element of surprise. But she had failed; she'd miscalculated. She'd thought herself so powerful, had waited, planned on perfect timing, but even so, she'd failed.

Her timing had only been off by seconds, but those seconds had cost Mary her life. She couldn't have brought others along tonight, not when she had failed so badly last time. After all, tonight, he was expecting her. Waiting for her.

She gritted her teeth. Win or lose, she had to believe in her own power, had to believe, perhaps even more important, in the rightness of what she was doing.

She smiled. "It won't really begin here," she said matter-of-factly, desperately groping, since she had no idea what the Master had planned. Certainly, if he had arranged a place, as he had done in Transylvania, it would be much farther from the city lights than this. But she didn't know where, and she needed to get this man to talk. "The Master doesn't like things...messy."

"No, I know. I've heard there will a dozen coaches waiting. He can command those around him to blindness, march down the street in daylight and not be noticed. Tonight he will take us to a place where we can savor all that we thirst for.... but then, you know that."

There would be no coaches, she thought dryly. Not here. The Master was too smart to be that obvious. There would be a few limousines, probably, but they *would* move in darkness and shadows. As her companion had said, somehow they would not be noticed.

"You are the dominatrix, are you not? In Transylvania, we had word that she would be there, would welcome us, then finally give us permission to strike." He paused then moved closer. "Beware. Someone impersonated the dominatrix that night.

She killed many. There was a warrior who appeared, as well." He shuddered, as if at the memory.

"But we will be safe tonight," she said, feeling the muscles in her jaw grow tight at the word "warrior." She still didn't know where the event was scheduled to take place, and she was growing frustrated, but she had to play this carefully. "Where have you traveled from?" she asked. He had the hint of an accent, but it wasn't one she could place.

He waved a hand. "France. Immediately after the battle in Transylvania, we knew the Master would plan a grand event right away. We all seek revenge," he said. "Sadly, many an ancient vampire fell, but even against deceit and treachery, the Master survived. He will not be defeated." He moved closer to her. "We've not had the pleasure of meeting." He bowed, a breath away from her, his smile sensual as he rose and faced her again. "I am Henri, Comte de Vallier. It is my pleasure to make your acquaintance." He came closer still, whispering against her ear, "I have been around a long time. I have so much experience."

"Do you?" she asked.

"Indeed. I have sucked many a beauty dry, yet she has died whimpering my name in sheer ecstasy."

She touched his face. "You have taken the lives of innocents? Relished the cries of the dying?"

He smiled slowly, as if they had become best friends, conspirators. "They say that it is different today. That we have to think of the greater good. That we do not have to be monsters. But I say we are what we are. Still, I have found ways.... I often prey upon those who are not long for this world, anyway. Still, I do admit, I have a weakness for women. Beautiful young women. But what I can do for them in turn…"

He drew a finger along her arm with tremendous insinuation. "I know that you are beloved of the Master," he whispered. "Everyone says so."

"Do they?" she asked coyly.

"But you are free, are you not? I've heard that you are more than pleased to…entertain your own kind, as well as dine upon the blood of our prey. The Master knows what we are, what we need, how we must live. Our so-called king is an idiot. He believes humans will accept our kind if we learn to live in their world. What is their world but a vast feeding ground for us? The Master understands this, and so I worship him. Though I am tempted beyond sin by you, I would not trespass upon what the Master considers his."

"I am not his, I am my own," she said, strangely torn. Henri had killed and killed again—would continue to kill. She was heartsick, thinking of the beautiful women who had died because of his depredations.

Women like Mary.

No, not like Mary. The Master had allowed Mary

to rise again to serve his purpose. Henri, she was certain, seldom, if ever, left a victim with the capacity to come back to life—no, not life, existence. Was that better? She would never know. She had meant to send Mary back to the grave, yet in the end, she had been unable to carry out that plan.

Yet there were things he said that echoed painfully in her heart. In what world would they ever be accepted? In what world could they ever be regarded without fear?

They heard a giggle from the shadows down a dark path lined by ornate mausoleums. He smiled, licked his lips. In the strange moonlight, a fang glowed with the bloody color of the night.

"Tempting," he murmured. "And I *am* hungry. Perhaps just a taste, before it all begins."

"Careful," Jessica warned. "We can't leave bodies strewn about, just waiting to be discovered."

His smile deepened. He slipped an arm around her. "There is nothing like the feel of a beating young heart, the beauty of youthful, living flesh. I can all but taste the blood now. In fact, I believe I must, but, my dear dominatrix, I will allow you the first taste."

She pretended to consider his words; then she reached beneath her cape.

She struck before he knew what happened. The stake was small but very sharp, carved from strong oak. She slipped it straight between his ribs.

He stared at her, not comprehending at first.

Then, for a fleeting second, a look of rage, of incredulous disbelief, swept through his eyes. He opened his mouth to speak. His lips curled back, fangs glistening.

Then, without a sound, he crumbled.

Dust…to dust.

The last things to go were the shimmering red teeth and the fire of fury in his eyes.

It was as if she had been alone all along. The dust that had been the vampire lay at her feet, mingling with the dirt, as she stood in the shadow of the silent, shimmering, houses of the dead. An angel with broken wings held her silent vigil atop a mausoleum, seeming to weep in silence. All was still.

She looked around the cemetery, her dark-adapted eyes picking out deeper shadows in the night.

Some eager for a feast.

Some the innocents, lambs for slaughter.

Sleight of hand, tricks of the eye. The forte of the Master.

The limos began to arrive. Dozens of them. Bryan kept his distance, watching from the cover of a society tomb created in the form of a pyramid.

It began with the mist, a damp fog the color of blood. It didn't settle over the cemetery; it came as if it had a life of its own, swirling, rising, creating a fantasy of mystery, a sense of the unreal and the spectacular. It spread to the streets, hiding the arrival of the long black, vehicles. There were hushed whispers, some of wicked amusement, some of sheer excitement.

The sheep and the wolves. Together.

He watched. They wore all manner of dress, making it difficult to tell the hunters from the hunted. There were the Goths in black, their long, sweeping cloaks brushing the ground. There were beautiful women in fitted dresses with regal purple velvet and lace. There were those in simple street wear, clothing for a night on the town, for barhopping and listening to the best jazz New Orleans had to offer. Some were surely in costume, Casanova-style, colonial, medieval. Street toughs, lovely waifs, all entered the limos, some giggling at the delicious daring of what they were doing, others in calculating silence. Strangers flirted with one another. Old friends linked arms, eager and wide-eyed. All disappearing into the blood-red mist.

He waited, watched. The last of the cars was filled. He bided his time, took a long and agile leap, and lay spread-eagled atop the last of the cars.

Like wraiths, the limos traveled the streets, following the path of the mighty Mississippi.

He looked back, and it looked as if the moon had

brought the statues to life. Winged angels seemed to struggle to move. To cry out.

And in the end, to weep.

Their destination was a plantation, old and abandoned. Jessica was surprised that some enterprising corporation hadn't rehabbed the place and turned it into an inn or a restaurant.

The drive that led to the house was rough, once a grand path, now an overgrown trail of tree roots and leaves. Jessica was sure it couldn't even be seen from the road, so far had nature encroached.

The red mist had followed them. When the limos came to a stop, it seemed as if they had reached the end of the world, a fifth dimension, a place of crimson fantasy.

People began to pour out of the cars.

Even the trail to the decaying porch was covered with vines and overgrowth. From within the plantation house itself, a red light created a glow of invitation. The partygoers hurried on, anxious for the unique and elite festivities to begin.

Jessica pushed her way forward, anxious to become oriented as quickly as possible herself.

It was a true plantation house, doorways built to allow the air to flow from porch to porch, upstairs and down. No doubt there were slaves' quarters, a smokehouse, barns and more somewhere on the property.

A large-screen TV played in the parlor off the main entry. Obviously a generator was running somewhere to provide power. A once grand and sweeping staircase led to the upper floor. In the great foyer, a bar had been created of old butcher-block tables and stocked in advance. A young man, the look in his eyes vague, was ready to serve drinks, including, of course, Bloody Marys.

Jessica made her way to the bar. The bartender greeted her. "Hello, you're the dominatrix, of course. I'd heard you were coming."

"Oh?" Her heart hammered. The Master *was* expecting her tonight.

The bartender stared at her and swallowed, his Adam's apple bobbing up and down.

She leaned over the bar, very close to him, fixing him with her eyes. "You need to leave. Now."

"Leave…" He was ready to obey. "How?"

"Go out the back. Head to the river and walk along it until you find a boat. Just get out of here, and do it quickly, do you understand?"

He looked at her gravely and nodded, then began to make his way out through the crowd.

She assessed those milling near her. She waited a moment, judging each individual. She caught a man by the lapels of his Edwardian-style suit. She made a point of glaring as she drew him near. "You—tend the bar," she said.

He seemed about to protest.

She curved her lips into a smile. "Do you want to be whipped?" she demanded. "Or will you obey? You know who I am," she said. "And you *will* do as you're told."

He bowed and almost fell to his knees. She tried not to shake her head in wonder at how easily he could be controlled.

"I beg to serve you," he said at last.

"Good. Get back there."

She left him scrambling behind the bar, ready to serve.

She stayed in character as she made her way through the crowd, her commands both sensual and demanding, separating the sheep from the wolves. The sheep had to remain below, where they could escape. The wolves...

"Attention, please," she announced. "We are all waiting for the Master, and, while we wait—" she lowered her voice to a husky growl "—I will see you all, of course, in turn. Those of you who are attending your first party will wait. Those of you who are... experienced will visit me first in my chamber upstairs. One by one or, if you prefer, in couples. But seniority will be respected."

With a sweep of her hand, she said, "The bar is open. Please, indulge yourselves, and then come see me. We will indulge one another."

She started back through the crowd again, counting and assessing. She needed to find the worst of the wolves. The oldest first, those who would select the sweetest, ripest, victims. She whispered invitations to them while she commanded the sheep to remain below, to wait their turns. Upstairs, she wondered how long it would be before the Master made his appearance. She waited in the darkness, and when her first guest arrived, she didn't bother with the least attempt at seduction unto death. She simply opened the door and staked him.

Like Henri, he disappeared into dust, mingling with the antique remnants of time already covering the floor.

She had chosen the room next to the one she was certain the Master would use. The set-up was the same as in Transylvania: the elaborate bed; the more elaborate dressing table. She listened carefully, aware that at any minute the trap might be set.

A giggling pair came to her next. Sheep. She ordered them below to wait their turn.

After the sheep…

More wolves. She heard the boasts of those who claimed they had killed again and again. And every time they spoke salaciously of the death and destruction they had sown, it became easier for her to wield her stake.

The dust on the floor grew thick.

She had to wonder at the stupidity, the ego, that kept sending them her way, one by one. And still... there were so many left. But at least she had tipped the odds more in her own favor. The trick now, however, to stop *him* and get the others out.

At last she opened the door and slipped down the hall. She had guessed correctly. A sense of darkness far beyond the black of night emanated from behind the door.

He was coming soon. Very soon. She could tell.

There was always a viewing room. It had to be just on the other side of the one in which the Master had chosen to enact his seduction scene. She hurried to it, stepping in.

Yes. There was the one-way window on the seduction chamber, the camera on the elegant set, the stage. *His* stage. The stage on which he performed his finest act: the death of an innocent, the demonstration of his own great power. He thrived on his performance, on the fear, and on the fact that he was watched, that those watching were enthralled and ready to bow down before him.

She wasn't too late. The scene was set but there was no innocent at that dressing table, decked out in white, brushing her hair, throat bared, waiting....

Had he come? Where was he?

There was a terrible scream from downstairs. She jumped. Had she miscalculated again? She bolted for the door. As she ran, she was jerked to a stop when a hand fell upon her shoulder.

A hand with fingers of steel, a vise of sheer power.

A heated whisper followed.

"Now you die."

14

David felt good. So good, in fact, that he didn't know just what the hell he was doing in a hospital, but so far, they hadn't shown any sign of letting him go.

And the cop on duty seemed to be a little bit of a wacko. He had hung something along the inner frame of the window, and though David tried not to think that New Orleans' finest might be really and totally nuts, he was pretty sure that it was garlic.

This guy's name was Santini. Officer Giovanni Santini. Aside from being crazy, he was a nice guy. But David wasn't at all sure why he needed an officer watching over him. It had something to do with the fact that the corpse had disappeared on his shift. He still couldn't remember much about it. He had a feeling, though, that there had been a woman. A really beautiful naked woman with great breasts.

"You okay, kid?" He almost started; Santini had

been so quiet over in his chair, that he had thought the man was sleeping.

"Yeah. I just wish I could go home."

"Soon enough," Santini said cheerfully, fingering the big cross he wore on a chain around his neck, twin to the one David had found himself wearing when he woke up the first time after the...incident.

"If you need anything, you just let me know."

"I need to go home," he told Santini mournfully. "I need to sleep all night without a nurse waking me up to take my temperature."

Santini laughed. "Sorry, kid. But if you wake up and need anything, you let me know right away. Now go to sleep," he said.

"Yes, sir."

David tried to. He even drifted off at one point, but before he fell deeply asleep, he woke again. He wasn't sure why, at first. He just sensed something.

This time, though, it wasn't a nurse. It was a doctor, and he was one huge guy. He had David's arm in his tight grip when a light came on, aimed straight at David's face, keeping him from seeing the man, who became a silhouette against the glare.

"Turn the other way, kid," the doctor said. "I've got to take some blood."

"Why are you taking blood in the middle of the night?" David asked. He wanted to shield his eyes from the light, but he felt as if the sleep he couldn't quite get was somehow hanging on to him, rendering his muscles useless.

"I need it," the doctor said. "Turn aside, I'll get my pints, and then you can go back to sleep."

He turned as bidden. Then the words hit him.

I'll get my pints.

Pints—with an *S*.

He turned—and screamed.

The doctor held his arm, and his teeth were sunk into his vein.

Instantly, Santini was out of his chair. Without even looking up, the doctor flung back one of his arms, slamming Santini against the chest and sending him flying across the room.

The door to the room burst open. A second uniformed cop had appeared. The doctor still didn't ease up on David's arm.

"Stop or I'll shoot!" the officer warned.

The doctor turned at last. David never saw him move, but somehow he was in front of the officer and the gun was on the floor. There was a horrible keening sound. The officer was off his feet, held one-handed by the doctor, who had bitten his neck, and was sucking...smacking his lips, sucking more.

Santini was up, shaking his head. He headed for the doctor's back, but once again the doctor knew he was there. He threw out an arm, and Santini dropped to the ground.

The awful sucking sounds continued, seeming to

go on and on as David tried to scream and the world faded to a sea of red-tinged black.

"No!" Jessica cried, turning around in a fury, the stake in her hand. The room was dark, filled with the red mist. She couldn't see her attacker, but it hadn't been the voice of the Master that threatened her; she knew that much. As she prepared to strike, a massive blow caught her arm; her stake went flying across the room.

She felt her attacker coming for her again, but she knew how to fight, and as split seconds flashed by, she waited. Then she lashed out with a hard kick, catching her opponent off balance, sending him staggering back.

Another scream.

She found her stake, wrenched open the door and went racing down the hall. She took the stairs in a single sweep, coming to the landing crouched and ready.

She had destroyed many wolves, but many yet remained, and they had not waited for any command to strike.

Directly in front of her, a painfully thin woman dressed in a skintight black dress stood with her fingers twined into the hair of a young man in Gothic attire, ready to sink her fangs deep into his neck. Others were on the attack all over the room.

She went for the vampire in the black dress first,

since she was closest. A quick plunge of the stake into the back of the temptress and she was dust. Jessica heard a furious hiss and turned; an ancient vampire with gray hair and long skeletal arms was preparing to leap at her. She ducked, letting him fly overhead, then jumped atop him and sent the stake plunging downward. She saw a body go flying by—and burst into fragments of dust and bone as it passed.

Stunned, she turned in a rush.

The man in the low-brimmed hat and frock coat was back.

As she stared, he reached under his coat for a small crossbow as a vampire rushed at him. An arrow caught the attacker when he was just inches from the dark man's face, and he fell.

The doors were open, screams rode the sudden wind of violence whipping through the crumbling manor, and the lambs were spilling out of the plantation house in terror.

Jessica whirled, watching as the man in the low-brimmed hat strode through the room, arrow after arrow flying from his small crossbow. She turned again, under attack, ducking when a knife would have sliced through her neck, then rising to stake her opponent.

Suddenly there was silence. The room had emptied. The wolves were dust. The lambs had fled.

There were only the two of them left: herself and

the man with the crossbow—which was aimed at her as he felt in his jacket for an arrow.

She flew across the room, slamming into him just as his fingers closed around the arrow. He flew backwards, and she flew with him. This was the man, she realized, who had attacked her upstairs. And he was about to kill her if he could.

He had landed hard against the wall, and she had landed on top of him, gasping for breath. She pushed against his chest, scrambling up, then turned to flee.

Too late. His arm shot out, his hand catching her ankle.

She fell hard to the floor.

In a second he was atop her, his weight bearing her down. She wedged an arm between them, throwing him off again, and tried to scramble away. She made it to her feet, but he was up, as well, and caught her by the shoulder. Without effort, he threw her across the room, sending her crashing against the newel post. Stunned, she nearly fell, then braced herself against the newel post and kicked out with all her strength as he came near, forcing him back.

Again she spun away in an attempt to escape, but he was there, in front of her. She tried to strike; he caught her arm. Off balance, she fell to the floor and landed next to the knife, one of the vampires had used against her earlier.

She reached for it as he followed her down, straddling her.

She had the knife. She could have used it, but something, some sixth sense, stopped her.

He was no longer on the attack, either. He simply straddled her, staring.

She stared defiantly back at him.

"Sweet Jesu," he whispered. "You." And the sound of the words was worse than any agony she had known in years and years…and years.

Sean had practically been crawling up the walls. He knew something was about to happen. He just didn't know where.

Then the call came, and he moved as quickly as he could.

When he reached the hospital room, one of the rookie cops was coming out of it, throwing up all over the place. George Mendez was there, too, having come as quickly as possible when the call went out. He followed the rookie from the room, and Sean called to him.

"Mendez," Sean said. "What have you got so far?"

"I was in my car when the call came. We've got the M.E. on his way up, and a crime-scene unit. I had to walk in—" He paused, taking a deep breath. "I knew our men were dead, but the kid was alive. I carried him out. The only other person who's been in the room is the nurse who found the bodies. She was on duty and she heard a scream and saw the officer on duty in the hallway go in. When he didn't come back she called Security and went to check. She was standing there screaming when Security got here, and they called 911."

Sean looked through the doorway. The bed was empty. There was a smear of blood on the sheets. Just a smear.

As for the rest of the room...

It was a bloodbath.

"It's been made to look as if Santini and Clark—those were our officers, I know you can't recognize them now—went after each other. They're...a mess." Mendez paused. He was a toughened officer, but he was also one of the most humane and religious men with whom Sean had ever worked. There were tears in his eyes. "Santini...he was one of my best friends. And he was a good cop. Clark, too. Someone went to a lot of trouble to make it look like they attacked each other with scalpels, but it's bull."

"Gloves, shoe covers, sir." Another officer offered Sean the required crime-scene gear. He didn't even look toward the doorway.

"Thank you, Rohan," he murmured.

"I—I didn't have gloves or shoe covers," Mendez muttered. "I...uh..."

"It's all right. You said the kid is alive?"

"Yes. They're giving him a transfusion now."

"Right," Sean murmured. "Maybe...maybe he'll survive."

"Maybe." Mendez didn't sound as if he believed it for a minute.

Sean walked carefully into the hospital room. It was just as Mendez had described it. The two officers had died almost on top of each other, each of them with his fingers loosely wrapped around a scalpel.

He hunkered down and shook his head, gritting his teeth. The men's throats were both deeply cut, almost to the bone.

Carefully, Sean inspected the bodies. Santini's throat had been slashed through clean and hard, with tremendous force.

But Clark's neck...

Clark's neck hadn't been neatly slashed. It had been cut again and again.

An attempt, Sean was certain, to hide the marks left by the killer's fangs. He started to rise. The crime-scene unit would come, but they wouldn't find any answers, only more puzzles. There would be no footprints, no fingerprints. Nothing would explain this.

Suddenly he hunkered back down again. By Clark's outstretched fingers, something was written in the blood.

Sean stared at it.

Swearing silently, with a sinking heart, he pretended to take another look at Clark's fingers.

He smeared the single word written in blood.

The *name*.

Then he rose, stepped out of the room. Mendez was staring at him dully.

Mendez *knew.*

"Should I stay with the kid?" Mendez asked dully.

Sean lowered his head. "It would be good," he said. He looked the man straight in the eye. "But you can't fall asleep. You can't be taken by surprise. And you have to be prepared."

Mendez offered him a hollow, humorless laugh. "Oh, Sir. I have been prepared. Trust me, I'm prepared. Hey, I was here with the young lady, Mary. Take a look at my hair, sir. I practically bathed in holy water." He took a deep breath. "Santini really fought. You can tell. You think he's an angel now?"

"Maybe," Sean said. Hell, what else could he say?

"You better get going, sir," Mendez said. "I won't leave."

As Sean left, he wondered.

Mendez had seen the name printed in blood, but did he know what it meant?

"You," Bryan repeated, looking down at her.

"Professor MacAllistair," she murmured back.

He reached down, and she almost cringed, but all he did was toss the black wig and cat's eye mask aside. He let out a sigh. "Contact lenses, I presume?"

She shrugged where she lay.

"*You're* the dominatrix?" he demanded sharply.

"There is no real dominatrix," she replied.

He reached under his coat. Reaching, she was certain, for one of his deadly arrows.

"Listen to me," she pleaded. "The dominatrix is all an act. I created her with rumor. I had to find a way to get into the Master's parties without appearing to be suspicious. I swear to you, the dominatrix never appeared in the flesh until Transylvania."

He sat back, his weight on his haunches, but his thighs like iron. "So you were at the debacle in Transylvania. Feasting?"

"No, you idiot. How could you have missed what happened here tonight? I killed more of those evil creatures than you did," she told him.

He hiked a brow. "I hardly think so. And what does it matter? Vampires have a habit of turning on one another when the need arises. And you *are* a vampire."

She stared at him, then swallowed hard. Her voice, when she spoke, was barely a whisper. "There are good vampires."

She watched the agony streak across his rugged features. "There is no such thing as a good vampire."

"But there is," she whispered. "There is. I swear it."

Her mind raced. He knew she was a vampire. Was that all he knew? "How do you think all those people escaped while you were battling the Master in Tran-sylvania? How do you think so many survived?"

"You?"

She met his eyes defiantly, as if daring him to doubt her.

"So where is the Master?" he demanded harshly.

"Oh, God," she whispered.

"You have no right to say that name."

"You bastard! You know nothing," she charged. "And while we're here fighting each other…it was a setup," she said. "He's out there somewhere, killing, and we're here. He probably intended for us to kill each other. Damn you, I came here to kill *him*."

Perhaps that convinced him at last; she would never know. They were both distracted by a blood-curdling scream from the yard just outside the house.

He was up in a moment, and she leapt to her feet a split second later. They both tore for the door, but he was ahead of her, racing into the red darkness. She saw him, moving as if he flew. Then she heard a hollow cry and a roar of anger, saw a figure go flying….

An arrow stuck the figure, and it burst into dust in mid-air.

There were sobs, and then the harsh demand, "Were you bitten?"

"No, no…I don't think so," a feminine voice said pathetically.

Whatever else went on there that night, Jessica

decided, Bryan could handle it. It was time for her to make an exit—as speedily as possible.

He was, after all, a warrior.

And the Master was out there...somewhere.

The young girl, wearing too much makeup and a too-short skirt, stared at Bryan blankly. She was ashen and shaking, and looked as if she had gone entirely stupid, as if her mind had burned within her skull. She'd been drinking, maybe taking drugs. Would she even remember this?

"Come over here," he commanded impatiently.

"Are you...one of them?" she stuttered in fear. Mascara streaked her cheeks.

"Come here. For the love of God, I'm out of time. I've got to get you out of here, but I have to be certain—"

"I swear I wasn't bitten. Don't stake me."

He sighed, gripped her arm and pulled her close. She didn't struggle. He saw a bruise on her neck; it was amazing she had managed to scream when she had been so nearly strangled by the vampire's grip.

He searched her arms, any bared flesh. She just stood there, shaking.

He could find no marks.

"You look clean. If you're lying to me..."

He held her for a minute, praying that instinct would kick in. He could usually trust his instinct.

Usually.

He had failed with Jessica. He had heard a heartbeat when he held her. She had been as warm as fire. He had, in fact, never felt such a fire.

He swore suddenly. "Where are your friends? Who did you come here with?"

"I...I...Cindy and Jean. They're gone. They ran... faster. My shoe caught in a tree root. I..."

She trailed off, staring at him. Then she burst into tears, threw herself against him and passed out.

"Shit," he swore.

He had to get her back to people and light and safety.

There were no cop cars coming tonight. Tonight had all been a sham. The Master was somewhere else. They had all been conned.

He sighed deeply. He couldn't leave her.

And whatever the Master had been planning, Bryan was certain, had already been accomplished.

He lifted the girl into his arms and turned back toward the house. He didn't even bother calling Jessica's name. He knew she was already gone.

15

Jessica burst into Montresse House, terrified that everything had gone wrong, that the Master had come and called out to Mary, who was still under his thrall, and had been unable to fight back, even with Gareth's help. Jeremy and Nancy would have been useless, and against the Master, what hope could Stacey and Gareth have had?

Gareth was at the front door. He stared at her with concern, then slowly arched a brow. She knew why. She never returned to her own house in leather, lace and latex. Tonight, however, she had been in far too great a hurry to worry about a costume change.

"The others...they're all right?" she demanded.

He nodded, looking perplexed. "Of course. You were the one at the party. The Master—"

"The Master didn't show," she said briefly. With disbelief, she added, "He didn't come here?"

"Everything's fine," he assured her. "I was down here most of the night, but I just checked upstairs.

Stacey and Jeremy are awake—and Mary, of course. Nancy is sleeping like a babe in arms."

Frowning, Jessica started up the stairs. She heard Gareth setting the locks again in her wake.

As she had ordered, Mary was confined to one small area, encircled by bowls of holy water, strings of garlic and crosses. She was apparently comfortable enough; they'd provided her with a pillow and blanket, and plenty of O-positive.

Stacey and Jeremy were seated across the room from her, wide awake. As soon as he saw her, Jeremy leapt to his feet.

"Jessica!" he cried with relief.

Stacey, too, jumped up. "Jessica...thank God you're here. But you look like hell. What happened? Is he...?"

Jessica shook her head. "Tonight was a setup," she said flatly. She walked in, then sank down on the bed.

Jeremy was still, staring at her. "My God," he breathed.

She had forgotten that Jeremy hadn't known that she was the dominatrix.

"You never saw the Master?" Stacey said.

"No. He never showed."

"But you're...pretty beat-up," Stacey said.

"Yes."

"All right." Stacey quickly became her efficient self. "A shower is in order. I'll tell Gareth to make you something to eat. It's nearly dawn. Nothing else is going to happen tonight—I hope. And you have to get some rest. And soon…" Her eyes moved to Mary, looking angelic inside her strange prison. "Soon Mary will sleep. Then we'll have to—" She broke off with a startled scream. The bedside phone had started to ring. "I routed all calls in here," she explained. "But who the hell would be calling now?"

"I've got it," Jessica assured her. She rolled over and picked up. "Hello?"

"Jessica? Thank God."

It was Maggie.

"Yes?"

"As soon as the sun rises, get over here."

"Maggie, what's happened?" Her heart sank. "It's the Master, isn't it? What did he do?"

"I'll tell you about it as soon as you come over."

"I'm on my way."

"No! Wait till it's light. He's still out there."

Jessica winced, tightening her fingers around the phone. "How many?"

"Two," Maggie said softly. "They were found with their throats slit."

"Where?"

Maggie hesitated, took a deep breath, then said, "The hospital. They were cops. Jessica, stay there till sunrise, do you hear me? I swear, I won't tell you anything if you don't listen to me."

"I'll see you soon, Maggie." She hung up. Stacey was staring at her. "Well, I know where he was tonight," she said softly.

"Where?"

"The hospital. He killed two cops. That's all I know so far. I've got to go."

"You have to change before you go out again," Stacey told her. "Get in the shower—quickly. It's nearly dawn."

"All right." She started toward the bathroom, then froze. She should go now. Bryan MacAllistair was out there somewhere, as well. Would he come here? Would he believe her if she told him what was going on? Worse than that…could he possibly be…?

No.

But *if* he was, did he know that she…?

No.

Because he *would* have killed her already if he knew. But how long would it take him to figure it out?

As Bryan brought the girl to the hospital, he saw the police cars and commotion going on. There were already news crews prowling the perimeter. And despite the fact it wasn't quite daylight, people were beginning to appear on the street, anxious to know what had happened. With that much of a crowd, there were rumors in abundance.

He had shed the old coat that held his weapons,

then hung around after he set the unconscious girl down in the emergency room to make sure an orderly found her quickly and called for a doctor.

"Drug overdose," he heard someone say wearily.

The girl was going to be all right. He could go outside and grill the lookie-loos.

"What's going on?" he asked the people around him.

"No one really knows yet," an anxious matron told him. "Someone said a couple of cops were viciously killed. Someone else said they got in a fight and killed each other."

Behind him, a girl, hugging her arms around her chest, offered, "They say they were nearly decapitated."

Bryan had a feeling there was only one way to get close to the scene. He walked around the growing crowd and found a place where a group of uniformed cops were hovering, waiting for orders.

"The whole thing is creepy. First there was that corpse that disappeared," one officer grumbled.

"Screw the corpse," another cop said bitterly. "Two of our own are dead."

There was silence for a minute.

The first cop said, "Do you believe what they're saying? That they killed each other? Santini couldn't ever stand to hurt a perp when he cuffed him. How the hell could he have gone after Clark?"

"Maybe Clark went after him," a third cop said.

A fourth chimed in then. "It's bullshit. It's all bullshit. How the hell could they *both* have their throats slit?"

That brought on a real silence. The first cop sighed. "I've got to find a john."

He had been leaning on his patrol car; now he straightened and headed toward a staff entrance to the building.

Bryan followed him inside.

The corridors were empty. Bryan followed the officer down a hall with a sign that bore a number of arrows. One pointed to "Out-patient radiation, vending machines, billing and restrooms."

He decided to let the man pee.

He waited. When the cop came out of the bathroom, Bryan caught him with a quick blow. He fell without so much as a whimper. Bryan dragged him back into the restroom.

"Sorry, buddy. I just need the uniform."

Upstairs, he found crime-scene tape blocking off the room. Pretending to ask about his assignment, he got close to the door.

They hadn't moved the bodies yet.

"You there. Harrison," a big cop called.

"Yes, sir?" he answered.

"What are you doing up here? You're supposed to be downstairs. They'll be assigning you to crowd patrol soon. The mayor is going to be giving a state-ment, and things might get ugly."

"Yes sir. Sorry. I was told I should report to you… Sergeant Mendez," Bryan said, reading the man's badge.

He stared at Mendez, who stared back, fingering the crucifix around his neck.

A strange look entered Mendez's eyes; he crossed himself. "You're not Harrison," he said softly.

"I'm not," he said, keeping eye contact. "But I need to see the bodies," he said.

"You—you shouldn't be impersonating a cop," Mendez said, but there was no conviction in his words, and he stepped aside to let Bryan pass.

"I want you to block the hallway," Bryan said. "Do you understand?"

"Yes," Mendez replied tonelessly, then stood firmly in the hallway.

Bryan saw that a reporter had just slipped in, and everyone was busy keeping him at bay. Good.

He moved quickly, surveyed the bed, then the bodies. He knelt beside them, checking them out thoroughly. He saw the scalpels. The blood.

And then he saw the smudge in the blood where something had been written.

He tensed, then rose quickly, slipping out past the still-dazed Mendez and the crowd holding off the reporter.

As he left the building—through the front doors this time—he saw a number of cops again and frowned. He recognized one of them.

Bobby Munro. The cop Stacey was dating.

Jessica reached Maggie's house just a few minutes after daylight. The children were still sleeping. Maggie looked as if she'd been pacing for a very long time.

"What the hell happened last night?" Jessica demanded. "Two cops dead?"

"Yes, made to look as if they'd gotten into a fight and killed each other. But no way could two guys have slit each other's throats like that."

"You saw them?" Jessica asked weakly.

"No. Sean described the scene. And it wasn't any newborn creature seeking a meal, I can assure you. The Master was there. In the hospital."

"We were conned tonight. He set it up perfectly. The would-be vampires, the real thing, the old house… But the whole thing was a ploy. It's as if…"

"It's as if it's been planned from the start," Maggie said. "He's found you. All these years, all the deception, the elaborate masquerade you set up yourself, and he's found you, anyway, and wants to show you his power, make you suffer."

"To have discovered I was in New Orleans, practicing psychology, to have found out about a conference, found out I was going, then planned the party, knowing I'd come...."

"He's had years to plan all the revenge he wanted," Maggie reminded her.

"But why bother?" Jessica murmured, but she knew the answer. Because he hated her with a passion that had outlasted centuries.

"So what happened? You were there, you staked a bunch of the bad guys...?"

"More or less," Jessica murmured.

"Did Bryan make an appearance?"

"Yes."

"When you were the dominatrix?" Maggie demanded.

"Yes."

"And he didn't try to kill you?"

"Yes."

"Oh, my God. You didn't kill *him*. You didn't kill a warrior, did you?" Maggie asked.

"No."

"Then...?"

"We came to an impasse."

Maggie stared at her for a long moment. "Kitchen," she said. "There's coffee on." She held her peace until they were in the kitchen, until she had poured coffee. Jessica took her cup to the table and sat in silence. Maggie joined her. "All right. Now, what the hell happened? In detail."

"I was waiting to capture the Master in his performance room. I'd…'entertained' a few vampires while I was waiting, someone was there already."

"Bryan?"

"Bryan."

"Go on."

"There was still no Master, but then the feasting began downstairs. There were screams. We both ran down, fought…them, then each other, and then… we talked."

"You just stopped fighting and you *talked?*" Maggie asked incredulously.

She leaned forward intently. "Jessica, Bryan is the king's warrior."

"I just…I just can't believe that."

"What do you mean, you can't believe it? You were lovers once."

"Almost a thousand years ago," Jessica protested.

Maggie looked at her dryly. "Since you've only indulged in an affair every couple of hundred years, you should be able to recognize the one great love of your life."

Jessica stood, started to pace, then stopped, spun, set her hands on the table and stared at Maggie. "If he is…" She paused, wincing. "If he *was* Ioin MacDuncan, why didn't I hear hundreds of years ago that he was alive?"

"Whoever said warriors were actually alive?" Maggie asked. "You know all about life without life."

"Existence," Jessica said. But Bryan is alive. He's no angel. He's flesh and blood and fire. *Alive*."

"Maybe in a way," Maggie conceded. "I don't know. I've never known a warrior before. But then, I didn't even spend two hundred years as a vampire, and I've never heard of anyone other than myself who's been bitten, then recovered more than a century later."

Jessica sat down again, deflated. "I don't know. He knows *what* I am. He doesn't know *who*."

"You're just going to have to tell him."

"What?"

"Look, we're in real trouble here. First Mary, now two cops have been slaughtered. That wasn't the act of a vampire doing his best just to survive. It was vicious. *Staged*. Just as the parties have been staged. Jessica, you're the only one, human or vampire, who managed to injure him so severely that it took him hundreds of years to heal. He hates you. He'll go to any length to torment you, to destroy you."

Jessica shook her head. "No…no. I can't believe he knows I'm here. That I'm alive. The whole reason I created the persona of Kathleen, Countess Valor, was to make him think I'd been evil, then that I was dead."

"The truth has a strange way of being discovered. Think about it. You've been living quietly for several hundred years now. You have no idea how long he's been back. I know you took every precaution, that you barricaded the crypt with crosses. But there must have been a quake...something. He—"

Maggie stopped abruptly, her eyes suddenly widening as she stared past Jessica toward the doorway.

Jessica froze, then turned slowly.

Bryan.

He hadn't knocked. And she could tell from the look in his eyes that he wasn't surprised to find her there.

She stared at him unflinchingly.

Maggie rose. "I didn't hear you knock," she said, her voice regally cool.

"I didn't." He smiled knowingly. "I don't have to be asked in. I'm not a *vampyr*. And even if I were, you've already asked me in." He stared hard at Maggie. "Just what is the story with you, Mrs. Canady? You're not a vampire, and neither is your husband, but you're both aware of their existence. And there's something about you, about this house...."

"You've just barged into my house unasked. Why don't you start by explaining *yourself*?"

"What is there to explain? I have but one purpose. To kill vampires," he said very softly, and his gaze fell upon Jessica. "There is one in particular for whom I've been searching for years. And years," he added dryly. "But then, you're both aware of that particular creature, aren't you?"

The two women stared at each other, barely daring to breathe. Maggie widened her eyes at Jessica, silently suggesting that she confess to everything.

Jessica still balked at the idea, her mind racing. It couldn't be. Wouldn't she have known, somehow, even after all these years? Yet hadn't she felt the familiarity, felt the sense of…

"We didn't know about the Master until I reached Transylvania. He had been…out of commission, I suppose you'd say, for hundreds of years," Jessica said.

Bryan strode over to the table and stared hard at her. "So you brought the dominatrix to life in Romania?"

"I could hardly walk in looking like Sister Golden Hair," she said, then let out a sigh. "You're so wrong about us. You have no idea how many of us fight against what we are."

"And you walked in to kill the Master?"

"Yes."

He spun on Maggie so suddenly that she jumped. "And you help Jessica with…with whatever it is she's doing? Your husband obviously knows and understands everything that is going on?"

"I understand *exactly* what she's going through," Maggie said. "*I* was a vampire once."

"*Was?*"

"I'm…not one anymore. It's a long story."

"I believe I have some time," Bryan said calmly.

Both women just stared at him.

"What's the deal with Sean?" Bryan asked.

"He's a cop, exactly what he looks like," Maggie said firmly.

"All right, so is this just a small party going on, or are there more of your kind around here—*good* vampires, as you claim?" he demanded, turning to Jessica again.

"There are more," she murmured.

"You didn't kill any of your friends the other night?" he queried.

"No. And I didn't start a staking campaign just to impress you, either. It's what we do. We don't kill indiscriminately—that's apparently your cause in life. We know the difference between good and evil."

"Where are your buddies, then?"

She looked at Maggie. "Lucien and Jade are somewhere in Africa, in pursuit of a very old demon," she said.

"Lucien," he snapped. "You're one-time king?"

Jessica held her breath. He knew more than she'd realized, even that Lucien had been hailed as the king of their kind—until he had become a champion for justice, rather than a creature to be dreaded.

"Listen, Professor, I refuse to allow this grilling to go on in my house," Maggie cut in. "If we're going to answer your questions, you're going to have to answer a few of ours. We think we know what you are. A warrior. So does that make you an…angel?"

Jessica offered a very unladylike snort. "Angel?"

He cast her a sideways glance. "No. Not an angel. A warrior as you said. I exist to fight the evil in the world." He stared at Jessica.

"I am not evil."

"So how do you survive?" he asked.

"Good Lord, this is the twenty-first century," she informed him. "Haven't you ever heard of blood banks?"

"And where do you keep this blood?"

"If you're so brilliant, why didn't you search my house?"

"I checked the refrigerator," he informed her.

"Apparently you weren't brilliant enough to find the secret drawer," she said.

"So what now?" he asked softly, pulling a chair and sitting down. Jessica sat across from him, and for a long moment they just stared. "It's apparent that everyone was conned last night. The party was a setup. The Master never intended to show. I'm a little surprised his plan wasn't to find Mary and force her into joining him in killing everyone at Montresse House, but he had something even more vile in mind. Not only were those two cops in the wrong place at the wrong time, the way he killed them sent a message as to just how evil he really is."

"You know what happened at the hospital?" Maggie asked.

He nodded gravely, then returned his attention to Jessica. "I think he's playing with you, showing you what he's capable of before he comes for you."

"What if he is baiting you?" Jessica suggested. Then she waited, not breathing. If he wasn't the man she thought, he would deny it with a shrug. But there had been few men the Master had hated more in life than the king's right hand, the knight named Ioin.

He didn't deny the possibility.

Maggie, typically straightforward, said, "I know exactly who you are."

His gaze riveted to her face and his brow arched. "Do you?"

Maggie nodded. "Ioin, champion of Robert the Bruce, who escaped a sure death at the hands of Edward III only because of your heroics. Robert was devastated by the loss of one of his illegitimate children—" She broke off abruptly and managed not to look at Jessica. "Anyway, you died so he could live. You stood alone against dozens of men while the king made his escape." She inhaled deeply. "Your body was never found, though. And there was a priest who disappeared, too."

Bryan stared back at Maggie, then, to Jessica's surprise, looked down as if ashamed. "It wasn't a matter of bravery," he said simply. "I don't believe I was sane at the time."

"So it's true?" Maggie whispered.

"You…" Jessica said, trying not to give herself away. "You…you didn't die? You became…what you are after the battle?"

"Not after the battle," he said, frowning as he studied her. "Not exactly. I didn't awaken for hundreds of years. And when I awoke, Gregore, the priest, was still with me." He was quiet for a long moment. "He lived long enough for me to learn to make my way in a new world. Long enough for me to understand the evil let loose in the world by a man who had been my most loathsome enemy in life, a man who brutalized women and children not on behalf of king or country but purely from a desire to rape, mutilate and kill. That was why I existed—to find him, however long it might take." He looked at Jessica and added softly, "And to hatchet my way all others of his kind, so he could take no strength from them and evil might be utterly eradicated."

"So you have sought the Master all these years," Maggie murmured.

"I had another goal as well," Bryan murmured, clenching his fingers. "And that was to find and destroy the king's daughter. I loved her, you see. She had been a warrior herself, because villagers across our country had been victims for years, butchered and destroyed anytime an advancing army crossed their land. She defended the children, the women.... But she had been lost to the Master, tainted by his black cruelty and savagery, compounded by his pact with the Devil, if that was indeed where he gained his power. There is, you see, such a thing as an immortal soul. And I meant to find her and bring peace to what the Master had destroyed." He lifted his hands in a gesture of futility. "I'm almost completely convinced she took on the guise of an English countess who found residence at the French court of Louis XIV. And that others saw to her demise. Still, I have sometimes wondered. There is so much evil in the world, so many places for her to hide if she is still in existence."

He leaned forward. "Now, Miss Jessica Fraser. Your turn."

She blinked. "Well...I was bitten, of course," she said.

"When?"

Should she lie? Or tell the truth? The truth? No, never. Not after what he had just said.

Jessica said, "Dublin, Ireland, the 1700s."

But even as she spoke, Maggie was offering, "Savannah, 1760."

Both women broke off, staring at each other with alarm.

"Oh?" Bryan said with deceptive calm. "The truth would be quite interesting, I'm sure."

But they never got a chance to attempt another lie, or even to offer up the truth.

They all froze as they heard the front door open and close and footsteps head toward the kitchen.

Sean.

From the hall, Jessica realized, he could see only herself and Maggie. "There you are! Thank God. Jessica. I didn't dare even mention this to Maggie on the phone." He strode over to Jessica, taking her by the shoulders, his back to Bryan, whom he clearly still hadn't seen. "This is worse than what we feared. Jessica, he knows you're here. And he knows who you are. He wrote your name in blood."

"Jessica?" Maggie whispered.

"No," Sean replied. "Her true name. In the blood of his victims, he wrote her true name. Igrainia."

16

Bryan gasped, and Sean spun around, aware for the first time of the other man's presence.

His jaw dropped. "MacAllistair!"

But Bryan was staring at Jessica. "*Igrainia*," he breathed.

She leapt to her feet, staring warily back at him. "Don't you dare judge me. I don't know what you *think* you know, but I can guarantee you're wrong."

"You really are," Maggie murmured.

Sean set a hand on his wife's shoulder. "Maggie," he cautioned, "they need to solve this themselves."

"Solve it themselves?" Maggie protested. "His solution is to kill her!"

Jessica didn't think Bryan had heard a word anyone had said since Sean had spoken her true name. He just stared at her. She felt an iciness, a fear she hadn't known in years. Not a physical fear. Something deeper. An attack against the remnants of her soul.

They all jumped when, from up stairs, they heard a little-girl voice call out, "Mommy?"

Jessica made an instant decision. She turned to Maggie and Sean. "We've got to get out of your house and talk this out between one another."

"Jessica, I can't let you leave here with him," Maggie insisted.

"I'll be all right," Jessica said firmly.

Maggie started to protest, but her husband cut her off.

"You two *do* need to work this out. Because we have a deadly situation on our hands. This Master has to be stopped, and both of you need to think about that before anything else. Am I making myself clear?"

Bryan turned to Sean. "You're right." He looked at Maggie. "Jessica has nothing to fear from me. At the moment."

"At the moment!" Maggie said, ready to do battle.

"It's all right," Jessica said, walking over to give her friend a hug.

"Mommy!"

Jessica slipped an arm casually through Maggie's, walking her toward the stairwell. "I swear to you, I'll be fine."

"You won't be fine," Maggie whispered back. "You're in love with him. You were before, you are now. And he'll lull you and seduce you—and kill you."

"No, Maggie. I'm not that foolish. I've survived this long."

"Because he hasn't known who or where you were."

"Maggie, it works both ways," Jessica reminded her. "I could kill him."

"You could, but you won't."

"Maggie, go take care of your daughter. I promise you, I'll be careful."

Maggie started up the stairs just as Sean and Bryan came up behind them. She paused, looking down in anger. "You need to find new accommodations," she told Bryan.

"Maggie," Jessica said, "Forget that for now. We need to focus on stopping the Master."

"Be back here by three this afternoon," Sean said. "I'll have gathered what and who I can by then. We need a better plan than just waiting to see what he does next. Or," he added softly, "who dies next."

"Right, back by three," Jessica said. She started out the door. Bryan followed her.

"You have your car, I see," he commented, walking around to the passenger side. "Is it your customary mode of transportation?"

"My *customary* mode of transportation? Are you asking me if I can turn into mist? If I can shape-shift?"

"I'm assuming you can."

"Can I? Yes. Do I? Not often. Only when necessary. I actually love my car. So get in, and let's get out of here," she said pleasantly.

"So," she murmured a moment later, glancing casually his way as she pulled out of the driveway, "what about you? Are you some superhero? Can you leap tall buildings in a single bound?"

"Only when necessary," he mocked. He was staring ahead at the road, frowning.

"What?"

"Jessica, someone close to you has to be in on this with the Master. How well do you know Stacey?"

"Don't you even dare suggest it."

"Why not? She knows you, knows your every move."

Jessica shook her head. "You don't understand. I met Stacey through my church."

"Your *church*?" he demanded.

"You really *don't* know anything, do you?" she said impatiently.

"Sorry, but I've come across very few vampires through the centuries who go to church."

"How many have you asked?" she demanded.

He didn't reply.

"It's not Stacey," she said heatedly. "Stacey and Gareth have looked out for me for years."

He stared at her, features drawn. "Jessica, don't be such a fool. Years mean nothing to the Master." He was quiet for a moment. "Dear God!" he exploded. "His hatred for me in life was madness. He didn't just want you dead, he wanted to turn you into pure evil simply because I loved you. Now his hatred for you is more powerful than any hunger. I blame myself for where we are now," he added bitterly. "I should have known he was here. I should have watched over Mary myself from the minute she was bitten. *I shouldn't have failed in Transylvania.*"

She was startled by his pained tone, by the fact he seemed far angrier with himself than with her. He had spoken almost as if they could be allies again, almost as if he believed that there could be those who, though touched by the hand of evil, could still resist it.

"I'm to blame, not you," she said. "Although blaming ourselves right now won't help anything."

"Right. So...who?"

"Who?"

"Who is close to you and is helping the Master to carry out his plans? Let's say its not Stacey, nor Gareth, even though they're closest to you. And human. Just how long have you known them?"

She looked at the road. "Gareth has been with me for a decade. Stacey, several years."

"Bobby Munro," he said suddenly.

"Bobby?"

"Why not?"

"Because I know him. He's always in my house, he loves Stacey. He's a good cop. You might as well suggest Big Jim."

She was startled when he remained silent. "No, no, no," she said. "He's one of the best men I've ever met."

Again Bryan was silent.

"Look, there's still the possibility we're looking for a stranger," she reminded him.

He looked at her. "True. As we both know," he added dryly, "almost anything is *possible*. But it's not probable."

"You really don't understand. I know the people around me. I've been…I've been around for centuries. I've learned how to judge human nature."

"None of us ever really knows anyone else."

"For an angel of goodness, you're quite a cynic," she informed him icily.

"I'm not an angel," he reminded her.

"Right. A warrior. For the forces of good. You might want to accept that there could be a little goodness in others."

They had reached her house; she pulled into the drive, turned off the engine, and they sat for a minute. He stared straight ahead, then finally he looked at her. "I'll grant you this, the place is well vampire-proofed. So how come you're able to enter?"

"You really don't understand anything at all."

She got out and headed straight for the porch,

shoulders squared, indignant. He followed instantly, grabbing her arm, spinning her around. She was about to tell him where to go when she realized he wasn't even looking at her. He was staring at the house. "Even here, you have to be careful." He frowned, jaw locked as he looked for danger.

"There's a vampire here, and I don't mean you," he said.

She set a hand on his arm before he could go racing in. "Mary."

"What?"

"It's all right. We have her under control."

He shook his head. "She has to be destroyed."

"No! Look, I would have killed her myself the night she turned—you know that. Even I was convinced that she was evil. But she's not, Bryan."

"There is—"

"Don't you dare go telling me again that there is no such thing as a good vampire."

She started in again, but he called her back.

"Jessica."

"What?"

"I'm trying. Honest to God. But you'd better warn Mary and all your little friends that one wrong move and they *will* be eliminated."

"And may I suggest that if you act against any us without provocation, I can be equally ruthless."

"I don't doubt it," he said.

She gritted her teeth, damning herself for feeding right into his beliefs.

"You do realize you're in even greater danger, now that you've let Mary in."

"Mary will be sound asleep all day."

"He can enter her dreams."

She froze, staring at him. Yes, the Master could enter dreams. He had entered hers, while she had foolishly imagined that it was Bryan who had somehow caused the nightmares of the past to plague her.

"You're in very serious danger here," he said softly.

"Right—from you."

"I don't lie. I said I wouldn't kill you."

"You're just a paragon of virtue," she taunted.

She was surprised when he actually laughed. "I wouldn't go that far. But my word is good."

She continued up the porch steps to the house. Stacey opened the door, and stared first at Jessica, then at Bryan.

"Is everything all right here?" Jessica asked.

Stacey nodded, still looking anxious. "Mary is as secure as…as secure as I know how to make her."

"Which is very secure," Jessica said firmly, a warning in her eyes.

"Right. And I saw to it that she was completely stuffed. I mean, if she feels like she's just eaten an entire turkey dinner, she's less likely to fall prey to his call, right?"

"Actually, she seems to have done a very good job of fighting him already. I haven't seen that happen before," Jessica said.

"But it *has* happened before," Stacey said. "You."

Bryan made a skeptical sound in his throat.

"Where's Gareth?"

"Watching over Mary, Jeremy and Nancy. No matter how much Jeremy objects, if Mary makes any trouble, Gareth will take care of her."

"Well, then, I'm going to get some sleep," Jessica said. "Stacey, make sure to wake me up by about two, all right?"

"What's happening now?" Stacey asked worriedly.

"Sean and Maggie are working a few angles," she said, and set a hand on Stacey's arm. "They know what they're doing," she said softly. She spun and stared at Bryan. "I'm going to bed. Good night."

With that, she started up the stairs. When she reached her room, he was behind her. She turned on him heatedly. "What?"

"Do you really trust Stacey and Gareth so completely?" he asked her.

She stared back at him, shaking her head. "Yes, I do. How have you managed to live so long without learning that sometimes you have to believe in other people? We don't exist alone. I don't. I *won't*."

She walked into the room and started to close the door, but he had followed her.

"I need some rest."

"Yes, and I won't leave you. You're in danger."

She looked up at him. "Maggie is certain that you are the greatest danger I'm facing."

"He's here for you," he said softly.

He walked around the room, looking in the closet, the bathroom and under the bed.

"Bryan, he's hardly likely to be hiding under the bed."

He rose. "Nice bed. No coffin?"

"No one sleeps in a coffin anymore," she said. "Well, all right, some do. But not the...the vampires I know."

He shrugged. "The old trunk under the bed? Scottish soil, I assume?"

Her turn to shrug. "I'm surprised you haven't already ripped my room to shreds to see what you could find."

"I really didn't know at first," he admitted. "My mind was on...other things. I should have known, though. Even after all these years..."

"I had no idea," she told him. "Time...well, time can heal a lot of wounds. Except..."

"Except what?"

I should have known, she thought. I should have known when I felt...something I had never felt before or since.

She fought the ridiculous desire to burst into tears.

She had survived this long. But she had never thought she would see him again. She had been sure he was dead, but now…

She shrugged. "Nothing."

He looked at her expectantly for a moment, but when she didn't say anything more, he stepped out onto the balcony and stared up at the sky. After a moment, she joined him.

"He isn't here," he said.

"You're certain?"

He nodded gravely. "He was, though. I thought it was my imagination that I was so intent on my pursuit I was conjuring him up, but it was real. It seems, however, that he can't enter." He looked at her. "Either that, or he hasn't chosen to yet."

"I think the first is correct," she said. "My *friends*, the people who care about me, are very good at keeping me safe."

"Ah, but did they keep you safe from me?" he asked.

Nothing could have kept me safe from you, she thought.

"You're not a vampire," she said dryly. "Anyway, it's daytime. He has to rest now."

"Does he? You don't always rest by day, and you're both ancient."

"Some women might take that the wrong way," she said.

He ignored the thrust. "The point is, you're both strong, with powers few others will ever attain."

"Right. We're *both* strong. He's not the only powerful one."

"I still fear for you," he said.

"Fear for me—or fear me?"

He shook his head but didn't answer.

She started back into the bedroom. He followed her, carefully locking the balcony doors. He took a long moment, staring at the garlic strings and intricate crosses that were strung there for protection.

"Interesting," he murmured.

"Don't you ever pause to think that if there is a supreme being who strives for peace that in the heart of every sentient creature, there is both evil and goodness?"

He took her by the shoulders, looking into her eyes. "I know what I have seen," he said.

"But faith means believing in what we *can't* see," she said softly.

"You don't seem to have much faith in me tonight."

"You've admitted that one of your key aims in life is to kill me."

"And I've said I won't do it."

"Now," she said.

"We have to defeat the Master. For good, this time."

His hands were still on her shoulders, his face close. Those eyes…

How had she not recognized those eyes?

Instinct had told her what memory had failed to see, but when she trembled now, was it because of Maggie's warning or from passion?

She had to resist him, dared not take a chance. But then he touched her face.

Still, she told herself, she would have resisted but for a single whispered word.

"Igrainia."

A name. And in that name, she heard a longing and poignancy that had outlasted the ages, the joy of what they had shared, what they had lost.

She couldn't have turned away then even if he had aimed a stake straight at her heart. He cupped her chin in his hands, his fingers moving with an infinite tenderness over her cheeks. She didn't even realize she had moved, but she was suddenly pressed against him. He bent slowly, and his lips moved over hers. It was a full, slow kiss, lips parting, the fire of the ages evoked in the play of their tongues. Passion, simmering, slow but explosive, awoke. She reached up, her fingers winding through his hair, and they kissed with a growing madness. She never knew how clothing found its way to the floor. It seemed the kiss never broke, but it didn't matter, because they were naked in each other's arms. Nothing, nothing at all seemed to matter, except the heat that infused their flesh, melded them together so they could sate the frenzied hunger that seized them both.

When their lips at last parted, she kissed his throat, feeling the pulse there, then his collarbone, the rippling expanse of his chest. His fingers stroked her hair as she moved against him, remembering, discovering, showering him with liquid caresses. She moved ever lower, reveling in the feel of hard muscle and sleek skin, noting a scar here, there….

It was as if time washed away. She felt a Highland wind as surely as if it touched her in truth. She drew her fingers around his hip, over his buttocks, and it was as if the colors of a distant valley lived with her again in springtime. She felt the roar of a storm, the crashing of the waves against the cliff, the hunger of innocence, trust…love….

She stroked and caressed with fingers, lips and tongue. She teased mercilessly, those distant memories rising in her with the shuddering of his flesh, each tensing of his fingers as they brushed her hair and shoulders. She took him in her hands, in her mouth; she felt him tremble, and then she was in his arms, lifted and carried, then lying on the cool sheets, but in her mind and heart she might have lain in an age-old field of mauve and green. Where she had teased lightly at first, she was met now with urgency and raw desire, his hands and mouth moving over her as if everything that had come before was but a prelude for this.

He had always been a magnificent lover.

And so he proved again, mouth upon hers, upon her body, raggedly teasing her breasts, her belly, between her thighs. Then he was atop her, within her, and the world beyond them was a storm, the sky blue and thunderous gray, the sheets a poignantly re-membered wool, cast upon the rugged ground, and theirs was the passion of youth, of a love that had grown, flown and entwined them forever....

In life, in death.

Yet this was the now, and what he did to her was raw and carnal and explosive. The sheets beneath her were real, the sun high, and he was flesh and thunder within her. When sensation reached the point of eruption, she felt a climax shake her as if she had died again, this time in a rapture and sheer physical ecstasy that was staggering. She clung to him, amazed at the joy that continued to grip her so sweetly as she seemed to drift on silver clouds, down to earth, down to the bed, the sheets, the room in the house on Bourbon Street.

And to him, beside her, there on the bed. Hold-ing her.

And then...the pain. Oh, God, the pain. Tears that stung her eyes. Tears she could not shed.

She spoke softly. "Perhaps, if you're going to do it, you should do it now."

"What?" he rose above her, puzzled.

"I am a *vampyr*. And you are a warrior."

He stared down at her for a long time. "Sometimes," he said at last, a rueful smile curving his lips, "we have to go on faith, to believe that which we cannot see, hmm?"

He eased back beside her, pulling her against him. She lay still, thinking that if he were to kill her now, it wouldn't matter.

She would happily die in his arms.

She felt his kiss brush her head, felt his fingers stroke through her hair.

"If only..." he murmured.

"If only...?"

"We could stay like this forever."

They couldn't. They both knew it.

She started to speak, but he pressed his fingers to her lips, drawing her closer still. "We have to rest."

She nodded. She didn't dare move.

She had thought him dead and herself alone. She had fended for herself, made herself strong, and she had learned that she could face any danger.

But now he was here. Alive.

Her greatest threat?

But his arms were around her now, and she felt, as she hadn't since they had last lain so, that she was cherished, protected, that...he would die for her?

He already had.

But tonight...

Whatever the future brought, she intended to savor the sensation, the belief, that she was loved, cherished.

She lay secure in his arms, desperately tired. And finally she slept.

No dreams plagued her, only his whisper as he moved against her.

"Igrainia."

17

Bobby Munro entered Sean's office. "We've tracked down the ownership of the plantation up the river," he told Sean.

"Yeah?"

Bobby shook his head. "No help. It's owned by the parish."

"Then someone knew it would be empty."

Bobby shrugged. "Sean, *anyone* could have known it would be empty. It's public record."

"Start with local bars, see who could have supplied the place."

"This is New Orleans, for God's sake. That's like looking for a needle in a haystack." Bobby cleared his throat. "And we're under a hell of a lot of pressure. Missing corpse. Two cops brutally killed. The press is breathing down our necks."

"And you know what to tell the press."

"No comment," Bobby said with a sigh.

"That's it."

"But, Lieutenant, we…"

"Yes?"

"Never mind," Bobby said.

"I know there's a lot going on, but when we find out who made the arrangements to host that party, we'll be ten times closer to the truth," Sean said. "I'm in charge here, huh?"

Bobby swallowed, looking at him. "Yes, sir. Of course." As Bobby replied, Sean was thinking he wouldn't be in charge much longer, not if the mayor didn't get a few answers.

He knew what he was doing, he reminded himself.

"Get help on it, Bobby. Assign a couple of teams. I'll be hitting the streets myself." And he would be. But first he had to visit the lockup.

When Jessica came downstairs, Bryan was already there, in the kitchen, pouring coffee for himself. So were the others, except for Stacey and Mary.

"Still sound asleep," Gareth said quietly, speaking to only her as she entered. "Stacey's watching her."

"Thanks," she murmured.

Jeremy looked at her happily. "Bryan says Mary should be safe for a while, anyway."

"Oh?" She looked over at Bryan. He was showered, handsome in jeans and a tailored shirt. His hair was still damp. Such a contemporary cut. But other than that…not so different at all. But then, neither was she. Yet time had come between them. Worse than that, belief had come between them.

And still hovered like an ax, ready to drive them apart.

"She can't be left alone for a minute," Bryan warned.

Jessica frowned. What made him think that Mary was "safe"?

"Pancakes?" Nancy said. "You need to eat."

No, she didn't actually need to eat. She did because it was part of her pathetic attempt to live a normal life.

"Pancakes sound wonderful. How much time do we have?"

"An hour," Bryan said.

"Before?" Jeremy asked.

"We have to go and see some friends," Jessica said.

"I'm going with you," Jeremy said staunchly.

"No," Jessica said.

"But I was there. In Transylvania. I can help you remember things. I—"

"Stacey and I know what we're doing," Gareth said. "Jeremy and Nancy might be helpful. You don't know."

"Actually," Bryan said, to Jessica's surprise, "if we're having a meeting to plan, to look for answers, I don't see why they shouldn't be involved."

Jeremy looked pleased, then frowned. "You're not trying to get me out of here so you can double back and kill Mary, are you?"

Bryan inhaled, exhaled and shook his head. "Do I think she should be destroyed?" he asked softly. "Yes. But I have no intention of doubling back here to do it. I have a bigger concern, and the Master is nowhere near this house right now.

"How do you know that?" Jessica demanded.

"I feel it."

He cocked his head slightly as he met her eyes. "Anything is possible, but I believe he's accomplished what he wanted here, for the moment. Maybe he hasn't gone far. Maybe he'll go back to the hospital for David Hayes. And no doubt at some point he'll come back for Mary. But right now, he isn't near this house."

"What do you think he's accomplished?" Jessica asked.

"If we're having a meeting with Sean and Maggie, let's save it, all right?" he suggested.

Jessica nodded. "You trust Stacey and Gareth, then—with Mary."

Bryan looked around the room. "Yes, because if they fail… Mary will turn them. And I will kill them. And they know it."

Whether it was true or not, Gareth turned ashen. He certainly believed it.

Jessica was proud of him when he stood up to Bryan. "With or without you around, professor, I live to protect Jessica."

Bryan acknowledged Gareth with a nod. "I believe you. Now let's get going, shall we?"

Cal Hodges and Niles Goolighan had been arraigned, and the assistant district attorney had seen to it that they weren't let out on bail.

To Sean's surprise, Cal Hodges agreed to see him without his attorney present. They sat in a dank green room, staring at each other across a scarred wooden table.

"You agreed to see me," Sean said.

Cal gave him a laconic smile. "Yeah."

"Why?"

"Because you should be squirming by now. I wanted to watch you. I heard about your dead cops, and you haven't got a clue. You haven't got dick."

"You should have seen how they died. Might be a lesson for you," Sean said evenly, and wondered if just a flicker of unease passed through the young man's eyes.

Cal lifted a hand. "I won't be here much longer, you know."

"Someone's going to get you out?"

"You bet."

"What makes you think so?"

"The time is coming. That's all I know. But—"

Sean leaned forward. "He's speaking to you when you're asleep?" he asked politely.

The frown Cal displayed for an instant assured Sean of the truth. He smiled. "When he's done with you, he'll chew you up into little pieces and spit you out." He paused briefly, then asked, "Did you attack Dr. Jessica Fraser on purpose?"

The change of tactic seemed to work. Cal frowned. "No. Yes. You're just a stupid dumb-fuck cop, you know? We were led to her. That bitch took my sister, you know." He started to laugh. "Thing was, I couldn't keep her and I couldn't shoot her, you know?"

"But now everything in your life is going to be just fine. Because *he's* going to get you out of here, because *he* cares about you." He saw small beads of sweat begin to appear on Cal's upper lip.

"What the fuck do you want from me? I wasn't in the hospital. I didn't kill your pals. And I sure as hell wasn't at that party."

"You knew about it."

Cal shrugged.

Sean moved in again. "How?" he demanded.

Jeremy sat tensely as they followed the elegant drive, lined by trees dripping with Spanish moss, that led to the Canadys' house. There were a number of cars there already. "Your friends?" he asked Jessica.

"Looks like it."

"Great. A whole pack of bloodsuckers," the professor said as the car pulled to a stop.

Jeremy was sure Jessica refrained from saying everything that was on her mind because he and Nancy were in the backseat.

"You want to defeat the Master," she reminded Bryan. "These people have gone up against some of the greatest evil out there and survived. Don't you see?" There was a plea in her tone. "We need the help."

Bryan MacAllistair didn't deny that. "Come on, kids," he said, getting out of the car.

Nancy looked almost as scared as she had the night she had sat with him at the hospital in Transylvania. He took her hand and helped her from the car. When he would have released her, she held tight. He smiled, maintaining a finger lock with her. He wasn't afraid himself. Not now.

A beautiful red-haired woman answered the door when they knocked. "Right on time," she said.

"Maggie, Jeremy and Nancy. This is our hostess, Maggie."

"Hello," Jeremy said, letting go of Nancy long enough to shake hands.

"Hi," Nancy said, staring. "Are you...?"

"I'm not a vampire," Maggie said.

"Of course not," Nancy murmured.

"But I *was*," their hostess said with a grin. "Come on in."

She led them to a huge parlor off the entry hall. Jeremy almost laughed in nervous relief when he saw that no one there looked undead or other-worldly. In fact, it looked as if they were at a photo shoot for the absolutely beautiful.

Bryan MacAllistair strode into the room, stopping dead center and staring at a tall dark-haired man. "Lucien? Known as the king of the vampires?"

"I'm Lucien, yes," the man said evenly.

King of the vampires? Jeremy thought. He felt Nancy cower behind him. Jessica wouldn't have brought them here if it weren't safe, he told himself.

Jessica slipped past the two of them then, positioning herself between Bryan and the other men. "Lucien, Bryan MacAllistair, Bryan, Lucien DeVeau. Oh, and Jeremy and Nancy." She introduced a very tall man as Ragnor and another man as Brent Malone. The women present were introduced as Jade, Lucien's wife, Tara, who was married to Brent, and Jordan, married to Raynor and taking notes on a notebook computer.

"A warrior," Brent Malone said, staring at Mac-Allistair with curiosity and respect.

"You're not a vampire," Professor MacAllistair said flatly.

"Werewolf, I'm afraid," Malone said with a grimace. "And fully dedicated to the destruction of evil in whatever form."

"This is entirely against everything I was ever taught," MacAllistair said.

Jessica touched his arm. "Times change," she said. "We're all part of what we call the Alliance, and we...oh, hell, I don't know any other way of explaining it. We're part of a continuing war against evil. A lot of us are vampires, and then there's Brent. Jade has some of our abilities, but not all. She was bitten, but she didn't die. Tara and Jordan are completely human."

Jade DeVeau said smoothly, "Time is of the essence here. We should start. Maggie, when is Sean due back?"

"I don't know what's keeping him," Maggie said.

Bryan strode across to the fireplace, facing Lucien DeVeau. The men studied each other. "I'd heard you were off demon hunting," Bryan said.

"We were. We're back," Lucien said flatly.

"And the demon?"

"Will wait. I've heard of the Master, of course," Lucien said, grimacing. "We had hoped he would never appear again. Now that he has shown his hand, he must be stopped."

"You're not afraid of me, are you?" he asked.

"Should we be?" Lucien asked.

"You know what I am," MacAllistair said.

"And you *don't* really know what we are," Lucien said evenly. "If you did, there would be no reason for any of us to fear you—ever. We are all determined that the Master must be stopped. Shall we go with that for now?"

MacAllistair kept his eyes on the man for a long moment. Then he said, "Let's start with the kids, then. They can describe that night in Transylvania, start to finish. I can throw in my part, Jessica can explain hers. God knows, maybe someone will see something we're missing." He took a seat on the couch, crossing his arms over his chest. "And I'm convinced someone out there is a traitor, someone Jessica knows. She won't even think about it. Maybe one of you can make her take a real look at the people she knows."

Jessica groaned softly, but Lucien looked at her assessingly. "Jessica, we have to take a long look at everything and every*one*."

"Coffee's ready, so the kids can start," Maggie said.

Jeremy realized all eyes were on him. His mouth was dry. He licked his lips. "It all started when Mary asked me to go to a party with her...."

Niles Goolighan lay in his cell, staring at the ceiling, regretting the fact he'd ever started believing in promises of a greater existence, power—and women.

Frankly, it had been the promise that women would find him irresistible that had sewed it up for him. Cal had always been bigger, braver and more assertive. He'd just followed along. But now he was rotting in a jail cell. The attorney they'd been assigned had suggested they might want to strike a deal; if they could give the cops information about who had killed two cops, they could get lighter sentences than they would receive if they were convicted.

He toyed with the idea. The information they wanted was really so simple.

A chill suddenly ran through him. He looked beyond the bars. A man stood there. He was tall, built like a brick shithouse. Strong features—he belonged in a movie about ancient Rome. Oddly he was dressed in a suit, the nondescript kind lots of attorneys wore.

"Niles."

"Yeah?" he said curiously.

"I'm here to help you. Ask me in."

"The guards have to let you in. They don't exactly give me a key," Niles said, tired and wondering what the hell the guy wanted. He laughed suddenly. "What the hell. If you can do it, come on in."

To his amazement, the iron door sprang open and the huge man walked in. He grinned, and Niles felt an icy terror curl around his heart. He sprang up, backed against the wall.

"You weren't thinking of betraying me, were you, Niles?" the man asked.

"Betraying you?" Niles felt his mouth fall open. "Are you…real."

The man smiled coldly. "Of course I'm real.

Here and in the flesh. And as for you…" He laughed softly. "I need you, Niles. So even if you are a pathetic coward, I'm about to fulfill your fondest dreams."

"No…I have no dreams," Niles protested wildly.

He opened his mouth. He couldn't believe it; he was about to scream for the guards. Scream? Cry like a baby, more like it.

No sound ever left his lips.

The man was suddenly right there, right in front of him. He had eyes like fire, eyes that burned as they stared into his.

And he had fangs.

Real ones.

Niles heard the terrible crunching sound as the man bit deeply into his neck.

Then…

Nothing.

"So that's it?" Lucien DeVeau said as Jeremy and Nancy finished.

"We didn't understand how we had survived, until…until we got home and Mary…Mary died, and we found out who and…what Jessica and Bryan are," Jeremy said.

"So," Bryan said, rising and pacing, "this is what I believe. The Master recently discovered who Jessica is and where she lives, and he planned carefully. When he found out she would be at the conference, he organized the party. He knew she'd come to find him." He flashed a glance at Jessica. "He didn't, of course, know she'd arrive as a dominatrix. And," he added thoughtfully, "I'm not sure he was aware I was trailing him, getting closer and closer, more and more aware of the way he worked. But when he came here, to her home turf, he had to have help. It's my guess that he's been creating havoc here for two reasons, to torture her, making her suffer, and to create a trap, so he can finally kill her. He never intended to be at the party here, but he knew we'd be there, and he'd have free rein to kill those cops and get to the morgue attendant. The thing is, he somehow knows what she's doing, and that means he managed to get to someone close to her."

"How can you be so sure?" Jessica demanded. It was the first time she had spoken since Jeremy had described the night in Transylvania.

"I think he's right," Lucien said.

Ragnor walked over to Jessica, bending down, taking her hands. "Jessica, perhaps whoever it is never intended to betray you. The Master's very powerful."

Sean suddenly came striding into the room, and everyone fell silent. "You're not going to believe this," he said.

"What?" Jessica demanded.

"If you'll let me at the computer…"

Everyone moved away. Sean sat down and quickly pulled up a web site that promoted vampirism as a solution for those looking for something better in life: money, power, sex, even a place to belong. As they all stared over Sean's shoulder, reading, he suddenly stood. "It's coming," he said. "And since I've seen it once and I'm only human, I'm getting out of the line of fire."

Frowning, Bryan peered more closely at the screen.

Then, in an instant, a blinding light flashed across the screen, followed by a red darkness, and then a face.

The Master's face. The words he spoke seemed to ring directly in the viewer's head.

Serve me. Welcome me. Bow down before me. Obey my every command.

Bobby Munro was exhausted. He'd worked back-to-back shifts, and he didn't know how many bar suppliers he had seen. He didn't know if they'd been straight with him, or if they had lied. But now, new teams were taking over and he had to call it a night.

Walking home, he passed the bar where Big Jim played. He could use a drink. He walked in, ordered a beer and took a seat at a table in front of the band. Big Jim saw him and waved. Barry Larson grinned. Bobby smiled back, then closed his eyes. Damn, but he loved good jazz.

His head was pounding. The music helped, but all too soon the band went on break. Big Jim joined him at the table; Barry Larson followed. "Tough day, huh?" Big Jim said.

"Yeah, must have been," Barry added sympathetically. "Two of your own guys. I was really sorry to hear what happened. There's a real psycho on the loose, huh? I mean, they don't think those guys really killed each other, do they?"

Bobby stared at him. He didn't like him much. He followed Big Jim like a puppy and tried too hard to be a part of the group. "No, they didn't kill each other," he said.

"How are you holding up?" Big Jim asked.

"I'm okay. I could use a few long hours just lying in the sun somewhere with Stacey," he said. "But she's been busy lately." He brightened suddenly. "Hell, I'm only a few blocks from Montresse House. Why am I sitting here staring at you? I'm going to walk over and see her for at least a few minutes." He rose, putting his money on the table. "Get yourselves a couple of beers, huh?"

"Sure thing. Thanks, Bobby," Big Jim said, grinning.

Feeling a lot more cheerful, Bobby started down Bourbon Street. There was a big crowd out that night. He loved to see his beloved home busy again.

His good mood faded a bit as he heard snatches of conversation. People were talking about the maniac on the loose. About the dead cops. About the missing corpse.

About the force's in ability to stop what was going on. Inwardly, he groaned. He was caught up in his thoughts, barely aware that the crowd was thinning as he moved alone.

Suddenly he paused. He could have sworn he was being followed. Followed? On Bourbon Street? Hell, he was more tired than he had imagined.

He reached Montresse House and walked up on the porch. He knocked, then saw Gareth looking suspiciously out past one of the drapes. A second later, the door opened. As it did, Bobby sensed once again he was being followed. He spun around, ready to reach for his firearm.

"It's you," he said, letting out a sigh. "Shit, you shouldn't follow an armed man like that."

"Bobby Munro, what are you doing here?" Gareth asked.

"Just wanted to see Stacey for a minute, Gareth, that's all. Didn't know my friend was joining me."

"Stacey's busy," Gareth said.

"Come on, Gareth, I'm beat to shit. Let me see her for just a minute. Let me in."

"Hell, Bobby. Come in and wait. I'll see if I can get her."

Bobby stepped across the threshold, then turned to the man behind him. "Hey, what's up? Why were you following me?"

"Don't know. Felt nervous," Big Jim said. "Just

thought I'd say a quick hello to Stacey, too, then I'll
be on my way."

Bobby groaned. "Great. Just great. Your shadow is
behind you."

Big Jim swung around to see Barry Larson coming
up the walkway. "Hey, Jim. You went running out.
We're not done with the gig tonight."

"We're on break," Big Jim said, shaking his head.
"Damn it all, Barry, you don't have to go following
me around all the time like we're in a flippin'
nursery rhyme."

"Sorry, thought something was wrong," Barry
said, hurt.

"Ah, come on in. We'll head back together in
just a minute," Big Jim said.

"Yeah, come on in," Bobby echoed, forcing a
smile.

Barry stepped inside, looking around. "Lordy, this
is a great place, huh?" he asked cheerfully.

"Yeah, but close the door," Bobby said irritably.
"We don't want to let any bugs in."

Stacey sat in a chair, watching over Mary. She
had discovered that the girl was quite happy in her
little prison as long as she could watch TV and as
long as she was supplied with the sustenance she
needed.

Gareth was prowling the house, she knew. He

came by at least every half hour to check on them, then, nervously, went off to assure himself that the rest of the house was safe and well protected.

"Stacey?" Mary asked suddenly.

"Yes?"

"What's going to happen to me?" Mary asked softly, pathetically.

"Well…"

"Either *he'll* come and get me, or…someone will drive a stake through my heart."

"Mary, maybe not. It's…it's a matter of finding the right path," Stacey started to explain. Then Mary jumped up in alarm.

"What is it?" Stacey asked.

Mary pressed her hands hard against her ears. "He's out there," she whispered.

The way she said it gave Stacey the creeps.

"But I won't let him in. I won't, I won't, I swear it," she cried.

Stacey stared in alarm as Mary cried out in agony, fell to the floor and curled into a fetal position. "No!" she cried.

Stacey raced toward the door to the hallway. "Gareth!"

She was relieved to hear the pounding of footsteps on the stairway. Then she started. Gareth was there, but he'd been followed up the stairs by Bobby Munro, Big Jim and Barry Larson.

Gareth spun around on the other two men. "Get back downstairs. You were not asked up here."

"I'm a cop, and I heard screaming," Bobby announced, then charged into the room. Big Jim and Barry Larson were behind him.

Just great, she thought. All those people... This was a mess. They would see, they would all know....

Suddenly the French doors seemed to explode.

Stacey spun around. Shattered glass flew, momentarily filling the air with shards of brilliance.

There was a red-black mist, a miasma....

Then there was a man. Tall, with blazing eyes, massive shoulders, and cruel features.

"Thank you ever so much for the invitation," he said, his tone pleasantly conversational. Gaping, stunned, *terrified*, Stacey wondered what he was talking about, who the hell had asked him in.

"Now, clear away that rubbish. I have come for the girl."

Mary cried out again. Stacey wanted to turn, to see who there was about to do his bidding, but she was too afraid to turn her back on what could only be the Master.

Jessica stared at the image as it faded. Bryan stepped back from the computer, turning to Sean.

"I think he gains control with that image. Like

subliminal advertising—he has entered the modern age of communication," Sean said.

Bryan stiffened suddenly. "Damn it," he swore.

"I know, it's amazing, isn't it?" Sean said.

"Yes, but that's not it. We've got to get back to Jessica's," Bryan said.

"What's happened?" Jessica demanded, jumping up, eyes wide.

"He's on the move," Lucien said. "I sense it, too. Ragnor, you and I will go with them. Brent, watch over this house with the girls."

Bryan was already following Jessica out of the house. On the porch, she paused and looked uncertainly at him.

He understood.

"Screw the car," he said. "You go your way, I'll go mine. I'll meet you there. *Be careful.*"

She willed herself to change, and suddenly she was a shadow that tore across the sky. She knew that Lucien and Ragnor were right behind her.

She saw the shattered French doors before she reached the balcony and warned herself to be prepared.

She burst through into the room, regained her form, and then froze.

He was there.

Her house had been invaded by the Master, and he hadn't come alone. The scene was chaos.

She recognized the two creatures with him from the ruined castle in Transylvania, the hip-hop female from whom she had rescued Nancy and a tall red-headed man who had also stayed downstairs, attacking those watching the video. The hip-hopper had Stacey in her grip this time, but unlike Nancy, Stacey was fighting back.

Big Jim was kneeling on the floor, hands raised, chanting in an age-old tongue. The redhead was standing over him, hands stretched out, long nails ready to swipe at his throat. Bobby was there, too, his gun leveled. But he couldn't shoot, and Jessica knew they had stopped him, leaving him frozen, shaking, desperate to pull the trigger, but unable to do so, unable to stop what he saw happening to the woman he loved.

The Master himself was headed toward Mary. Tall, black-suited, dressed like any executive, he let the sound of his laughter echo through the room. He seemed enormous, like a shadow that filled time and space, controlling everything that was happening. Two bodies lay on the floor, Gareth and Barry Larson.

At that moment, Bryan arrived. Even as she stepped onto the broken glass that lay at her feet, he reached the woman holding Stacey, and Jessica was relieved at the way he had assessed the situation instantly and, despite his desire to destroy the Master, had known that if he didn't help Stacey, her life would be forfeit.

Jessica flew at the man standing above Big Jim, but she had acted too quickly. He turned on her, wrenching a stake from a belt around his hips. She backed away, ducking the first blow, vaguely aware of a body flying past, turning to dust in midair.

Bryan had dealt with the woman trying to kill Stacey.

The circle of protection that had kept Mary prisoner had been broken. And over the shoulder of the redheaded man, Jessica could see that the Master had Mary.

"Let her go!" Jessica screamed.

He let out a burst of laughter throwing Mary across the room with a strength that would snap her spine if she struck the wall. It wouldn't be a fatal injury for a vampire, but it *would* leave her paralyzed. There was no choice. Jessica leapt desperately to catch Mary before her fragile body was destroyed.

As she moved, the Master strode across the room, slamming a hand against Big Jim's head. He crumpled. Jessica cried out as the redhead's fingers threaded through her hair, whipping her around. She threw up an arm, breaking his hold. She was dimly aware that Lucien had arrived in time to grab Big Jim before the Master could finish him. Then he threw himself in front of Bobby before the Master could break the cop's neck. Ragnor was right behind Lucien, engaging the redhead, leaving Jessica free to act again. The Master went straight for Stacey.

He swept to the window, Stacey in his arms. Bryan was on him, landing a vicious blow against his throat. The Master was rocked by the force of it, then turned and let out a snarl of rage. He threw Stacey straight at Bryan, who was forced to catch her, then made good his escape in a swirl of smoke and mist.

Jessica heard a sound like a sigh.

Ragnor had killed the redhead. His dust was mingling with the broken glass on the floor.

She turned to Bobby. He was shaking, eyes wide. "Bobby, what the hell happened? How did he get in?"

She saw Barry Larson on the floor, struggling to rise. She didn't wait for a reply from Bobby. She was certain she knew. Fury rose in her like a geyser. "You bastard. You whiny bastard!" she cried, striding to Barry, ready to strike him back down.

"No...no!" Bobby managed to get out. "He tried to stop it."

"What are you talking about?" Jessica demanded. "If it wasn't Barry, then who?"

Bryan had laid Stacey down next to Mary's unconscious form. Then he walked up to Jessica, his eyes actually sorrowful. "For the love of God, Jessica, who's left?"

"Gareth?" she said, feeling ill. She shook her head in denial. Lucien had walked to the man and was turning him over. "It was that image, the computer image. He was controlled against his will. He..."

Bryan walked over by Lucien and stooped down beside Gareth. "He's coming to," he said.

Jessica shoved past the two men and knelt down. Gareth opened his eyes and looked straight at her. A crooked smile curved his lips. "You were beautiful," he gasped. "But he is the Master."

His eyes began to close.

"He's dying," she said. "How? Why?"

"Could be the fact that his head is caved in," Lucien murmured.

Bryan gently touched the dying man's face. Gareth's eyes opened again. "What does your Master want?" he demanded.

Gareth's mouth formed words. Barely discernible. Jessica leaned closer. "You...and Igrainia. As it was."

His eyes closed. This time, Bryan eased away. There would be no more questioning. The man was dead.

18

The French doors to the balcony weren't exactly repaired, but they were boarded up and once again bore all the trappings necessary to keep away monsters.

Since one of New Orleans' finest had been there, they'd been able to report the incident, and get Barry Larson to the hospital for the care he needed *and* explain the dead man in the house. Lucien and Ragnor had whisked Mary off, so there was no need to explain how the missing corpse had come back to life at the crime scene. Sean arrived and took over the official end of things, but to Jessica, the night seemed to stretch forever. Nancy and Jeremy remained at Sean and Maggie's, safe, with Brent Malone and the others.

As he watched the crime-scene team do their work, Bryan felt like an uneasy observer.

He had worked alone for so many years, and he told himself that was a good thing. Look at the way Jessica had been betrayed. And yet he couldn't help feeling he had lost out in some way, never really trusting anyone since Gregore's death. He was a warrior, and a warrior's solitary quest was the destruction of evil. Yet this group had also made that their aim, as unnatural—as impossible as that seemed to him.

Once, so long ago it didn't seem real anymore, he had known what it felt like to belong. He had fought for a king who had honored him, alongside stalwart comrades. They had worn leather, chain and steel, rather than cotton and denim, Levi's and Armani, but in a way, they were much the same.

He was quiet, watching the activity all around him, making a few plans of his own.

At least the results of the preliminary investigation were manageable from a PR standpoint. The perp had, obviously, come in through the French doors, and he'd worn gloves. No identifiable prints had been found, and no shoe prints in the garden below. By agreement, Bobby had described the attacker as a tall man who had fled when he'd arrived. Bryan was surprised to see that after his initial shock, the cop dealt with the situation quite well.

Bryan finally left Jessica's house, knowing she was safe in the hands of people who cared about her, and went to the hospital in the wake of the ambulance. During the hour he waited until he was allowed to see

Barry Larson, he checked on the status of David Hayes. One of the residents lowered his voice as Bryan questioned him, saying, "I never saw so much blood loss, but I think he's going to make it. Whoever attacked those cops ripped up the veins in his arm pretty good, though, which still that doesn't explain…"

"Explain what?" Bryan asked.

"He's convinced he was attacked by a vampire. Twice. The first time by a naked girl in the morgue, then in his room by a man in a doctor's whites."

"So he's conscious now? Is he allowed visitors?"

"It's up to the cops who gets in," the resident said.

Bryan thanked him. Mendez was on duty and let him past without comment.

"Hey, how are you doing?" Bryan asked.

The boy looked at him curiously. "Do I know you?"

"I'm a professor," Bryan explained. "I study ancient legends and beliefs—like vampires."

"They exist," David said gravely.

"Yes," Bryan said.

David looked at him, stunned that someone finally believed him.

Bryan smiled. "No one else is ever going to believe you. I'd give it up, if you want to become a doctor."

Hayes shook his head. "You don't understand. I'm…petrified."

"Do everything they tell you and you'll be fine.

The vampire who came after you is done here right now. He's moved on to his real target. They're pumping you full of new blood, so hang in there, and grow up to be a great doctor."

"That's…it?" David said.

"Well, it won't hurt you to eat a lot of garlic and keep religious symbols around your house."

"Like crosses?"

"Like whatever you believe in. Face it, whatever supreme power is out there, I'm pretty sure that in the end, what's going to be most important is how we treat one another while we're here on earth."

David stared at him blankly.

"You've got a real chance, kid. Use it," Bryan advised, then got up and headed toward the door.

"Hey, Professor? Are you going to be around? In case…in case I need some help?"

"Not for a while, actually. But don't worry. Someone will be watching over you."

He went back to Emergency and found out where they had taken Barry Larson, who wasn't in bad shape, suffering mostly from a concussion. He was amazingly happy as he greeted Bryan.

"I nearly stopped him. I tried, anyway."

"Good man," Bryan said.

"I've known something was going on at that house. I knew Big Jim knew it, too. No need to worry about me, though. I had my story down. I said I couldn't remember much, just that a really big guy broke in from the balcony and we tried to stop him." His face hardened. "'Course, Gareth will come out looking like a hero, dying to fight off a burglar, but that's okay, I guess."

After a few pleasantries, Bryan left. When he got back to Montresse House, Stacey was downstairs with Bobby, who still looked shell-shocked, but at least he was getting some colour back in his face. He looked at Bryan with weary eyes. "They're going to need a new maintenance man," he said dully.

"Yeah. Where is everyone?" Sean asked.

"Sean's been called back in. Niles Goolighan went wacko in his cell, attacked a guard. Most of the others are at Sean's place. They're making arrangements." He hesitated. "They decided it's too dangerous to keep Mary at a house where there are children, so she'll be staying with a guy named Malone and his wife until it's all figured out. Jessica's upstairs," he said. "Resting."

"She's not resting. She's busy blaming herself for everything," Stacey contradicted.

"Thanks."

Upstairs, he found Jessica pacing the floor in her room, which had been put back in some semblance of order. She stood still when he appeared and stared at him, as if holding her breath. Waiting.

"Hey," he said softly.

"Oh, God, Bryan!" She ran across the room to him, and he took her into his arms.

"All these years...Gareth came to me before I ever even moved here. A couple of punks trying to rob the manager of a convenience store, and he... saw me take them down. He told the cops then I'd just had a lucky break, coming up behind one and cracking him on the head with a bottle of wine. I was sure he'd seen the truth, but he was so convincing. A few months later he admitted that he knew what I was, but he said he wasn't afraid, he only wanted to help me. And he did. Bryan, he was with me for ten years. I left Stacey alone with him. I trusted him."

Helplessly, he smoothed her hair. "We all need to have faith in others. And sometimes we make mistakes." He hesitated. "Don't let it change you. I'm not saying that you don't have to be careful, but..." He lifted her chin. "Don't forget there is love out there, friendship, loyalty. You've got good friends. Big Jim, for one. And I have to admit, I really thought it might be him. And Barry. I'm pretty sure he's the real thing."

She smiled. "Go figure, huh?" She shook her head, then let out a deep sigh. "Sean went back to the station. Niles Goolighan attacked a guard."

"The Master intended to leave a mess in his wake, and I'd say he did a damn fine job."

"I don't know what you mean."

"He's moved on. He's caused all the trouble here that he wanted. Now he wants us to follow him. He never intended to have a full-blown battle here. We're not on his turf. And we have no choice. We *have* to follow him."

"Follow him where?"

"Where this all started. Sometimes I don't believe myself it all happened. I don't believe I was once a man, a knight fighting for a king and a cause, in love with the king's illegitimate daughter. That's what he wants, Jessica. He wants to relive that day. We have to return to Scotland."

She backed away and stared at him.

"It will be a different battle. But," he added slowly, "the odds won't be quite as bad as I'd always expected."

"Oh?"

"I suppose there *are* a few good vampires out there."

She smiled and moved into his arms again.

"You need to get some rest," he said.

"We don't have time."

"Yes, we do."

She looked up at him. "A little physical activity always seems to help before a nap."

Hell, he hadn't been born yesterday. He kissed her, his lips light, infinitely tender.

And he made love to her. Slowly, savoring every touch, whisper, glance between them. It wasn't until the end that they both gave way to the absolute passion and desperation of arousal, climaxing together in a bond as sweet as any the far distant past had ever offered.

Afterward, she slept.

He rose. Downstairs, he found Bobby and Stacey cuddled together on one of the sofas.

"Jessica?" Stacey asked.

"Is sleeping," Bryan said.

"I'd kind of like to go see Sean, then…" Bobby hesitated, looking disbelievingly at Bryan. "Stacey's tried to explain it to me."

Bryan grimaced. "Bobby, you can get explanations for a lifetime—hell, you can live several lifetimes—and still not really understand."

Bobby nodded. "I guess everyone needs to get some rest, but then we'll have to start making plans. And…" He barely missed a beat, then looked Bryan straight in the eyes. "We'll need all the help we can get."

Stacey smiled. "A major meeting. Here. Tonight. I'll see to it."

"I'll be here," Bobby said. "I won't fail again, I promise."

"You didn't fail, Bobby. And next time you'll be prepared. But nothing is going to happen here. I'm almost sure of it."

"I won't fail again," Bobby repeated.

Stacey curled her fingers around his hand, smiled grimly as she looked at Bryan. "*We* won't fail," she assured him.

Bryan shook his head. "I'm going to need you guys to provide support, and that's not because I don't trust you. But you're only human, like it or not. There's only so much you can do."

They both looked deflated, but Bobby only sighed and told Bryan, "Yeah. Sure. We'll make great babysitters."

Bryan found Sean Canady outside the entrance to the cells.

"How did you know I'd be here?" Sean asked him.

"Hunch," Bryan said. "Will you have trouble getting me in?"

"Usually I would have to pull some strings and do a lot of paperwork. But today…I don't think so. Come on."

Bryan followed close behind Sean as they made their way to the holding cell, filling the cop in on his theory about the final battle. Sean assured the guards they passed that he could handle things himself, though he shouldn't have been going in alone, much less with Bryan; it was totally against policy. But the guards were spooked. They didn't want anything to do with the entire area where Niles Goolighan was being kept.

Bryan remained out of sight when they first approached the cell. Goolighan grinned at Sean. The kid was covered in blood, His own? The guard's?

"Hey, piggy, piggy," Goolighan taunted in a singsong voice. "Come on in. I've the power now, and you're going to die."

"You're a punk, Niles. Always were, always will be," Sean said.

Goolighan shook his head. "No. He kept his promise. He came to me."

"Who's that?" Sean asked, as if he weren't the least bit interested.

"The Prince of Darkness," Goolighan said delightedly.

"He's not the Prince of Darkness. Just a punk follower—like you, He's had a little more practice, that's all, and he isn't quite as dumb," Sean said.

"I'm not stupid. I'm going to be all-powerful. I'm his ally."

"No, Niles, you may have asked him in, but you're still a punk. Cal talked, by the way. We know all about the Web site, and we know how he gets to you assholes."

Goolighan didn't seem to be listening anymore. He was liked a crazed hyena, laughing, chortling. "I'll be there. I'll be at the great battle. Come on in, pig. I'm going to kill you. Then I'll die and come back and be at the battle when it rages."

"You'll be the best punk there, I bet," Sean told him. "Where will this battle take place?"

"What do you care? You'll be dead. Come on, pig. You can't resist. Get in here and try to kill me."

"You're right. I can't resist. But humor me, first. Where is it going to be?"

Niles started laughing as if that were the funniest thing he'd ever heard. "It will be so cool there, in the mists."

"He'll be waiting below the high tor, huh?"

Niles giggled again. "Not bad, piggy, piggy. It's the bitch he wants. He's wanted her all along. Wants to kill her. I think once he wanted to fuck her, but she was like all bitches, wanting someone else. Some piece of highland shite." He gave the last the Scottish pronunciation, then went into gales of laughter. "Ah, laddie." he said, doing a creditable Scottish accent, "he'll bastion himself in the MacDonnough ruins, that he will. He'll command the valley and the highlands. And then it will end for those who made his life—and death—a hell."

"Great. Thanks," Sean said, turning the lock, stepping into the cell.

Bryan moved up behind him in the blink of an eye, and Niles saw him for the first time. He roared in sudden knowledge and fury.

Sean stepped back. There was no fight. Not really. Niles was a fool. He attacked Bryan, going straight for him, impaling himself on the small wooden stake Bryan held. He hadn't even needed to thrust it forward.

"I guess I'm going to have to answer a lot of questions," Sean said when it was over. "But I've done it before and, God help me, I'll probably do it again, somewhere down the line."

They both looked at Niles, crumpled on the floor.

"Rest in peace, you sorry punk," Sean murmured.

"There was nothing else we could do," Bryan told him.

"I know. It's just such a waste." Sean sighed, straightened. "Let's go."

This time they were all at the house on Bourbon Street.

They filled the kitchen, and at first glance they might have been any group of friends; Stacey and Bobby had gone to Sean and Maggie's to watch the children, but all the rest were there. Sean was explaining what had happened to Niles Goolighan.

"How did you explain killing him in his cell?" Jessica asked, pouring coffee for herself.

Sean hesitated for a moment. "I've had to explain far worse," he reminded her. "There wasn't a soul who didn't believe he'd attacked me. I said I was damn lucky Bryan had a stake on him."

"A *stake?*" Jessica said. "And how did you explain Bryan carrying a stake?"

"Easy. A prop for his lectures," Sean said.

"Somehow," Maggie said, "it will work out. It always does."

Sean smiled. "Hey, this is N'awleans. We've always been what we are, a little decay, a little voodoo, history, jazz…mystery. I had another interesting conversation today, too."

"With…?" Jessica asked.

"Florenscu," he said.

"Florenscu?" Jessica repeated. "The detective in Transylvania?"

"The same," Sean said. "I asked him to interview some of the partygoers about a hunch I had. He got back to me immediately, and damned if the information about the party didn't appear on the 'Master' site about twenty-four hours beforehand. If we'd known to look, I'm sure we would have found the same thing for the party here, even though the Master never meant to attend."

"We'll find it before the party in Scotland, then," Jade said.

"I can already tell you when it will be," Bryan told them.

They all looked at him.

"The Demon Moon, an occurrence that falls maybe once in a century. But the way the planets align, it's not an eclipse, it's a red moon."

"I've seen it," Maggie whispered.

"As have I," Jessica said dryly. "The Demon Moon, and the MacDonnough castle." She shook her head. "It wasn't all that well fortified. It wasn't even that big. There was a wooden fence around the clan homes, and the castle itself was stone, but…"

Jade DeVeau walked over to her with a sheaf of pages. "In the 1400s, the clan came into some money. They built a stone wall around the keep. You can see what remains of the courtyard. During the Jacobite uprisings it was abandoned, taken over by the Crown and forgotten. It's nothing but ruins now."

Tara walked over and showed Jessica the second page. "This is the original chapel. There are tombs beneath it. Lots of them. Apparently it was a big family. The catacombs run like tunnels beneath the place. There's a huge memorial room there. The chapel itself was deconsecrated a long time ago, though." She was silent for a few seconds, thinking. "I can't be sure, but there have been a number of unexplained disappearances in the area over the years, and I believe the Master has been using it as a base while he regained his strength. I'm willing to bet he's created an entire army there, and they won't all be newly made vampires who have no idea how to defend themselves." She looked over at Bryan. "You need to be careful," she said softly. "I gather you have superhuman strength and an ability to heal, but everyone has a weakness." She shook her head. "Frankly, I don't think you should go."

Bryan walked over and met Tara's eyes. "I have to go," he said flatly. He looked around at the group. "I have to go, and you know that. Perhaps it would be best if I go alone."

Tara sighed. "I knew he'd say that."

"No way in hell are you going alone!" Jessica protested.

"You know," Lucien said, "I'm not underestimating your power, Bryan, but we're talking about an army. I think more of us than just Jessica should go."

"I think this is a battle Bryan and I have to face alone," Jessica said.

Bryan inhaled. "Frankly, you're exactly the one who shouldn't go. I have to destroy him."

"*We* have to destroy him," Jessica corrected him.

"Jessica, don't you see? That's what he wants. Both of us there to be destroyed."

They were all startled when the doorbell rang. "Who is that?" Sean asked, frowning.

"Want me to go?" Ragnor asked.

"No, it's all right," Jessica said. "I'll get it."

Bryan followed her at a discreet distance. He was startled to see a very distraught woman at the door, then he frowned as he realized he recognized her, then tried to remember from where.

"I knew he was going off the deep end," the

woman was saying, nearly sobbing. Jessica had a hand on her shoulder, trying to soothe her. "He's been gone since last night, but I know he didn't run away," she said. "This is real. And it's not a ransom note, it's…I don't know what it means, but the police won't help, and your name is here…. Oh, God, what should I do?"

Bryan's memory clicked. It was Mrs. Peterson, mother of Jacob, the boy who thought he was a vampire. Without Jacob, he might not have been in the right cemetery that night.

The woman had brought Jessica a note hand printed on a torn piece of computer paper.

"Mrs. Peterson, we'll find Jacob," Jessica promised.

"You can find him?" the woman asked with desperate hope. "You think he's alive?"

Jessica nodded. "I'm sure of it."

She let out a deep sigh. "I'll find your son, Mrs. Peterson. And I'll bring him back to you. I swear it. Now go home, have a glass of wine, call a friend and leave this to me."

"Thank you. The police wouldn't even take a missing persons report yet—they said teenagers wander off all the time and he hasn't been gone long enough yet. But this note…it scares me."

Bryan realized someone was standing close behind him. Sean.

"I'll see her home. I can't leave New Orleans now,

anyway," Sean said softly. He walked past Bryan, meeting the woman at the door. "Mrs. Peterson, I'm Lieutenant Canady. I'll get you home and take down all your information."

Mrs. Peterson, looking so lost and scared, stared numbly at Sean.

As soon as Sean left with her, Bryan strode over to Jessica. "What does it say?" he demanded.

She handed him the paper.

He looked down at it. In pen, it said *For Jessica Fraser*. Beneath that three words had been scribbled in what appeared to be blood, one on top of the other, the middle word underlined.

Ioin

and

Igrainia

19

The land was no longer drenched in blood as it had been last time he saw it. For several minutes, standing atop the high tor, Bryan had been awed by the sheer beauty of the rugged landscape, the cottages on the slopes, the colors of fields and hills. White sheep and long-haired cows grazed on long rich grasses in the distance. Wildflowers grew in abundance. Only the remnants of old stone walls, some of them dating back to Roman times, divided the landscape. It was a magical vista.

Yet the night was coming, and with it, he knew, Father Gregore's Demon Moon.

Detective Florenscu had been the first to find a reference to the party. He had called Sean, who had called them. They had reported the possibility of trouble to the local authorities, realizing that in the end, when the party was over, there would be a need for official help.

Bryan looked back across the fields, savoring the

sight, the scent and the breeze. The pastel colors, in their soft radiance. Because soon, with the darkening of the day, would come different shades.

At first, a pale maroon. And then, just before darkness, red.

Tonight the land would appear once again to be drenched in blood.

"Well?" Lucien, standing by his side, asked.

"So little has changed here," Bryan said softly. "All these years...the countryside is still magnificent." He pointed. "That's where Edward III paused, the position his troops took when his raiding party returned with Igrainia. To our right is the path to MacDonnough castle."

Ragnor and Brent, who had gone scouting to the north, returned in time to hear the last. "To the west, the only escape is the sea," Brent said. "Just as you remembered."

Bryan nodded and looked past them to where Jessica stood alone, staring down at the field of battle. He could only wonder at her thoughts.

What had happened here had happened many lifetimes ago, and yet, standing against the ever present Highland wind, he could close his eyes, hear the clash of steel....

He wondered if those same thoughts filled Jessica's mind, *Igrainia*. Or was she remembering how she had been seized and tormented, how the fire had singed her, how the teeth of the vampire had ripped her throat, turning her forever into something less than human?

"It's time to go. We've only got a few hours before sunset," Lucien said.

They all knew that whatever they could do in that brief time might not mean much. The army they would face had been years in the making. Hundreds of years, perhaps.

And they were only a small force. Himself and Jessica, Lucien, Ragnor and Brent, and one more, called in at the last despite Lucien's unease because he was such a newly made vampire. Sean had argued that he was a cop, and he'd prevailed in the end. The man's name was Rick Boudreaux, and like the others, he was ready to face whatever came. Jade had argued furiously with her husband that she should come, but in the end, she had stayed back in New Orleans. There had been no question of the other wives coming, they were far too human.

"Bryan?" Lucien said. "Are you ready?"

"Yes," Bryan said. "A moment."

He walked over to Jessica. The breeze caught her hair, tossing it around her face. Her eyes were clouded and infinitely sad. She wore no wig tonight. She wasn't attending *this* party as the dominatrix. She was going as a wide-eyed innocent, hoping to be the chosen one. Bryan hadn't been able to argue her out of it, so all he could do now was watch like a hawk.

She was wearing glasses and a long white cloak with a fur collar. She was the picture of pristine innocence.

He had on his long railway coat and low-brimmed hat. He didn't give a damn whether he was recognized or not.

"So long ago," Jessica murmured.

He closed his hands over her arms, turning her to him. "I still don't think you should go."

She offered him a smile. "I have to go. Bryan... years ago, this very place was where I learned we all need to be strong." She touched his cheek. "You're ever the champion, the knight, ready to lay down his life for others. But you have to believe in me. My life and destiny were stolen here so long ago, too. You have to let me fight beside you."

"I don't have to like it," he told her.

Someone cleared his throat nearby.

Brent walked up, determined to sound light. "Party time, kids. Time to go."

Jessica eased from Bryan's hold. "One by one," she reminded him. "No need to announce our intentions from the start."

They'd ridden horses in this part of the country, transportation far more convenient for the turf than cars. He watched her walk away and mount up. Ever graceful, ever proud.

The king's daughter. Royalty in any age. And always in his heart.

He could not fail her again.

* * *

Jessica made her way through the crowd milling just outside the ruins. This was worse than Transylvania. With the sea to one side and great, ragged tors to the other, there was only one escape route

"Hey, baby."

She had barely seated herself at the bar set up just inside the ruined walls when the man accosted her. He had an Irish accent, and he was good-looking, with ink-black hair and startling blue eyes.

He was also a vampire.

She smiled. "Hi."

"You're American?" he asked.

He didn't know what she was, she realized. He didn't look all that young. He should have learned to recognize his own. Too many vampires were so interested in their own hedonistic pleasures that they didn't learn everything they should.

"Yes, American."

"You know, there's a special privilege for the most beautiful girl here," he told her.

"You're flattering me."

"Not at all. I wish I could keep you for myself tonight."

"Then why don't you?"

He leaned against the bar, his eyes rapt on her. Instead of answering her question, he asked, "Want a drink?"

"Thank you."

"Two Bloody Marys," he called to the bartender.

Tonight, she noticed, the bartender was also a vampire. He arched a brow, frowning as he looked at her companion. "Yeah, Bloody Marys," the Irishman snapped. Then he turned to her and offered his hand. "Bruce. Bruce Mayo. And you're…?"

"Jesse."

The drinks arrived. She sipped hers. It was a Bloody Mary, all right.

"Know what that is?" Bruce asked her, eyes gleaming.

"A Bloody Mary?"

"Yes. But it's real blood."

She gave a little shudder and stared at him wide-eyed. "Really?"

He nodded. Then he gave a little shrug. "Cow's blood, but it's the fantasy that counts right?" He took her hand. "Let me show you around. The best stuff is downstairs."

He led her into the ruined castle and down an ancient, winding staircase to the stone catacombs, just as they had been laid out in the computer printout. She had memorized every twist and turn.

"Do the dead scare you?" he teased.

"They sadden me," she murmured.

"They're all around us," he said, pointing out the rotted caskets in niches in the walls.

She knew what he was really thinking, that the

dead really were all around, not just the skeletons, but the vampires, just like him.

"Here we are. You just wait right here. Freshen up, if you like. You'll find that you won't be alone for long."

She knew the room. It was the same one the Master used every time. The bed on the dais, the dressing table. She sat down and began playing her part, brushing her hair, waiting....

She felt the shadow as it formed, felt the miasma, all that was dark and blood-stained and evil, and she was helpless to do anything but brush her hair.

Bryan made a low-key arrival, striding casually through the crowd, tipping his hat now and then as he passed a group of giggling girls. He took a seat at the bar.

Vampire, he thought, seeing the bartender, whom he knew could tell that he was not one. He ordered a beer and nursed it, aware of the covert glances he was receiving from around the room. Jessica was nowhere to be seen. He was sure she'd been chosen, just as she had planned to be. Bryan didn't like the fact that she was already gone, but he knew the layout of the ruins, and the minute the others entered to cover his disappearance, he would be in hot pursuit. And if they didn't show...

They did.

Rick Boudreaux and Brent Malone entered together, a pair of wandering Americans out for a good time. Lucien and Ragnor came in next, playing the role of exactly what they were—vampires.

Lucien sidled up to the bar and he and Bryan acknowledged each other briefly, like strangers sizing each other up.

Then Bryan rose. There were enough people milling around for him to make his way to the old chapel without being noticed. Once there, he hurried to the winding stairs leading to the crypts below.

There was a tall dark-haired man at the foot of the stairs. "Off-limits," he said harshly.

"Didn't hear you," Bryan lied, stepping into the raw earth flooring.

The man's lip curled. "Y'er fookin' off-limits." He shook his head. "I've half a mind—hell, who's to care?"

He started to laugh, exposing long, yellowed fangs. He reached out for Bryan.

He didn't even come close. Bryan speared him with one silent, powerful thrust, and the vampire burst into dust and ash.

"Old but stupid," Bryan murmured, shaking his head. Too easy. Too damn easy.

He hurried down the long corridor of crypts. He could hear music, and his pace quickened. There was a break in the wall ahead; light streamed from it.

He hurried in. There she was, the woman in the gossamer white. Jessica.

There he was. The tall, broad-shouldered, caped figure of the *vampyr*. The Master.

Jessica was sitting in front of the dressing table, brushing her hair while the Master stood behind her and stroked her arms. Her eyes were wide, like a doe in the headlights. The Master looked up at Bryan and laughed. "Can you begin to imagine what I will do with her before I behead her?" he asked. "You know, I had counted on you running down here, the great warrior to the rescue. Well, watch, for she is mine. Watch…if you can."

He heard the Master's voice, knew he was supposed to be in such a rage that he wouldn't have heard those coming up behind him. And he *was* in a rage, but he hadn't gone deaf.

He spun, small, double-edged swords in both hands. They had been honed to perfection. The first two vampires who came after him were sliced cleanly through the midriff at his first furious swirl of motion.

But there were more, breaking free of the rotting coffins where they had hidden. They came to life with a fever, with a will, ripping away the shrouds that had hidden them, shrieking out their battle cries. He couldn't keep count. Two from the left, one from the right, another crawling up the wall above him. He leapt to avoid the sword of what looked to be a cavalier, and in the same movement severed the head from the creature above. He managed to get his back to the wall, there better to oppose the horde that came at him. At first, they were like conceited schoolboys, wanting to best him on their own. But the pile of ashes grew before him— and, for those who were younger, bits of bone, decaying flesh, scraps of clothing—and they were still coming....

This was truly a land of the walking dead, he realized.

He got a brief glimpse of the Master, still touching her. His eyes had gone cold, his muscles rigid. He was going to take her away, Bryan realized, and she was still helpless to resist him.

"Igrainia!"

No longer fearing what might threaten from behind, he moved forward. All he feared was a future without her once again.

She wanted to cry out and couldn't, but it didn't matter. She knew. Sensed him behind her, behind the Master. Without seeing him, she knew he was a flurry of motion, faster than wind, sound, light. The vampires died, crumpling, before him. On and on, the battle raged.

She felt the viselike tightening of the Master's

fingers, just as she had felt them once before, so long ago.

She looked up, she saw his face. Saw the eyes change first, to something snakelike but evil in a way no snake had ever been.

It was as if his every hunger for power, wealth, brutality and strength was there, like glass shards filling his eyes. He drew her up, and she knew that she had no weapons against such strength, except...

Except her teeth, the teeth he had given her.

She could no longer sense Bryan; the power of the horde was too strong.

Just like it had been all those years ago....

"Come, my dear, we are leaving. I would prefer to enjoy the last of your so-called life and then your death at my leisure," he told her, smiling just as she had smiled once before, in a different lifetime. "Once more the great knight Ioin, champion of the wretched, traitorous Robert the Bruce, will be beaten. Sliced to ribbons by too many enemies for any creature to withstand."

Teeth!

She twisted her head and bit his hand, bit with no mercy. She tore at the flesh, and it felt as if she were tasting poison, but she didn't care.

He let out a howl of pain, and everything went dead still.

Then a roar of fury erupted from him, but it was too late. She was free and thinking fast. She lashed out at him with a tremendous kick, courtesy of the

tae kwon do studio off Royal Street. She caught him
with such force that he flew back against the wall,
then turned, ready to join the fray that now seemed
like a great gathering of flies atop Bryan.

Flies gathering atop a corpse…?

"Bryan!" she shouted. And then, "Ioin!"

The floor was then strewn with weapons. She
selected a sword, lifted it and tore into the crowd of
attackers. So far, the other vampire hadn't noticed
her. She raised the weapon as she had been taught
so long ago, and stepped forward, swinging.

Like flies they fell before her. She was ready when
they began to turn at last, realizing the danger from
their rear. Yet not one lifted a weapon.

She spun around.

Too late.

She felt his fingers, tearing into her shoulders,
dragging her around with impossible force. Once
again she faced the fiery eyes of the Master.

"It's begun," Ragnor said softy.

Lucien rose from his bar stool, drawing his sword
and dispatching the bartender, who had just picked
up a hatchet of his own. At the same time, Ragnor
turned with his heavy Viking sword and swung it in
a wide arc, catching three vampires at once. He slid
down from his stool while Lucien leapt atop the bar,
the element of surprise gone, and prepared for the
fight of his life.

People were screaming, running everywhere. Across the room, Lucien saw Rick Boudreaux calmly reloading his old police revolver. He had it rigged to fire bullets that contained wood, and he had excellent aim.

A fierce vampire roared, breaking off a leg from one of the bar stools, then racing toward Brent who let the man reach him, then snaked out an arm like steel, catching the chair leg and sending the burly vampire crashing into the fire that burned in the remains of the great hearth. "Sorry, not a vampire," Brent muttered.

"Get down!" Rick shouted to him.

Brent ducked. A silver bullet whistled overhead and exploded into the stone wall. Brent rose, surprised. A hatchet went flying, crashing directly into the neck and shoulder of the man with the pistol with the silver bullets. He went down.

"Thanks," Brent called to Ragnor.

"Don't mention it."

"Brent, Rick," Lucien called, "one of you finish in here, one of you get on the trail. Make sure none of the victims are followed."

"Right," Brent acknowledged.

"Hurry it up in here," Lucien told Ragnor. "I have a bad feeling about what's going on downstairs."

Ragnor glanced around quickly. No more vampires were in evidence. "I think we're just finished in here," he said.

"Then let's get below," Lucien said grimly.

* * *

This was so much like it had been before, except that this time he had seen her there, fighting. She was still alive. He was determined to live, too.

Bryan stepped forward with long strides, his senses so finely honed that he seemed to know the move of his every opponent. He ducked, spun, leapt and struck back with such speed and fury that it was as if he couldn't miss. Every enemy had to be sliced in half, beheaded or pinned through the heart or brain. Slashed to ribbons, they might still come back. Of course, if they were disabled enough, he could always finish them off later.

His arms were tiring, his muscles burning like molten steel, he didn't care. Then he heard her scream.

"Bastard!" he raged. He kicked the vampire in front of him, then staked him dead center in the heart. He fought his way through the crowd, slashing indiscriminately.

And then, just when it seemed they were about to descend on him again in impossible numbers, they began to fall away instead.

He had a brief glimpse of Ragnor, fighting two-handed, with both sword and ax. Behind him, Lucien, using double-edged swords, as he was himself.

"Go!" he heard Lucien shout to him. "Get her back!"

He burst through the battle lines, staring from side to side. He gritted his teeth, allowing his senses to guide him. The tunnel to the south...

He turned and ran.

Jessica had no idea how long he dragged her through the catacombs before they suddenly burst out into the night.

Beneath the Demon Moon.

There he threw her viciously across the ground.

She rose and realized she was standing exactly where she had stood hundreds of years before, the night bathed in the bloodred light of the moon.

And the creature staring at her, features contorted with a rage that seemed older than time, was lit with that crimson tint, as well.

She scrambled to her feet. She had lost the sword she had acquired. Now she had nothing. Nothing but her wits.

He lunged at her, his own blade so honed it seemed to drip blood, but it was only the reflection of the moon. She willed herself to become mist, and he slashed at nothing.

She materialized behind him.

He turned. "Clever girl. Too bad your father was a traitor," he sneered.

"My father was a man of his people, a great king."

"He was quick enough to watch you die," the Master said, the words barbed. "But then, you were just a bastard child."

"My father is dead and gone, and history has proved his worth," she said.

He stood still, staring at her, then smiled mockingly. "You have nothing. No weapon. How many times can you transform yourself before exhaustion overtakes you? Eventually, I will reach you. I will slice your flesh again and again. And when you are in such pain that you can no longer abide it, I will create a funeral pyre upon which you will burn. Unless…"

"Unless…?"

"You turn on him," the Master said softly.

"What?"

"He became a warrior," the Master said, and spat on the ground. "Warriors kill vampires. You are a vampire, you stupid girl. Do you think he can ever forget that? He's been fooling himself, glad to sleep with you again, but do you think he can *love* you again? He has used you to get to me, but one day, when you are sighing in his arms like the foolish strumpet you are, he will stake you straight through the heart. You can't change what you are, so choose to help me—and survive."

She stared back at him and smiled, amazed that there was only one tiny pulse of fear within her, before she told him, "You are as insane as you have always been. You think I'm your creation, but I'm not. Yes, you changed my form, but you didn't change what lies beneath. And I would die a thousand deaths before I would turn on him."

She watched his face contort again. It looked mottled, hideous, as if it were composed of bursting veins, red and black. He started toward her; she leapt aside. He swung; she became mist. She meant to disappear, flee, until she found a weapon, but he reached into the mist and somehow she was a woman again, and his fingers curled around her arm. "You have only one more life to give for him," he spat out. "And you will give it now."

Bryan burst out from the tunnel, instantly aware of the moon, the terrain, the exact location where he stood.

And there, exactly where, once before, he had tortured and taunted Igrainia, was the Master.

He was surrounded by mist, but then the mist became real. Jessica. *Igrainia.* The sweep of her hair was like a wave around her, golden against the white fur of her cloak, a shining sweep of all that was angelic. The Master had her in his grasp, but she was twisting, fighting, ever the fierce, proud spirit with whom he had fallen in love.

He let out a cry of rage that seemed to shake the very heavens.

The Master turned to him. His enemy in life and death. With a violent motion, the Master cast Jessica from him, then stared at Bryan.

"You and me, then. The final battle," the Master said.

"The final battle," Bryan agreed.

They circled each other warily. "But will you fight?" taunted the Master. "Think of those scores of vampires, my enemy, my minions, who get to live. Even as we fight, all those little innocent lambs who came here for a taste of the forbidden are running in an insanity of fear, desperate to escape. How many will die tonight, as you fight me?"

The Master lunged and thrust. Bryan parried and followed with a fierce attack, both swords swinging. The Master deflected each blow, and they both fell back, pausing as an unholy howling tore across the sky.

Bryan thought he saw a frown briefly flicker across the Master's brow.

He almost smiled. "Werewolf," he said with a shrug. "One that chews nasty vampires to little bits and spits them out."

The Master thrust forward in a fury of motion.

Bryan neatly ducked and struck back, sending one of the creature's weapons flying.

He lunged swiftly and expertly, trying to seize the advantage. The Master moved, as well, but not before Bryan caught his shoulder with the tip of his blade. A snarl of fury rose to the Master's lips as he clutched his shoulder.

"Hanging around with werewolves? Slumming it, for a warrior, aren't you?" the Master taunted.

"You know, this really is a brave new world," he said. "It seems we can all get past our prejudices."

The Master roared, feinted, then whirled, attempting to pick up his lost weapon. He managed the feat, and with his next strike, he caught Bryan in the arm.

Pain ripped through Bryan. He ignored it and bided his time.

"Come on, come on, let me finish this," the Master chided. "I will slice and bleed you, warrior. I will torture you, and I will force you to watch her burn, before I finish you.

Bryan saw Jessica move then. Out of the corner of his eye, he saw her stir. *She was alive.*

With a burst of speed, he tore into the Master, swords flying in a crisscross pattern. The creature leapt back, but too late. Bryan caught his arm, and again a sword went flying.

The sword never got a chance to hit the ground. Jessica was there, the wind whipping her hair, catching the folds of the cape. She might have been the goddess of justice. And she was holding the Master's sword.

"Lose something?" she taunted.

Again, he let out a cry of rage, and like a maddened bull, he leapt toward her. She raised the sword, parried his blow. He turned, going after Bryan again.

Bryan spun, catching the Master a solid blow in the midriff. Not a killing blow, but one that drained the creature of strength, forcing him to pause.

The Master let out a bone-chilling scream of rage, as if he believed that he could force Bryan to cower from the sound alone.

But Bryan only smiled. "I should torture you. Slice and bleed *you* for the agony and suffering you have brought to so many on this earth. But it's far more important that you die, that you be eliminated at last. Although," he said, taking a step forward, "I would like to skin you alive and roast each piece."

"Bastard! You will die slowly," the Master swore his rage propelling him forward.

Bryan stood still, waiting. Then he leapt neatly aside and swung his swords together in a huge arc.

Something flew through the night.

The Master's head.

It arced upward, a living thing for the beat of a second, its scowl of rage hideous. Then it burst into dust, just like the body that lay at Bryan's feet.

He stood, stunned. It was over. Really over. Then he heard her cry out his name as she raced into his arms. He buried his face against her hair. "Igrainia."

It would be the last time he called her by that name.

Epilogue

Cool jazz filled the air. The crowds in the streets were slightly rowdy, but Bryan knew Jessica was always happiest when her city was doing well, so he ignored the noise from outside. For the first time in perhaps forever, he was completely relaxed.

So what if a werewolf was buying the beers? And half of his new best friends were mostly vampires? At least a few were actually human.

Jessica was watching the band with a smile. Big Jim smiled back, and so did Barry Larson, who seemed to exude a newfound confidence.

No lives had been lost in Scotland. He considered that something of a miracle, but those fighting with him just called it a good night's work. The authorities had found a bunch of crazed kids running around and chalked it up to drugs.

Some would remember the truth. Some would learn from it. Some would spend the rest of their lives in therapy. But at least they had lives.

As for Mary, that had been tricky, but he had to admit that she had developed a real passion for good, so a story had been invented.

She showed up at the police station one day, claiming amnesia. Only seeing her own picture on television had reminded her of who she was.

Sean, sitting between Jessica and Maggie, looked thoughtful, unhappy.

"What's the matter?" Maggie asked him

"We lost two really good cops," he said sadly. "Nothing can ever change that."

Jessica's brow furrowed. "It was not your fault. Don't even start that."

Just then the werewolf appeared with the beers.

"Hey, Jessica, are you going to design your own wedding dress?" Maggie asked.

Jessica choked on her beer. "Maggie, no one's asked me to marry him."

Maggie stared at Bryan. He felt a smile curving his lips, and he stared at Jessica. "What do you think?" he asked softly. "Can a warrior and a vampire find happiness in this day and age?" he inquired.

She looked back at him, her eyes grave. "I don't know. What do you think?"

He rose, taking her hand. "I don't know. But we can all learn new things, right?" He pulled her up and into his arms. "I do know that I will love you for eternity," he whispered.

She kissed his lips.
And the jazz played on.
It was, after all, New Orleans.

* * * * *

Turn the page for an exciting excerpt from
THE DEAD ROOM,
the next paranormal novel by
New York Times *bestselling author*
Heather Graham.
Available in March 2007,
only from MIRA Books

There had been an explosion, she thought. Someone had screamed something about gas, and then a blast had seemed to rock the world. Yes, she could remember now, the feeling of being lifted, of flying…slamming hard against the wall. But…she wasn't leaning against the wall now.

She was looking down on a scene of absolute chaos. *And she was in it.*

She could see herself, who had been taken and placed in a line of sleeping people. She didn't recognize any of them. Matt…where was Matt? Others were hurrying around the room, moving with purpose. They were all in uniform, firemen and cops. The freshly painted walls of the room were blackened and scorched almost to the doorway, evidence of the blast.

She hurt! Oh, God, she ached in every bone. The scent of charred wood—worse, charred flesh—filled her nostrils. She remembered the terrible sound, the way she had been lifted and thrown as the room was rocked by the explosion.

Now she looked down on herself, contemplated the others near and realized that the people she was lying with weren't sleeping.

They were dead.

She could see the open, glazed eyes of the woman beside her. And then she realized that a man was hunched down beside her own body. And it wasn't Matt. The man had his fingers against her throat. Feeling for a pulse?

"This one is alive!"

Of course I'm alive.

There was sudden confusion.

People rushing over to her. Shouting.

"Quick! Move or we'll lose her! Her pulse is fading."

People rushed around her. She couldn't see past them to see what was happening.

"Clear!"

She felt fire in her chest.

Every bone in her body seemed to be in sudden, raw, agony. She knew she needed to open her eyes, to rake in a desperate breath.

She blinked.

"We've got her! She's back."

And she was. Back in her body, looking up at her rescuers, no longer staring down at the scene.

Recollection and awareness filled her, and her awareness of the scene around her was acute, agonizing.

There were four bodies against the wall. And one of them belonged to Matt.

Suddenly, there was no confusion, just knowledge.

Matt was dead.

She started to choke, to scream....

"Calm down," a medic said. "You're alive, and we've got to keep you that way."

Alive? Not really, not if Matt...

"No, you've got to help Matt. *He's* alive. I was just talking to him. You've got to help him. Help him!"

She saw the distress in the medic's eyes. "I'm so sorry...."

Matt...

She was vaguely aware of a needle in her arm.

Then there was only darkness.